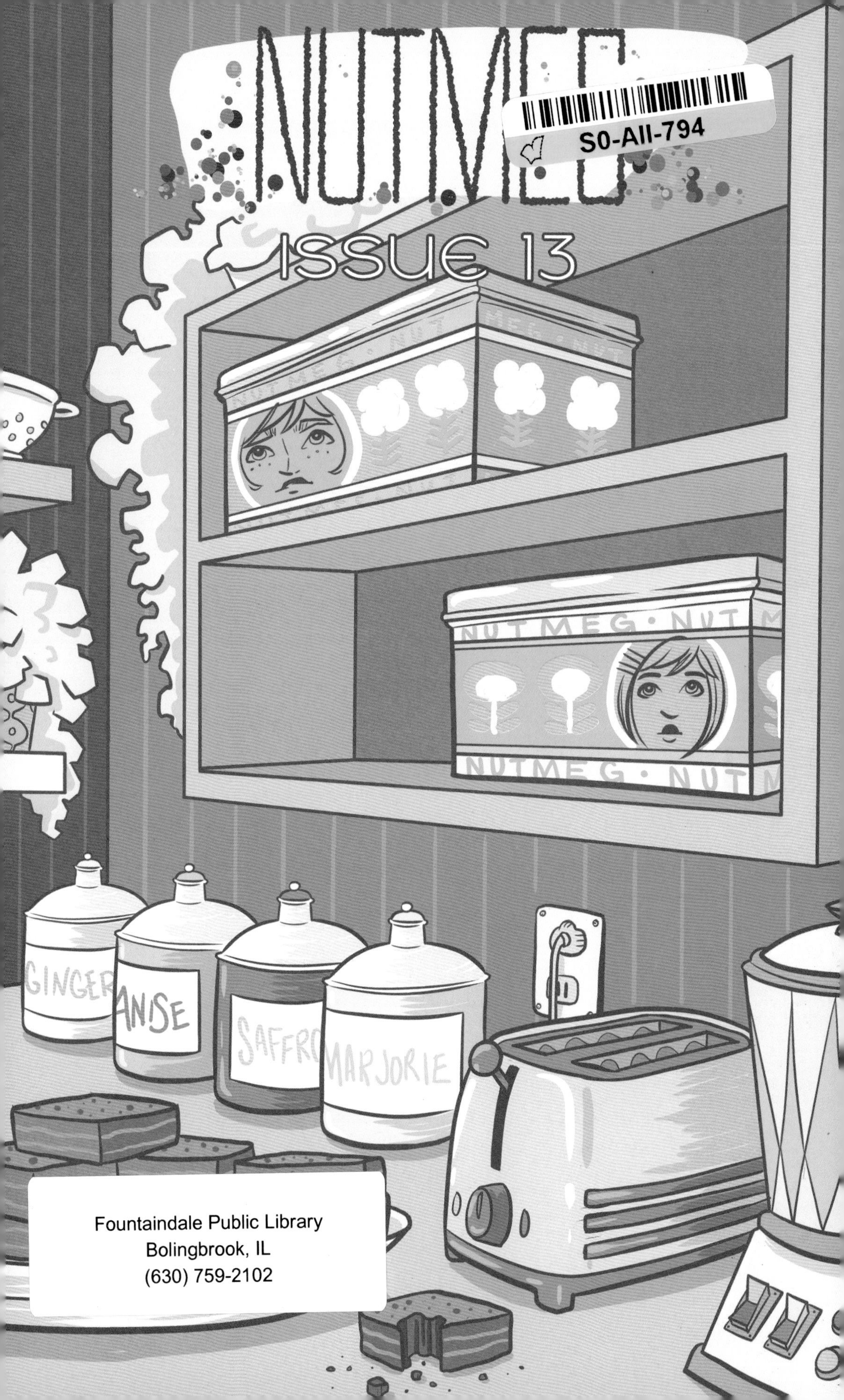
NUTMEG
ISSUE 13
NUTMEG · NUT
NUTMEG · NUT
GINGER
ANISE
SAFFRO
MARJORIE

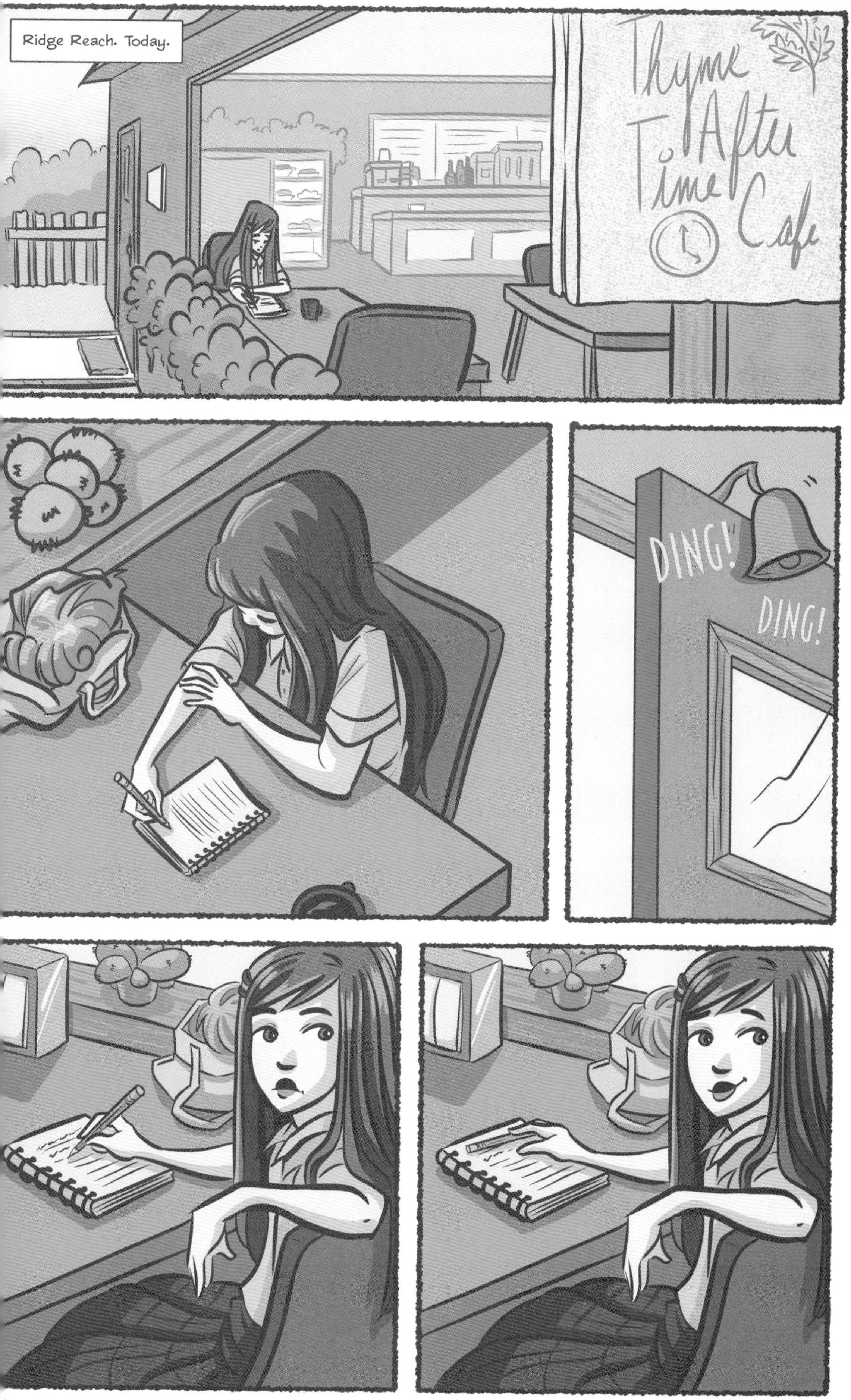
Ridge Reach. Today.
Thyme After Time Cafe
DING!
DING!

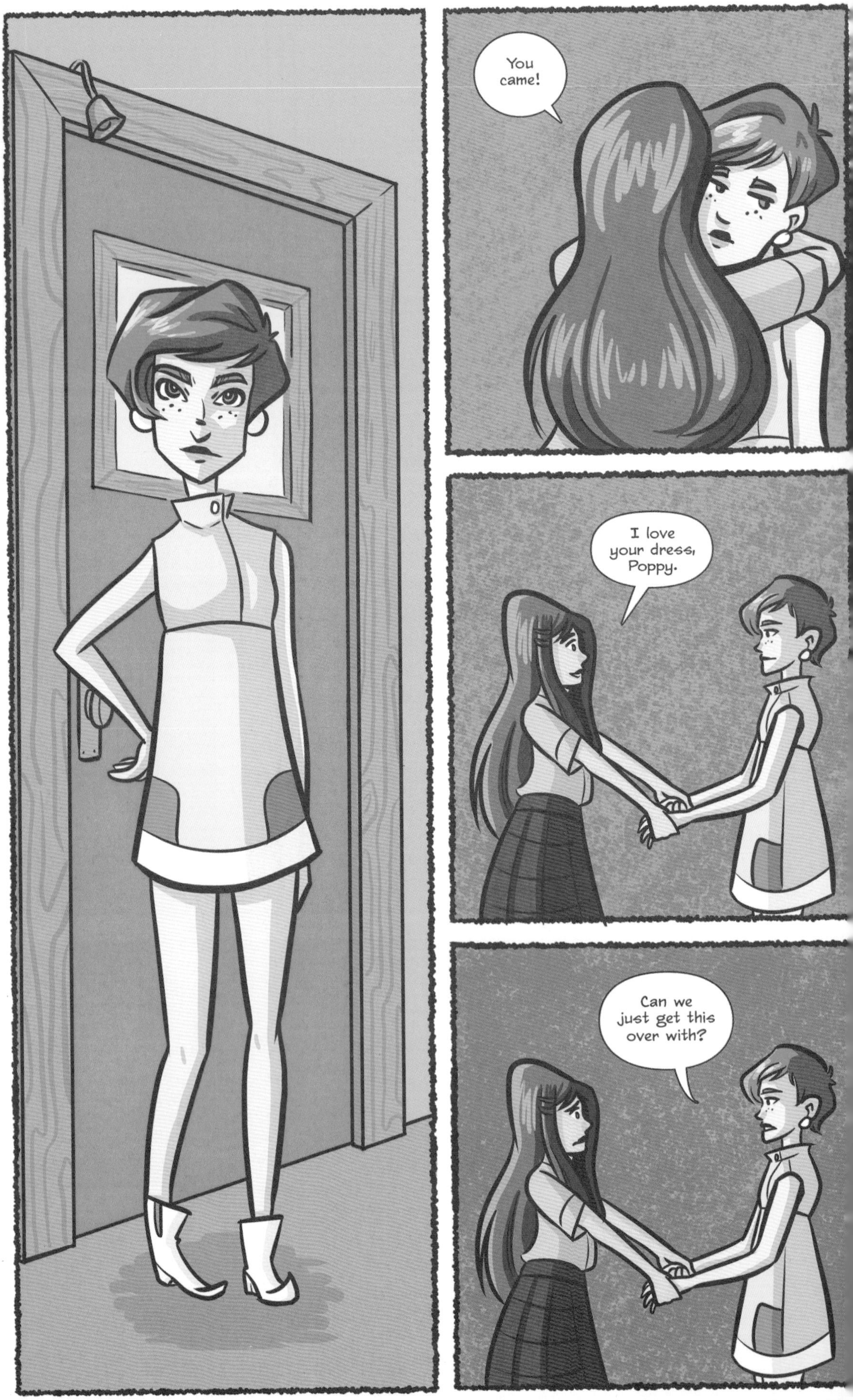
You came!
I love your dress, Poppy.
Can we just get this over with?

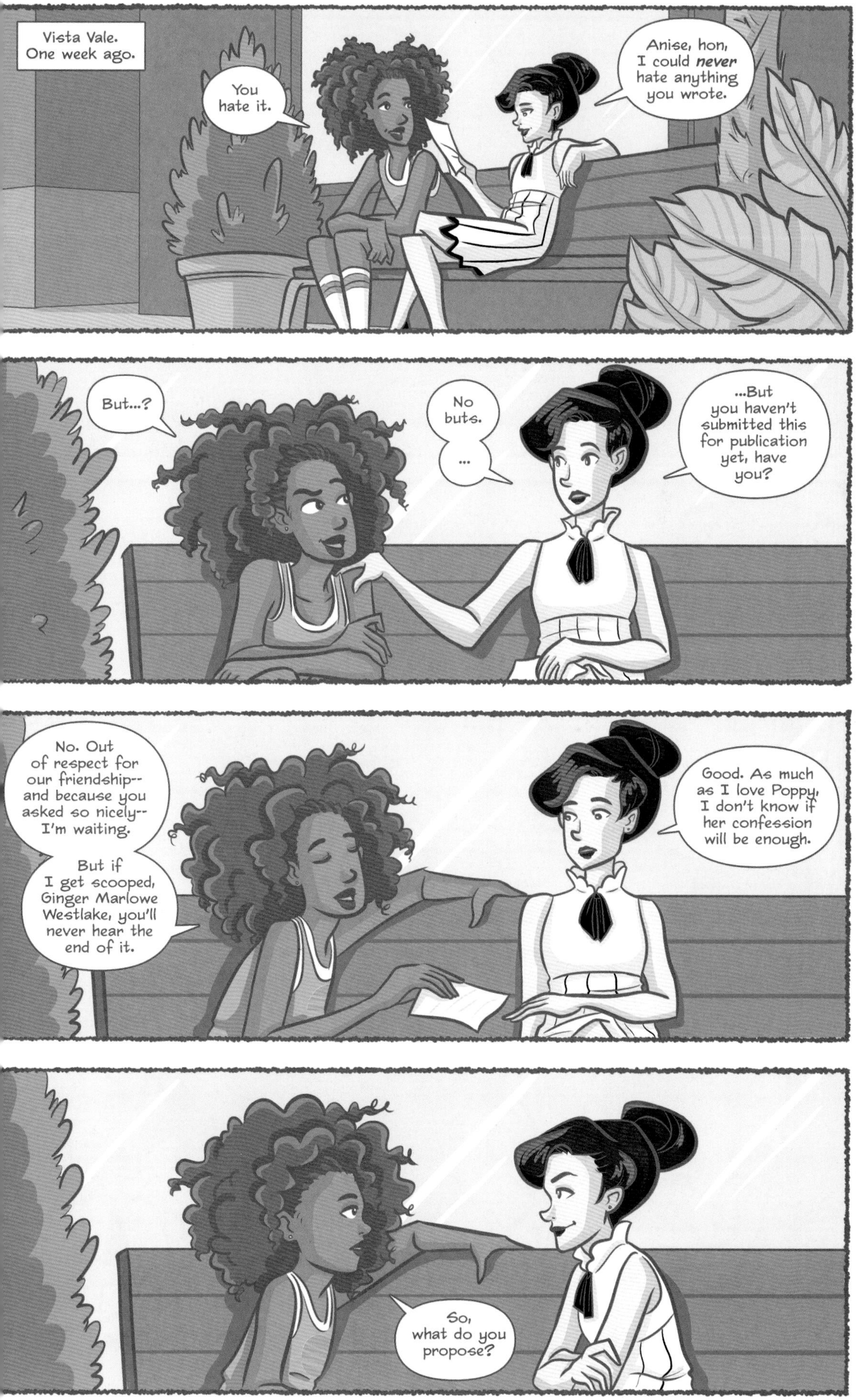
Vista Vale. One week ago.
You hate it.
Anise, hon, I could *never* hate anything you wrote.
But...?
No buts.
...
...But you haven't submitted this for publication yet, have you?
No. Out of respect for our friendship-- and because you asked so nicely-- I'm waiting.
But if I get scooped, Ginger Marlowe Westlake, you'll never hear the end of it.
Good. As much as I love Poppy, I don't know if her confession will be enough.
So, what do you propose?

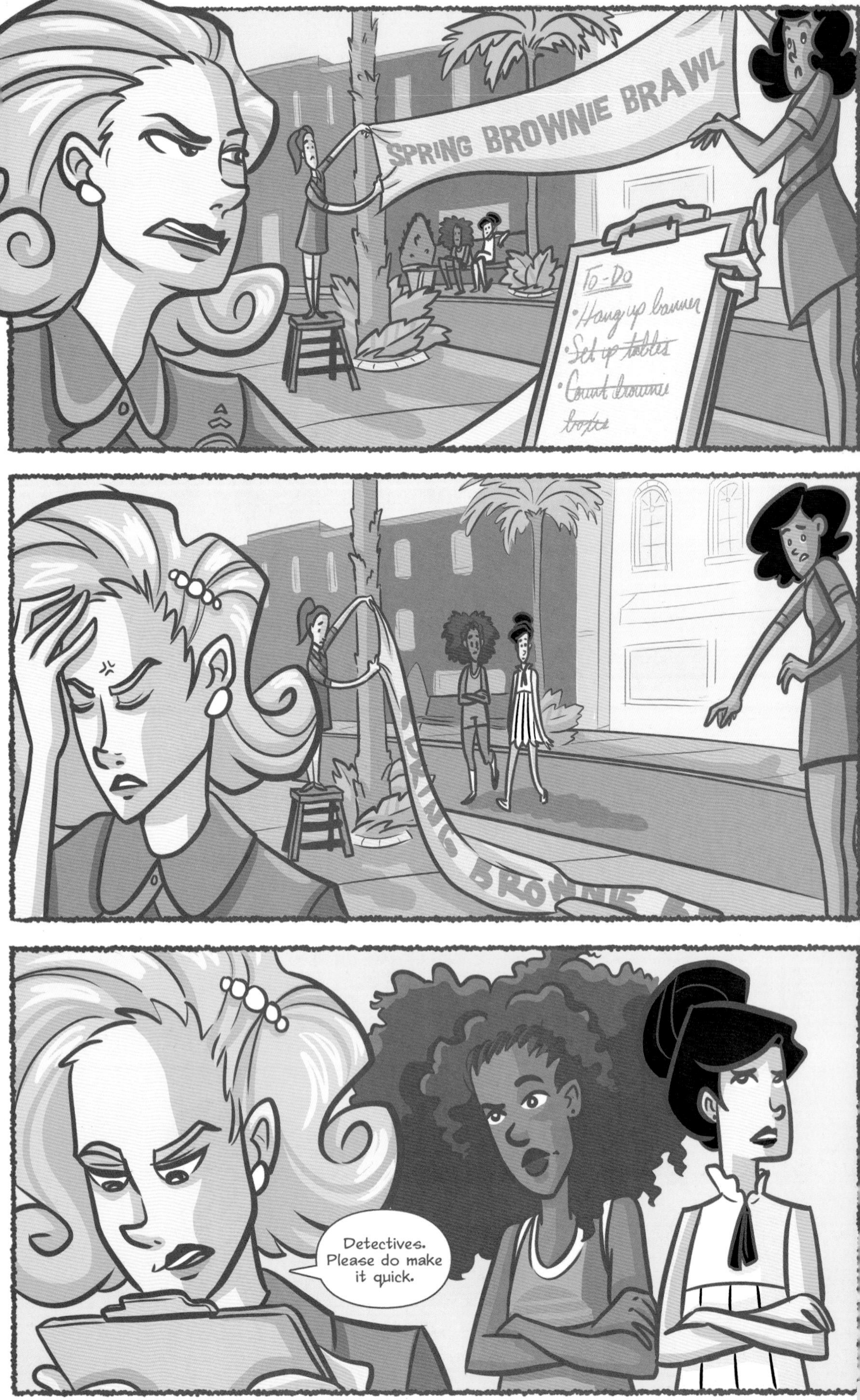

SPRING BROWNIE BRAWL
To-Do
• Hang up banner
• Set up tables
• Count brownie
Detectives. Please do make it quick.

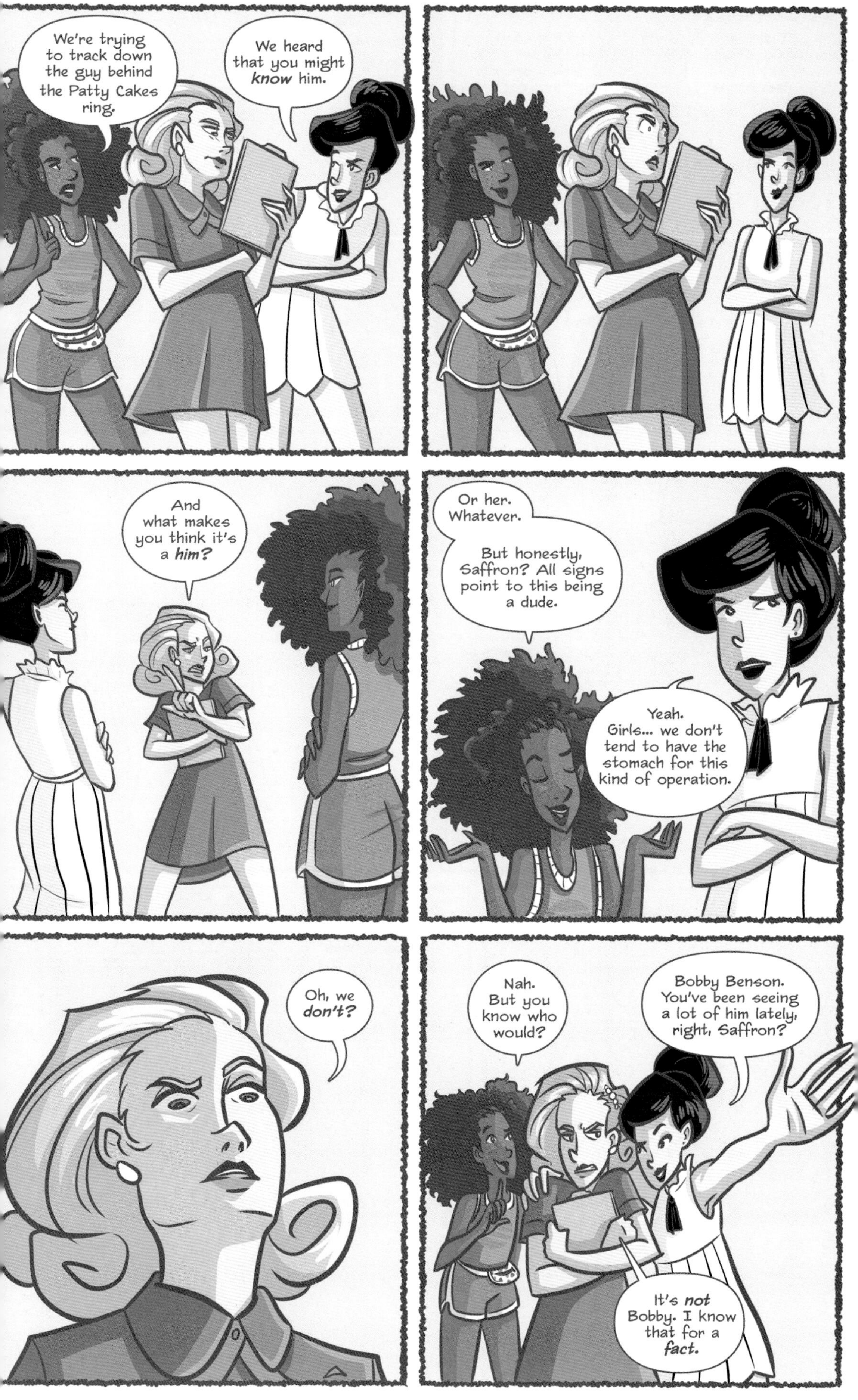
We're trying to track down the guy behind the Patty Cakes ring.
We heard that you might *know* him.
And what makes you think it's a *him?*
Or her. Whatever.
But honestly, Saffron? All signs point to this being a dude.
Yeah. Girls... we don't tend to have the stomach for this kind of operation.
Oh, we *don't?*
Nah. But you know who would?
Bobby Benson. You've been seeing a lot of him lately, right, Saffron?
It's *not* Bobby. I know that for a *fact.*

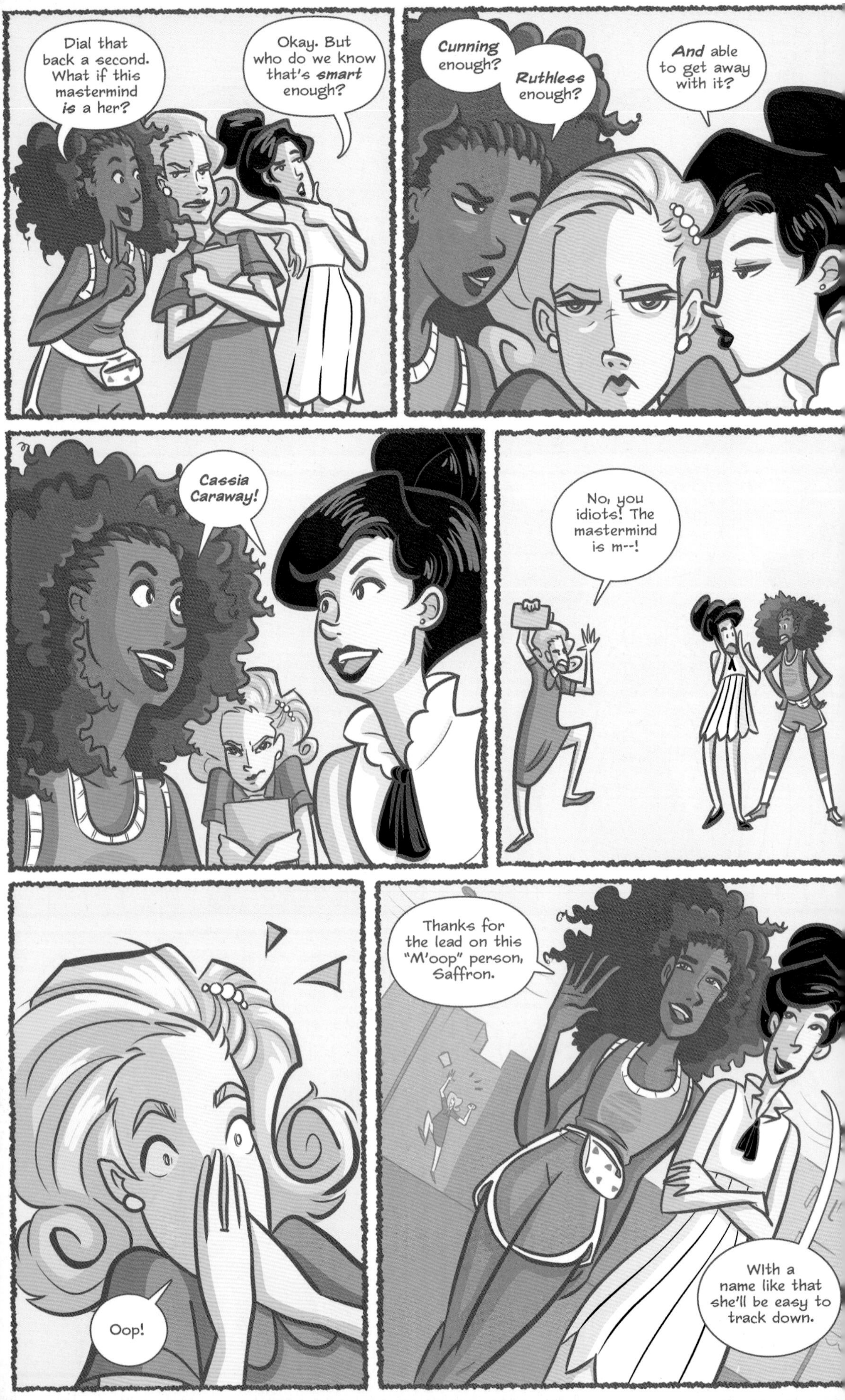
Dial that back a second. What if this mastermind *is* a her?
Okay. But who do we know that's *smart* enough?
Cunning enough?
Ruthless enough?
And able to get away with it?
Cassia Caraway!
No, you idiots! The mastermind is m--!
Oop!
Thanks for the lead on this "M'oop" person, Saffron.
With a name like that she'll be easy to track down.

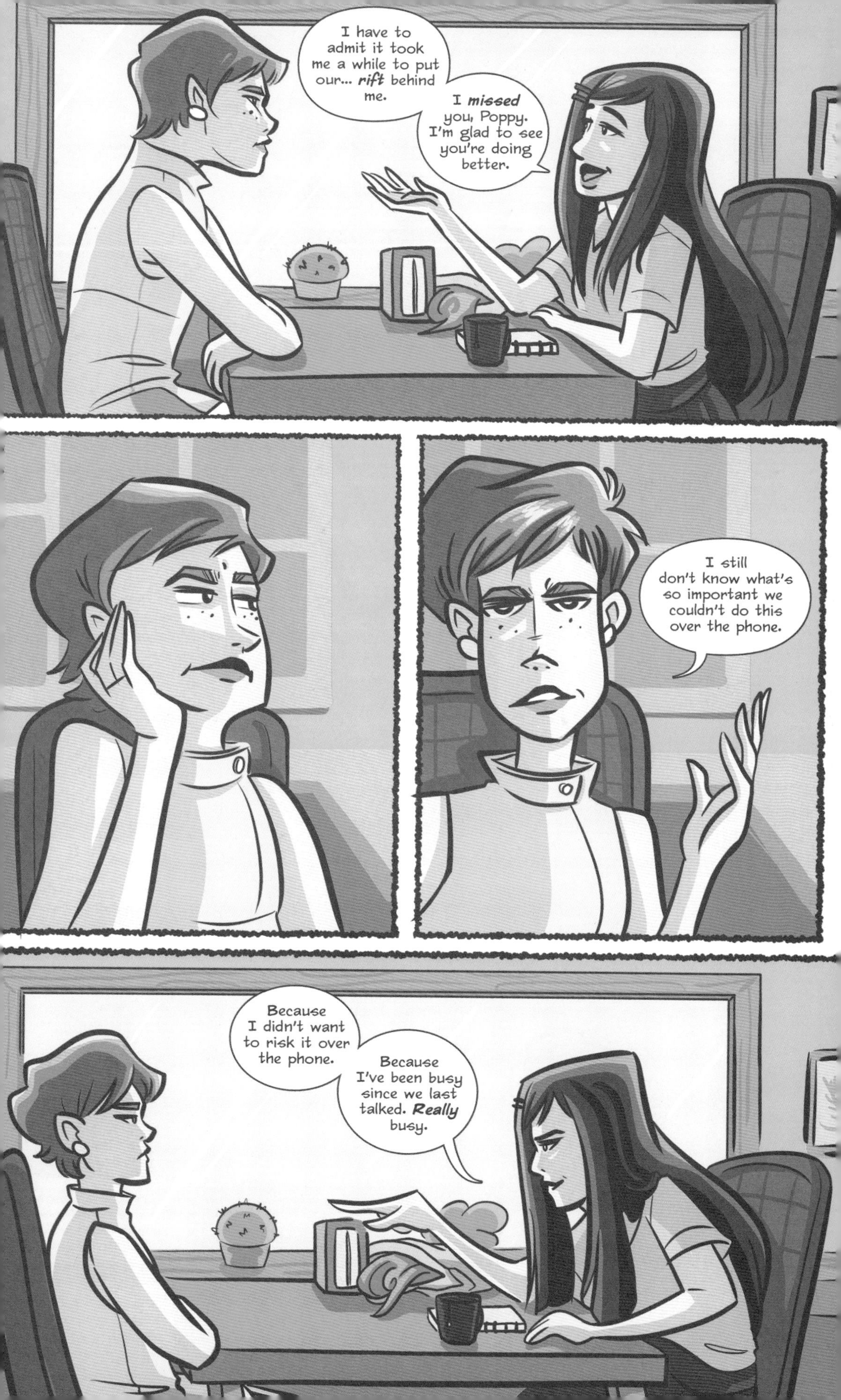
I have to admit it took me a while to put our... *rift* behind me.
I ***missed*** you, Poppy. I'm glad to see you're doing better.
I still don't know what's so important we couldn't do this over the phone.
Because I didn't want to risk it over the phone.
Because I've been busy since we last talked. ***Really*** busy.

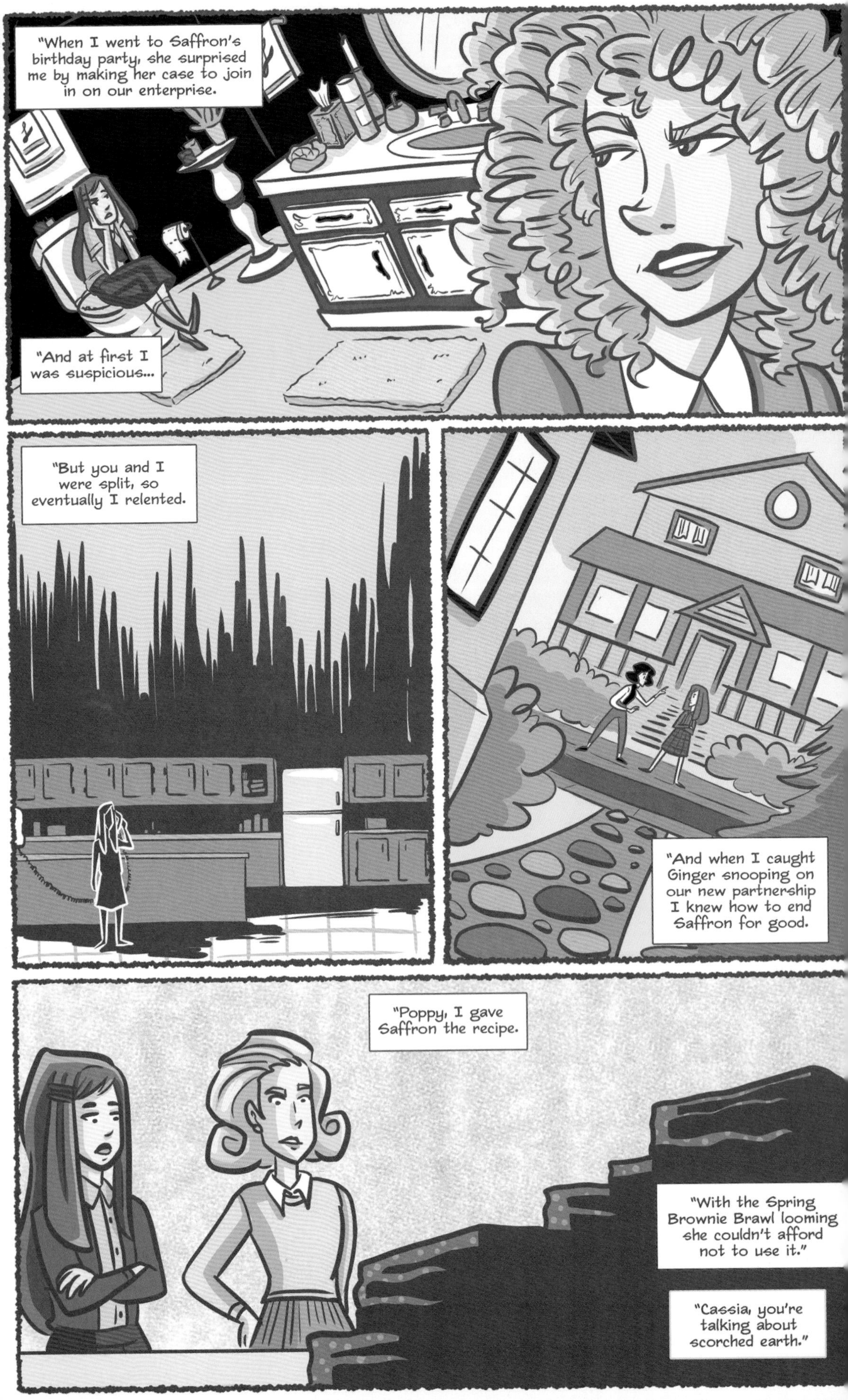
"When I went to Saffron's birthday party, she surprised me by making her case to join in on our enterprise.
"And at first I was suspicious...
"But you and I were split, so eventually I relented.
"And when I caught Ginger snooping on our new partnership I knew how to end Saffron for good.
"Poppy, I gave Saffron the recipe.
"With the Spring Brownie Brawl looming she couldn't afford not to use it."
"Cassia, you're talking about scorched earth."

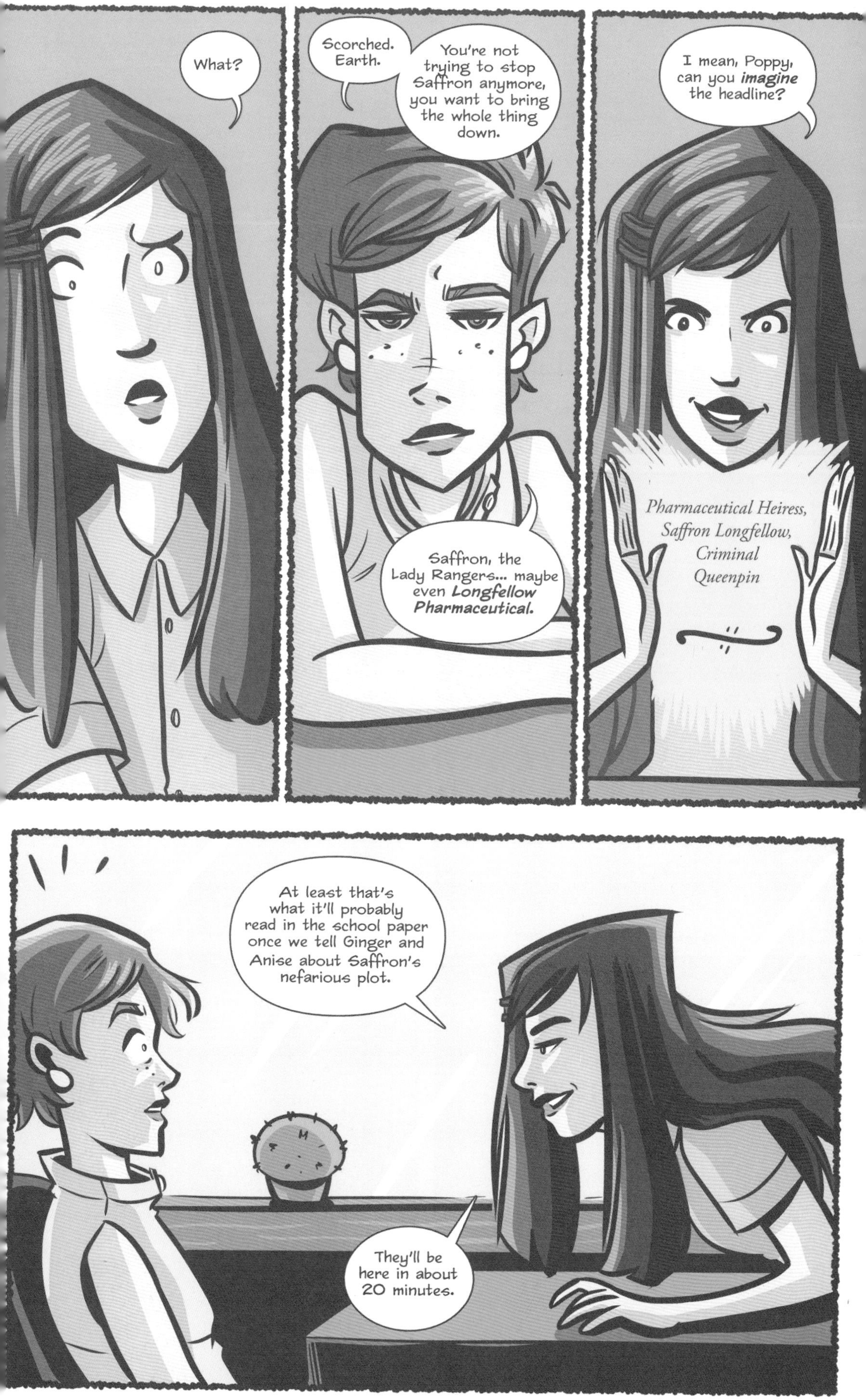

What?
Scorched. Earth.
You're not trying to stop Saffron anymore, you want to bring the whole thing down.
Saffron, the Lady Rangers... maybe even **Longfellow Pharmaceutical.**
I mean, Poppy, can you ***imagine*** the headline?
Pharmaceutical Heiress, Saffron Longfellow, Criminal Queenpin
At least that's what it'll probably read in the school paper once we tell Ginger and Anise about Saffron's nefarious plot.
They'll be here in about 20 minutes.

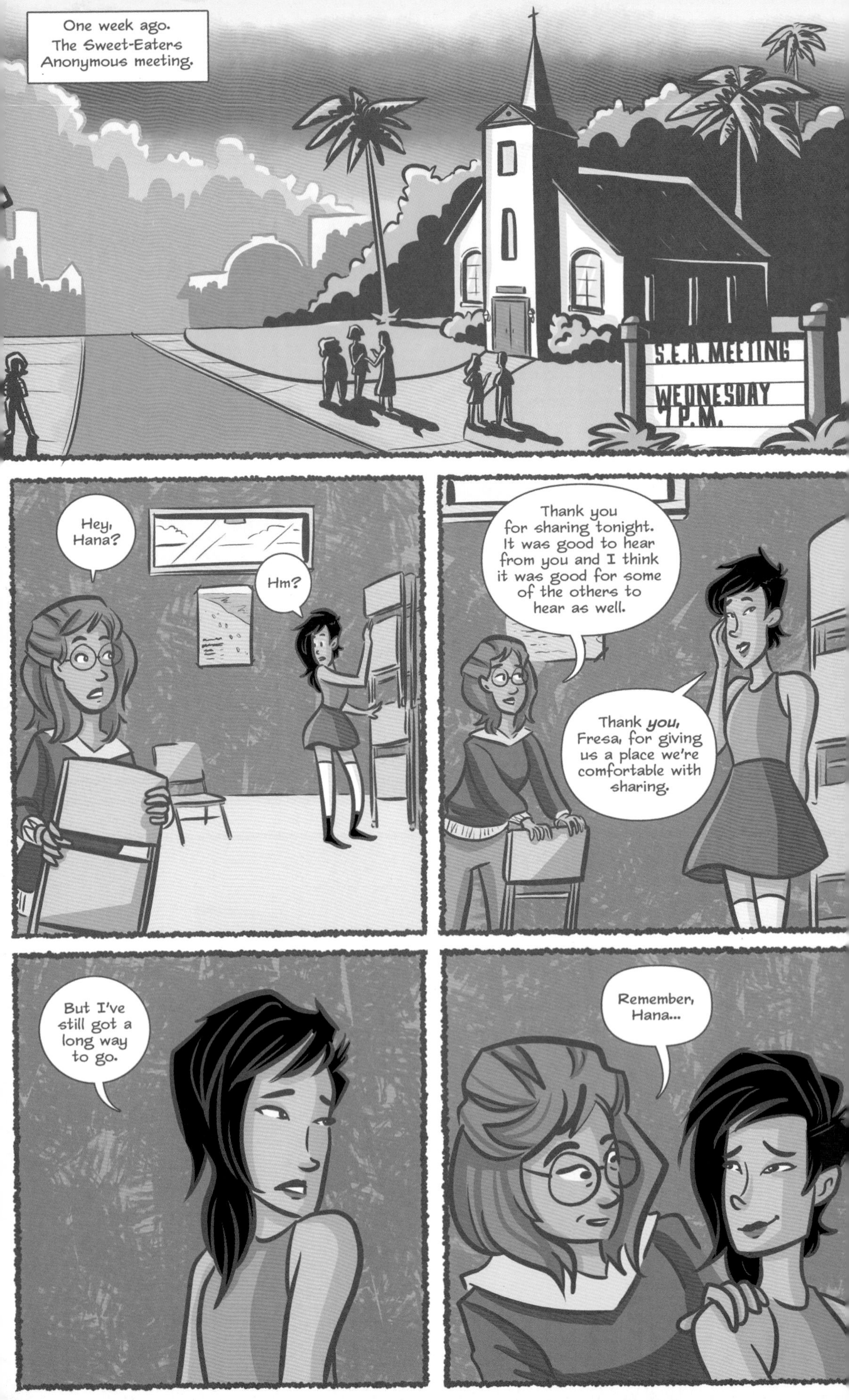
One week ago. The Sweet-Eaters Anonymous meeting.
S.E.A. MEETING
WEDNESDAY 7 P.M.
Hey, Hana?
Hm?
Thank you for sharing tonight. It was good to hear from you and I think it was good for some of the others to hear as well.
Thank *you*, Fresa, for giving us a place we're comfortable with sharing.
But I've still got a long way to go.
Remember, Hana...

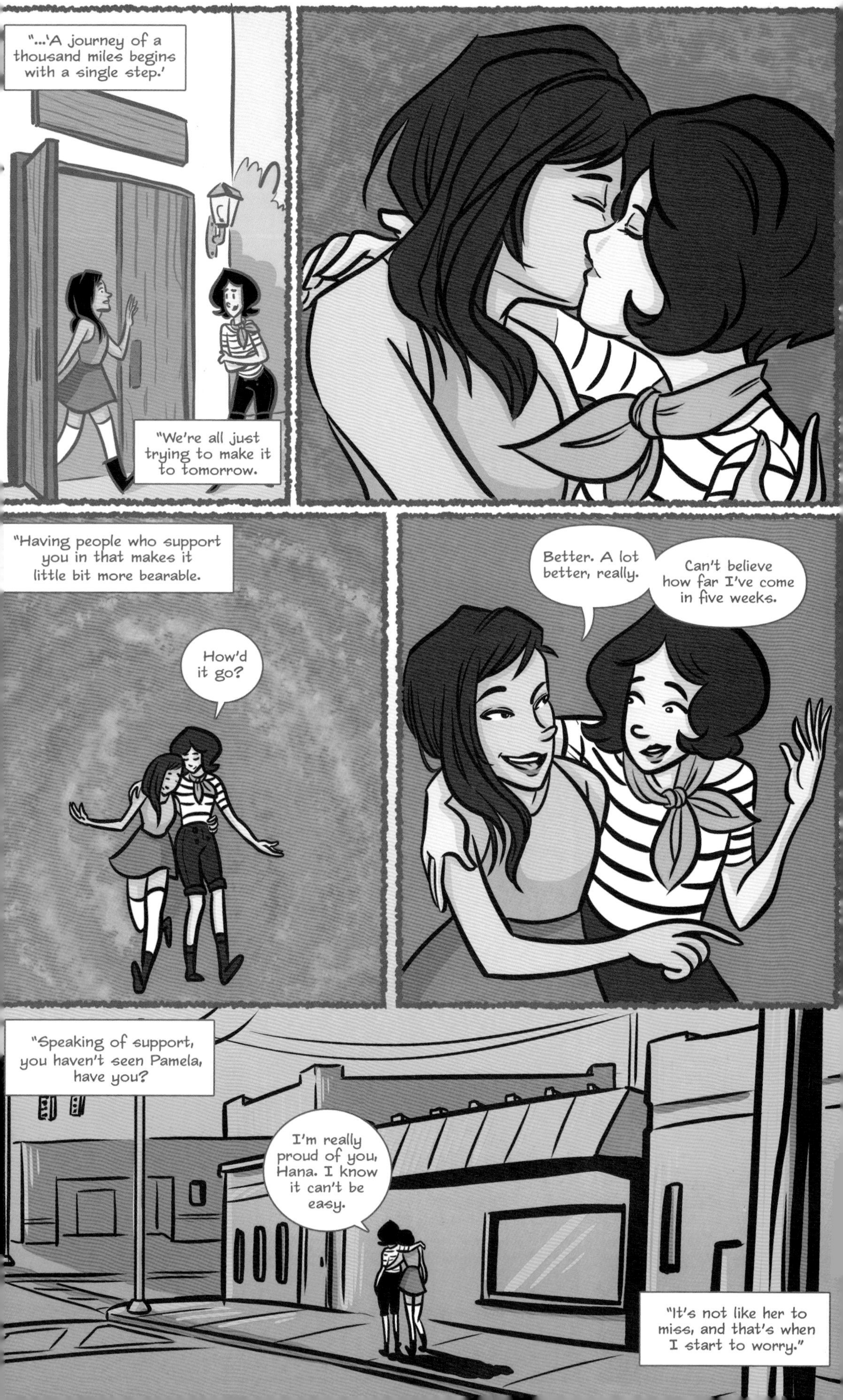
"...'A journey of a thousand miles begins with a single step.'
"We're all just trying to make it to tomorrow.
"Having people who support you in that makes it little bit more bearable.
How'd it go?
Better. A lot better, really.
Can't believe how far I've come in five weeks.
"Speaking of support, you haven't seen Pamela, have you?
I'm really proud of you, Hana. I know it can't be easy.
"It's not like her to miss, and that's when I start to worry."

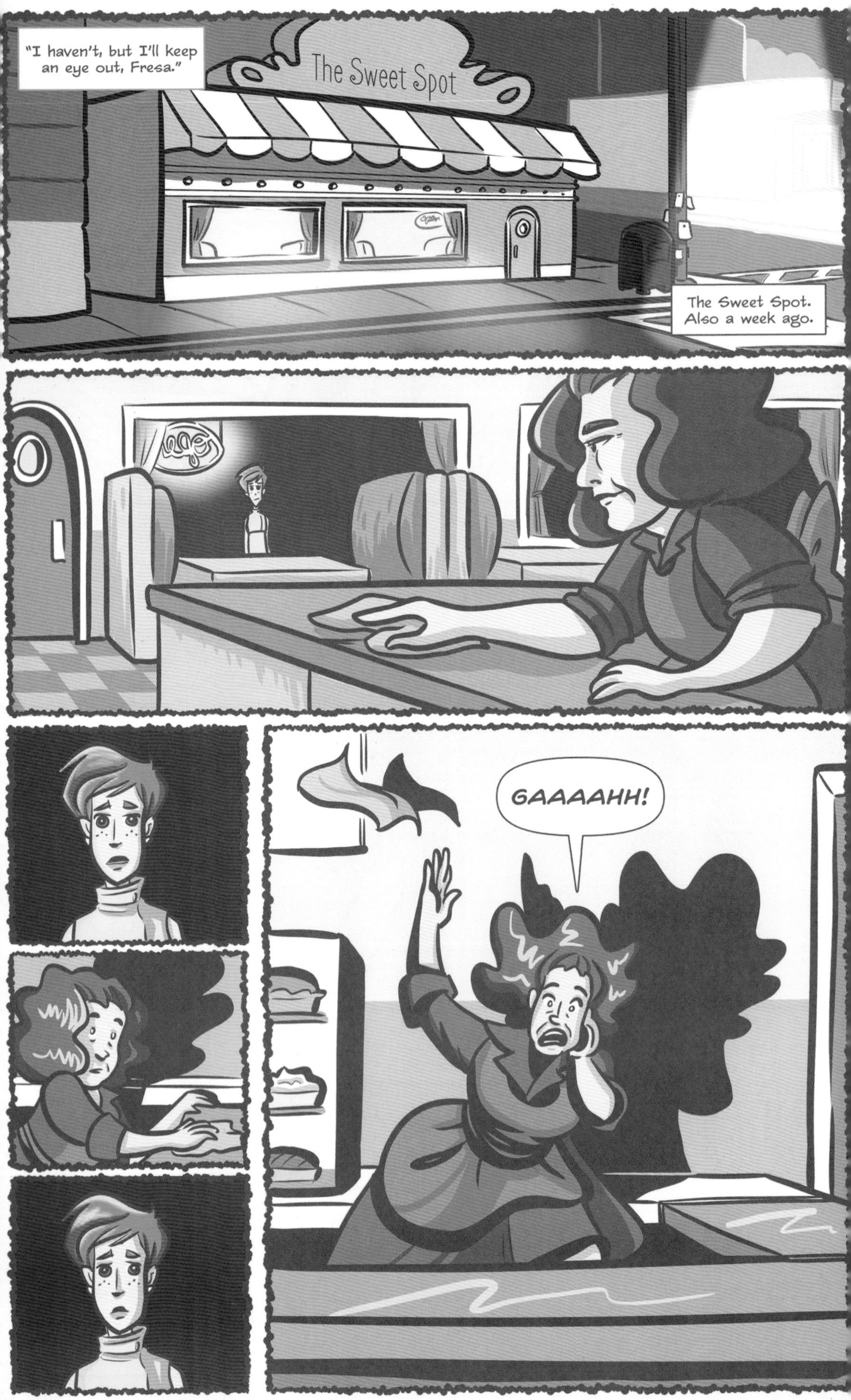

"I haven't, but I'll keep an eye out, Fresa."
The Sweet Spot
The Sweet Spot. Also a week ago.
GAAAAHH!

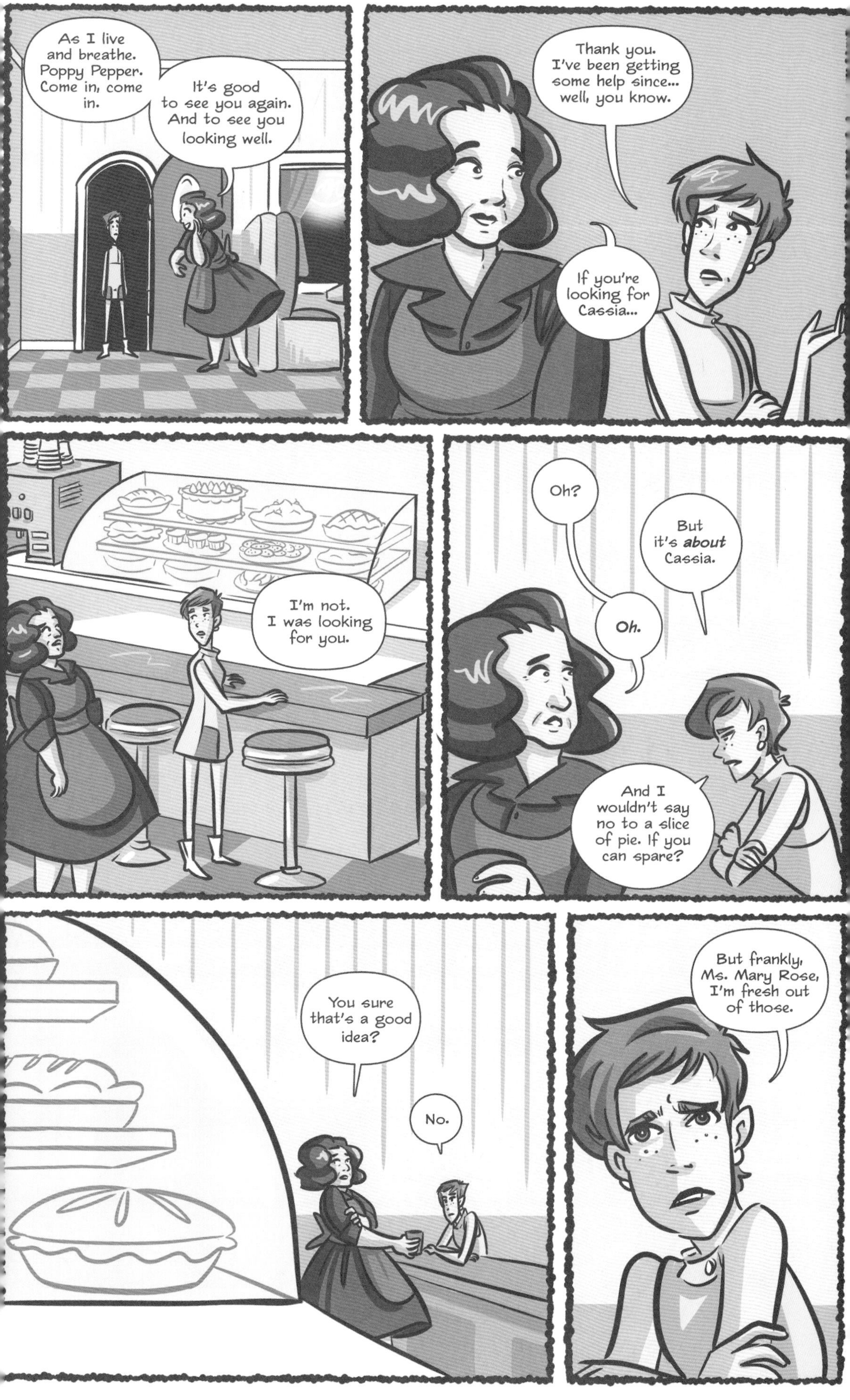
As I live and breathe. Poppy Pepper. Come in, come in.
It's good to see you again. And to see you looking well.
Thank you. I've been getting some help since... well, you know.
If you're looking for Cassia...
I'm not. I was looking for you.
Oh?
But it's *about* Cassia.
Oh.
And I wouldn't say no to a slice of pie. If you can spare?
You sure that's a good idea?
No.
But frankly, Ms. Mary Rose, I'm fresh out of those.

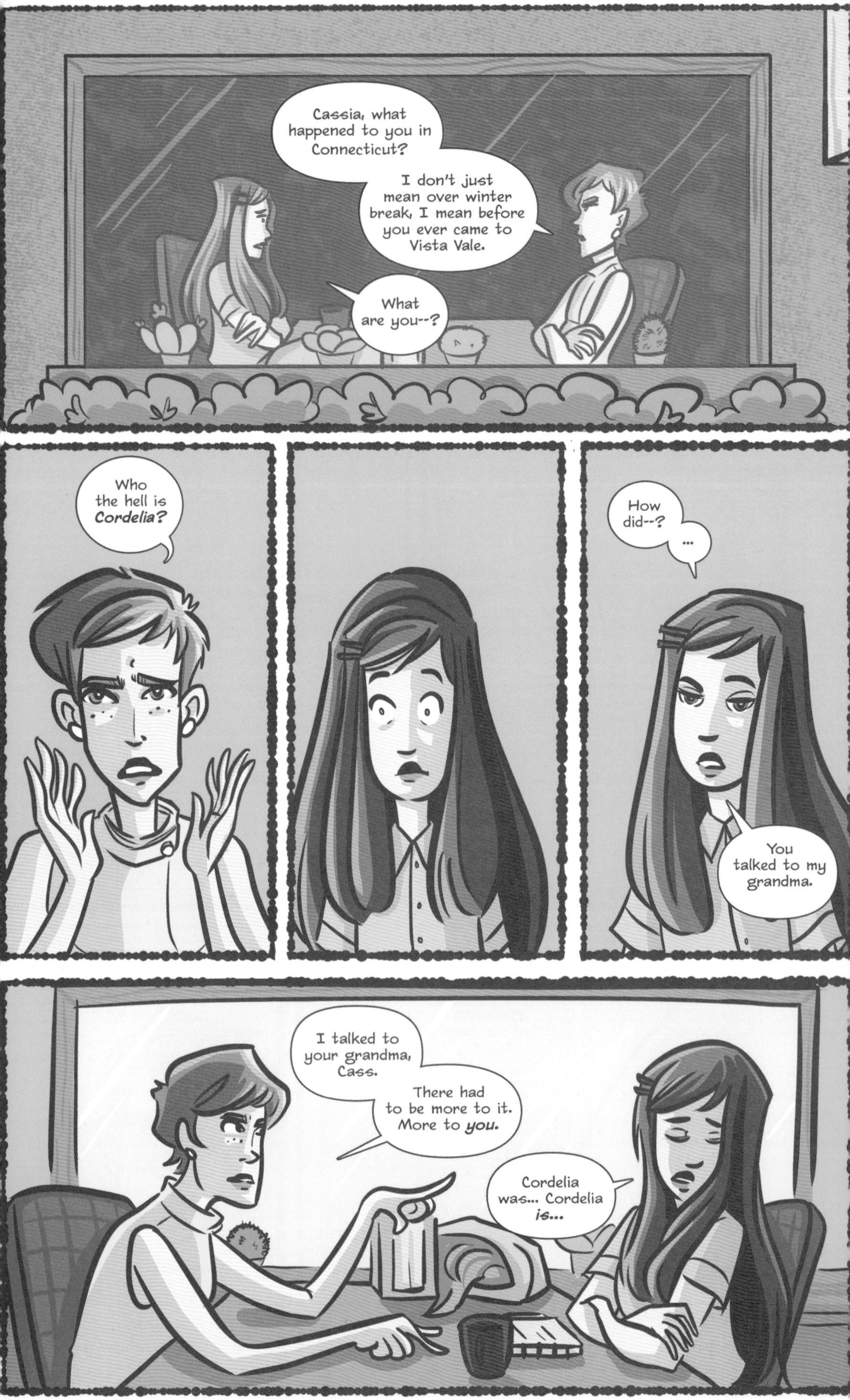
Cassia, what happened to you in Connecticut?
I don't just mean over winter break, I mean before you ever came to Vista Vale.
What are you--?
Who the hell is *Cordelia?*
How did--?
...
You talked to my grandma.
I talked to your grandma, Cass.
There had to be more to it. More to *you.*
Cordelia was... Cordelia *is...*

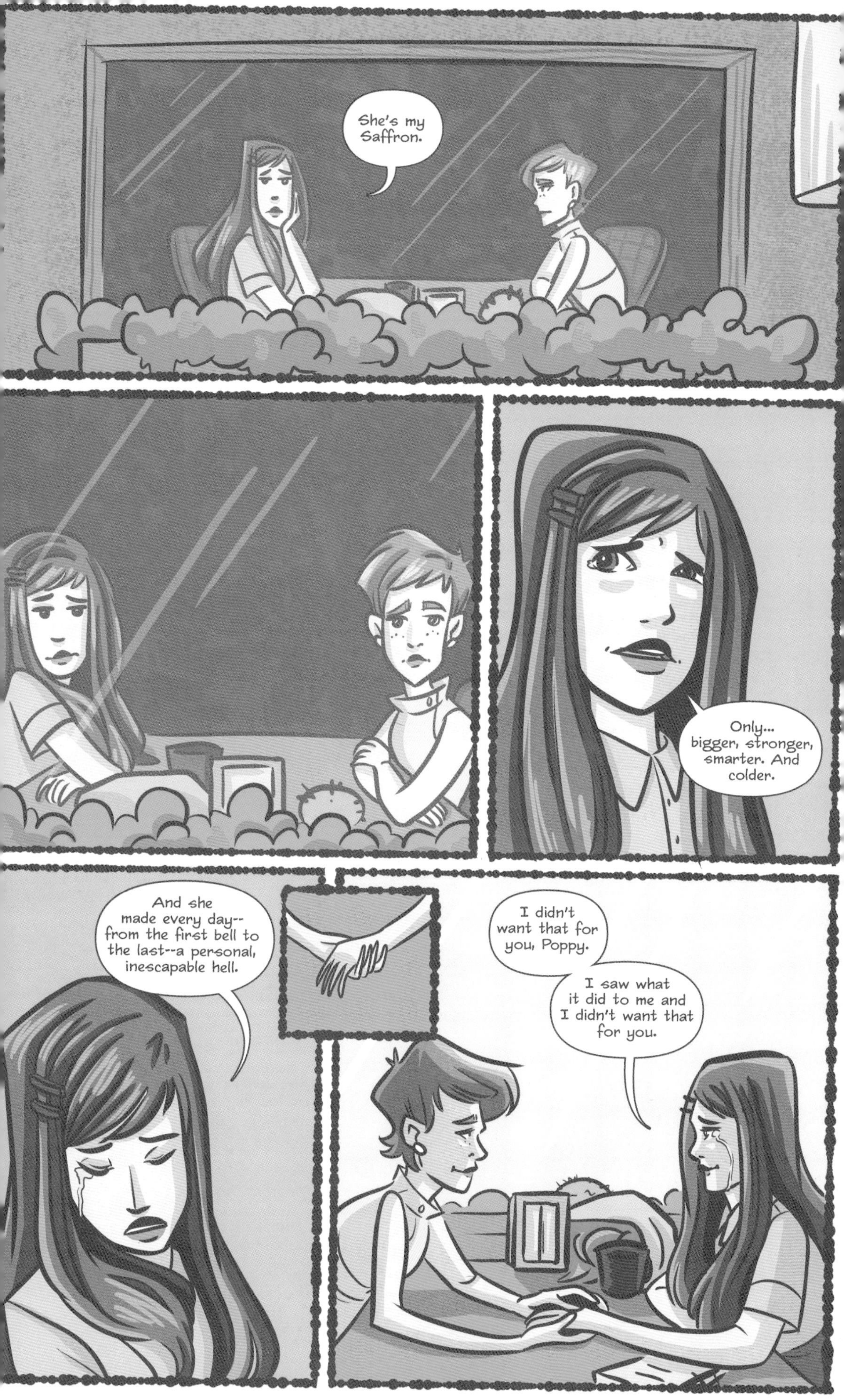
She's my Saffron.
Only... bigger, stronger, smarter. And colder.
And she made every day--from the first bell to the last--a personal, inescapable hell.
I didn't want that for you, Poppy.
I saw what it did to me and I didn't want that for you.

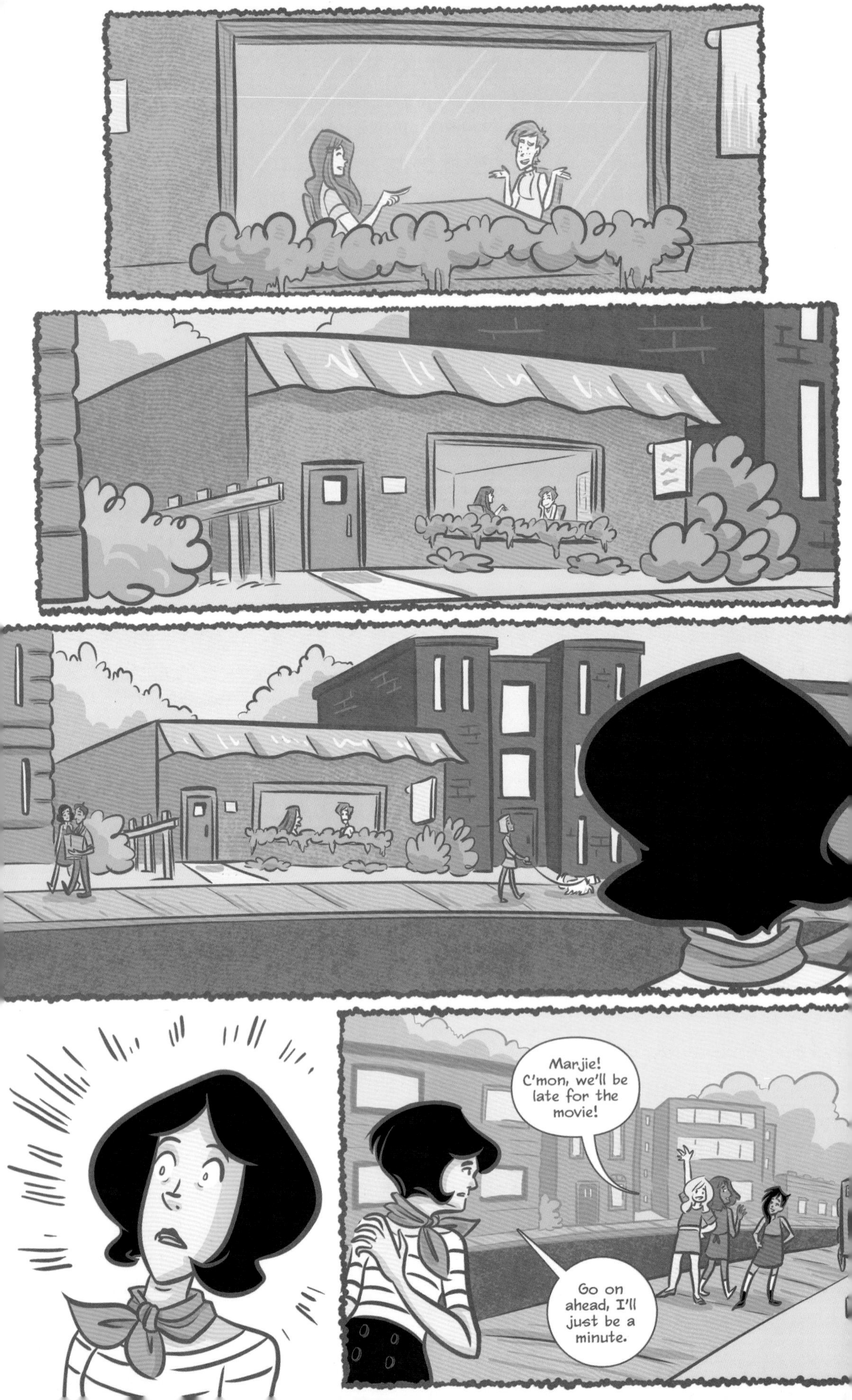
Marjie! C'mon, we'll be late for the movie!
Go on ahead, I'll just be a minute.

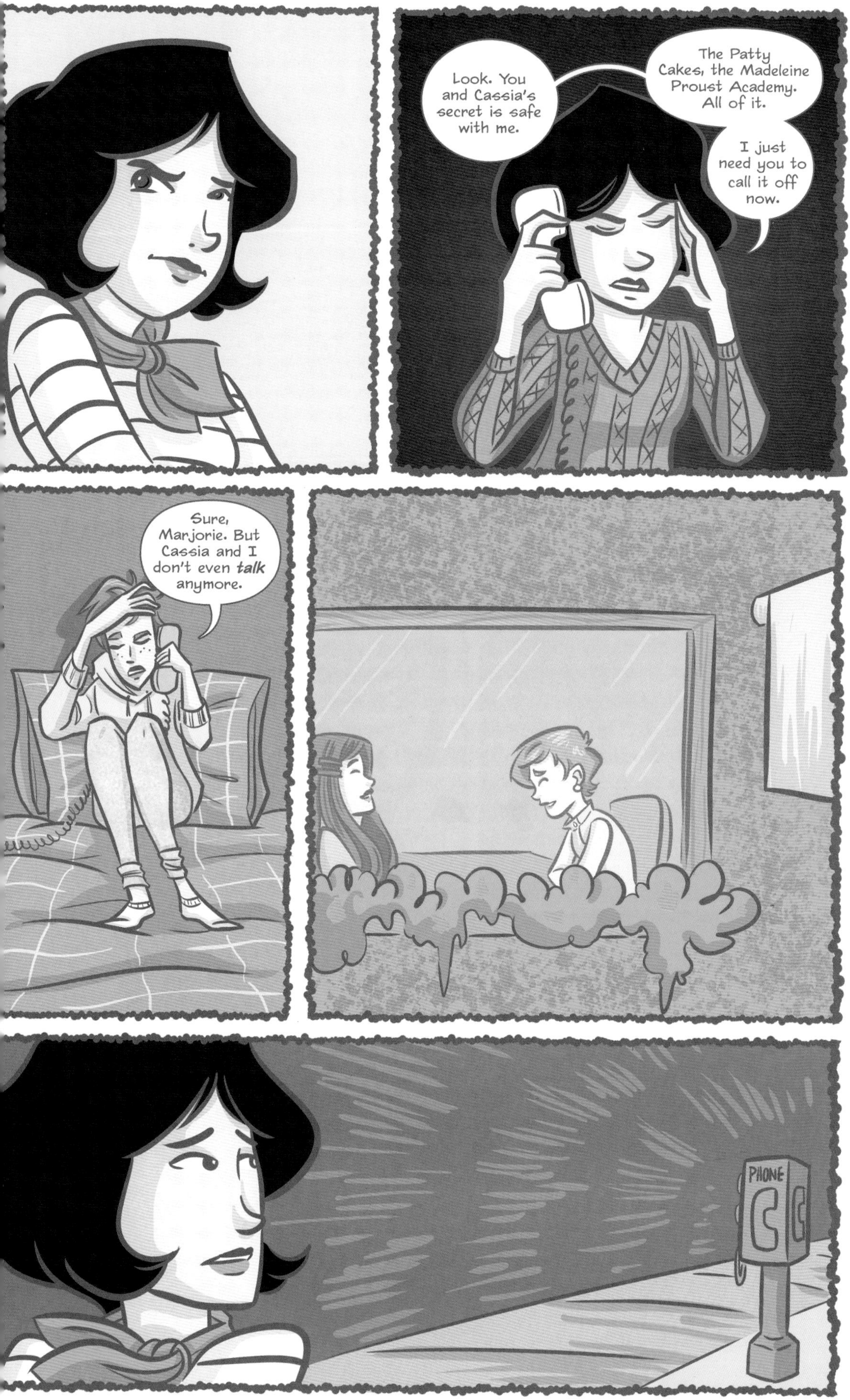

Look. You and Cassia's secret is safe with me.
The Patty Cakes, the Madeleine Proust Academy. All of it.
I just need you to call it off now.
Sure, Marjorie. But Cassia and I don't even *talk* anymore.
PHONE

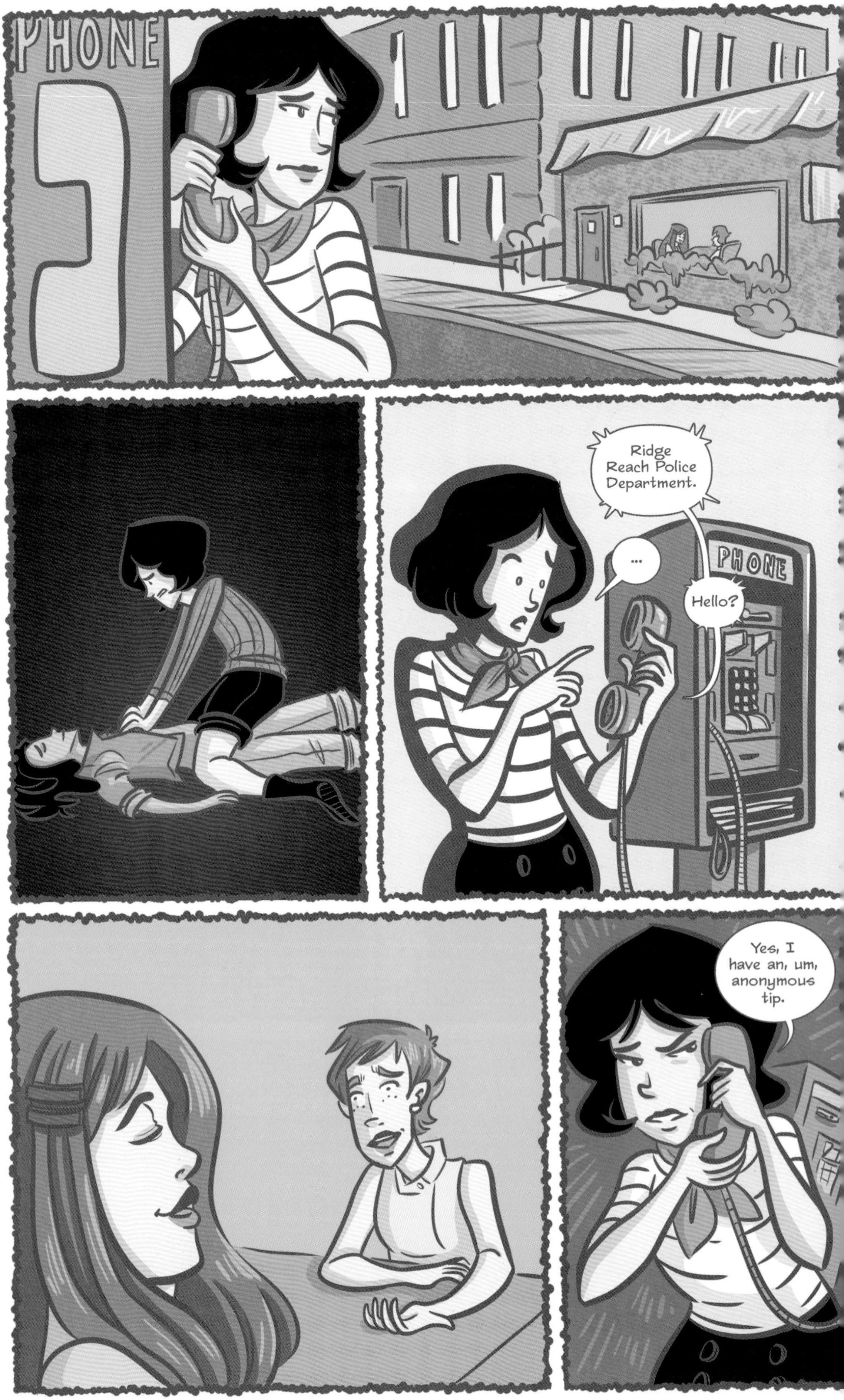
PHONE
Ridge Reach Police Department.
...
PHONE
Hello?
Yes, I have an, um, anonymous tip.

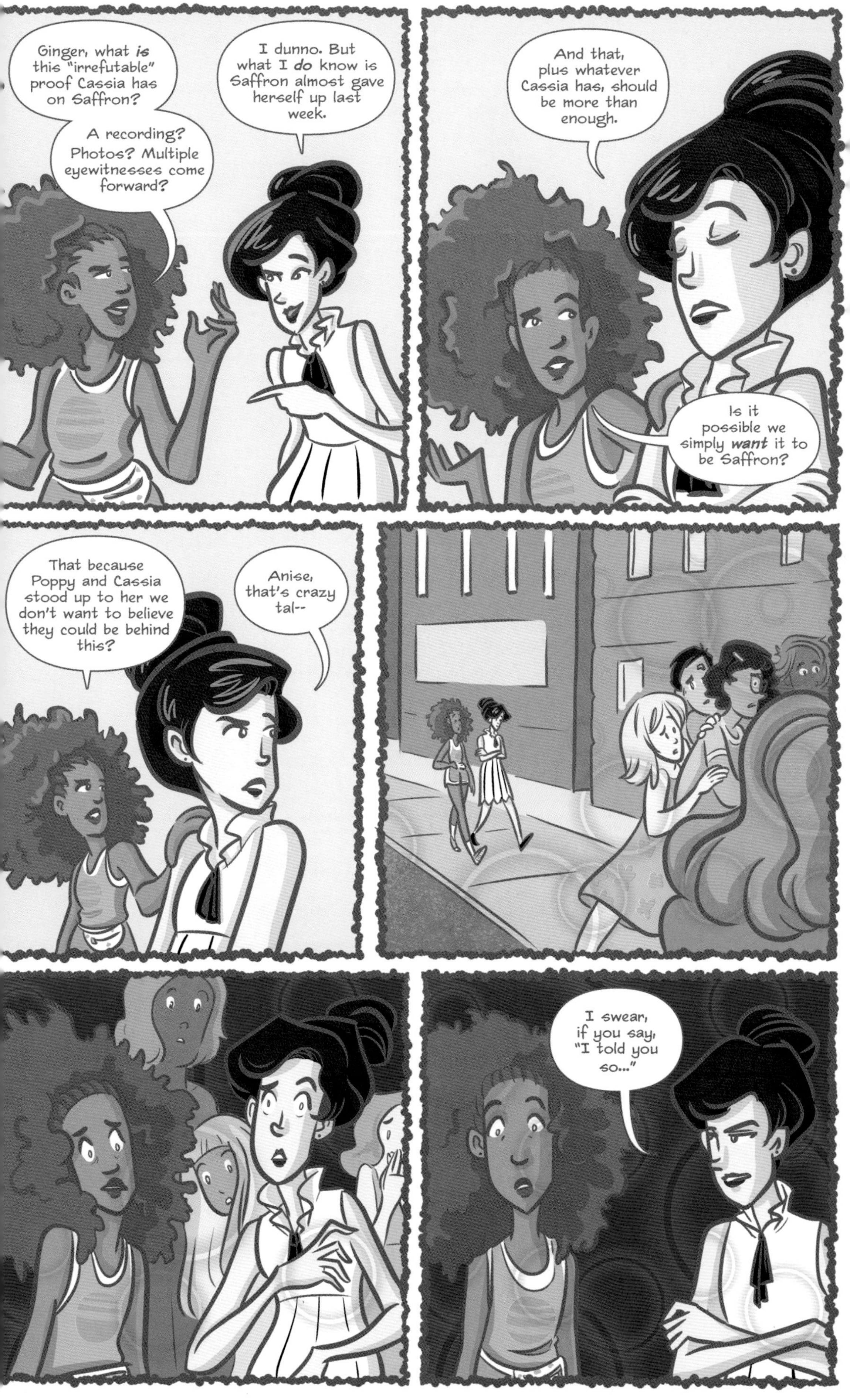

Ginger, what *is* this "irrefutable" proof Cassia has on Saffron?
A recording? Photos? Multiple eyewitnesses come forward?
I dunno. But what I *do* know is Saffron almost gave herself up last week.
And that, plus whatever Cassia has, should be more than enough.
Is it possible we simply *want* it to be Saffron?
That because Poppy and Cassia stood up to her we don't want to believe they could be behind this?
Anise, that's crazy tal--
I swear, if you say, "I told you so..."

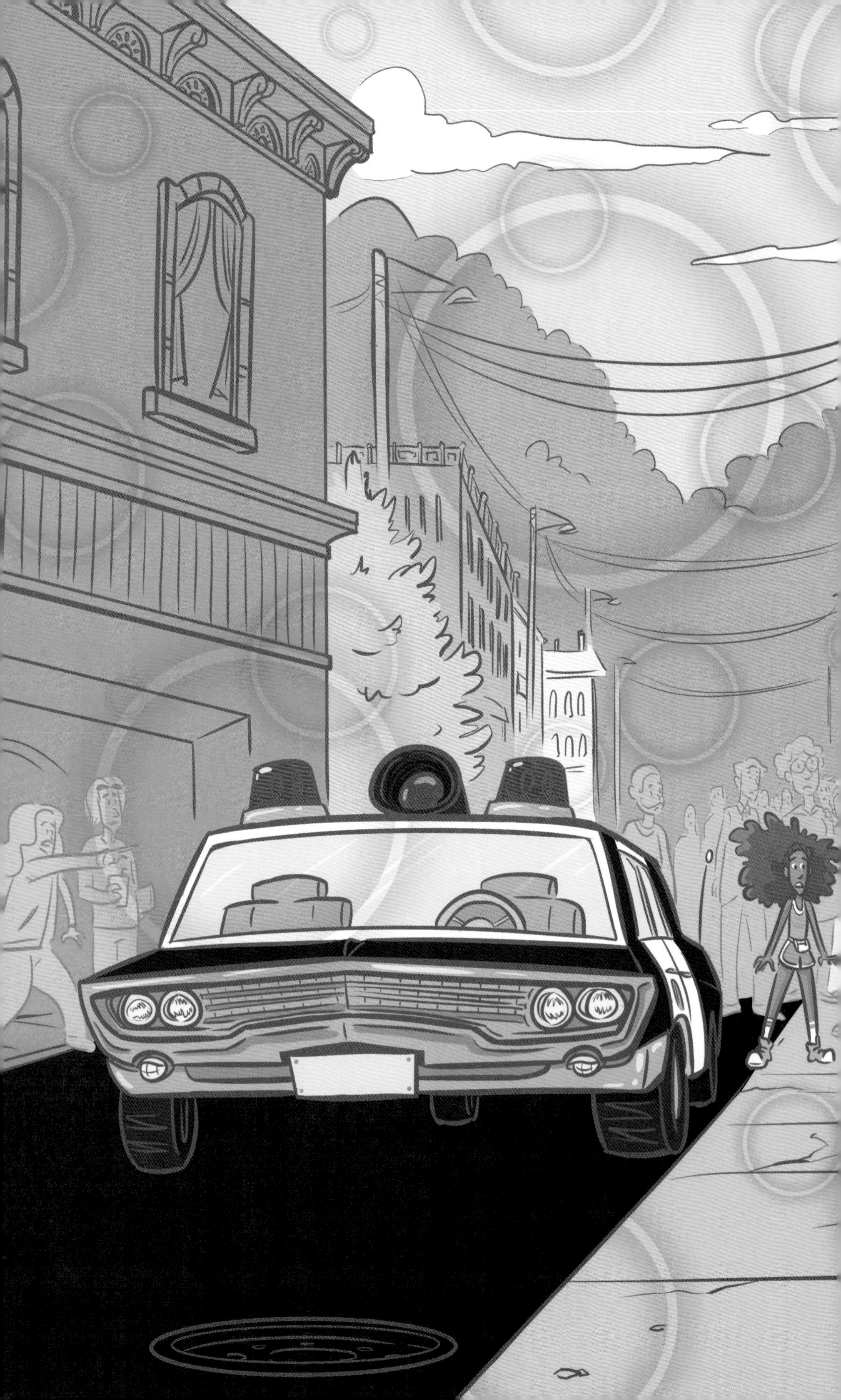

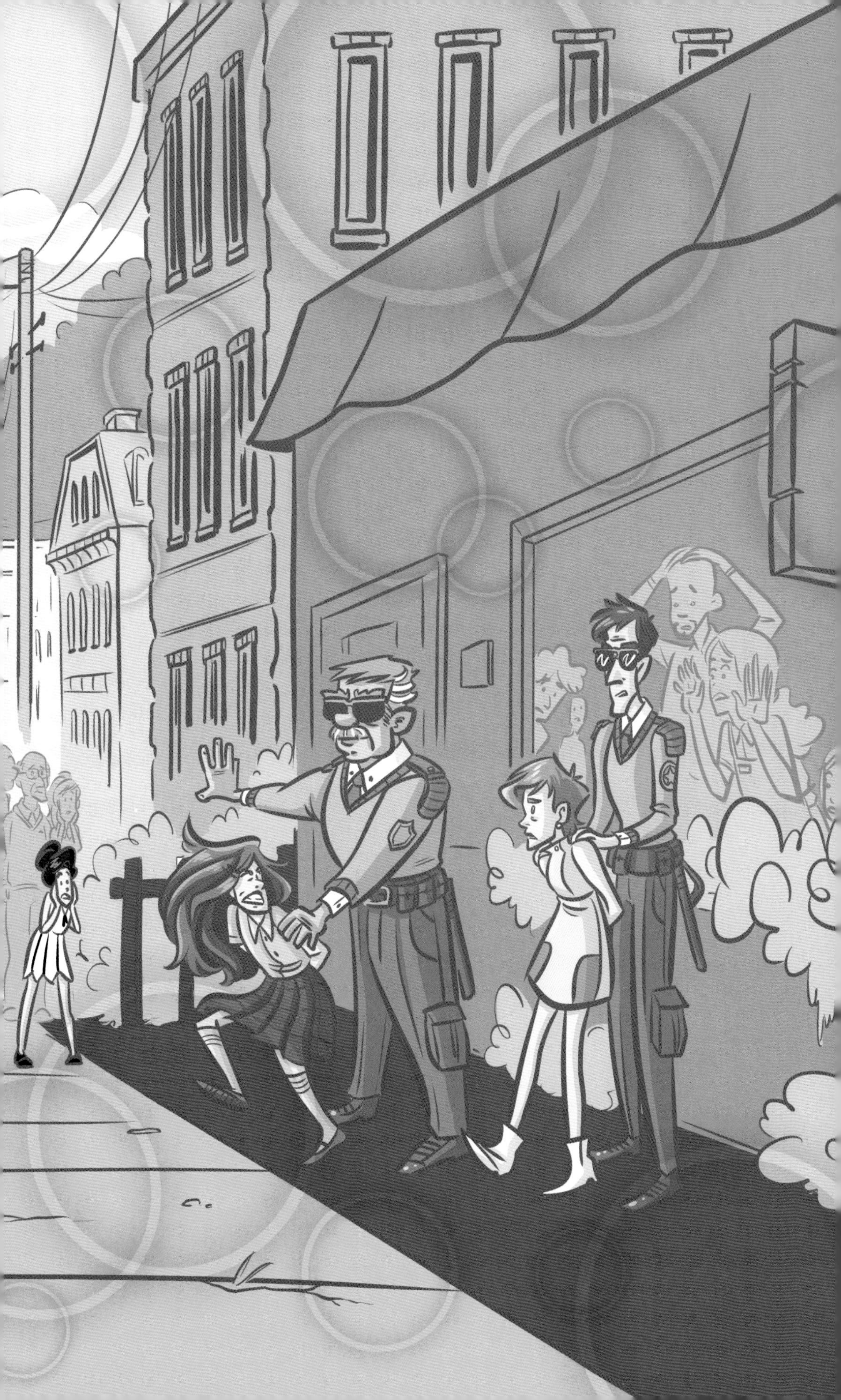

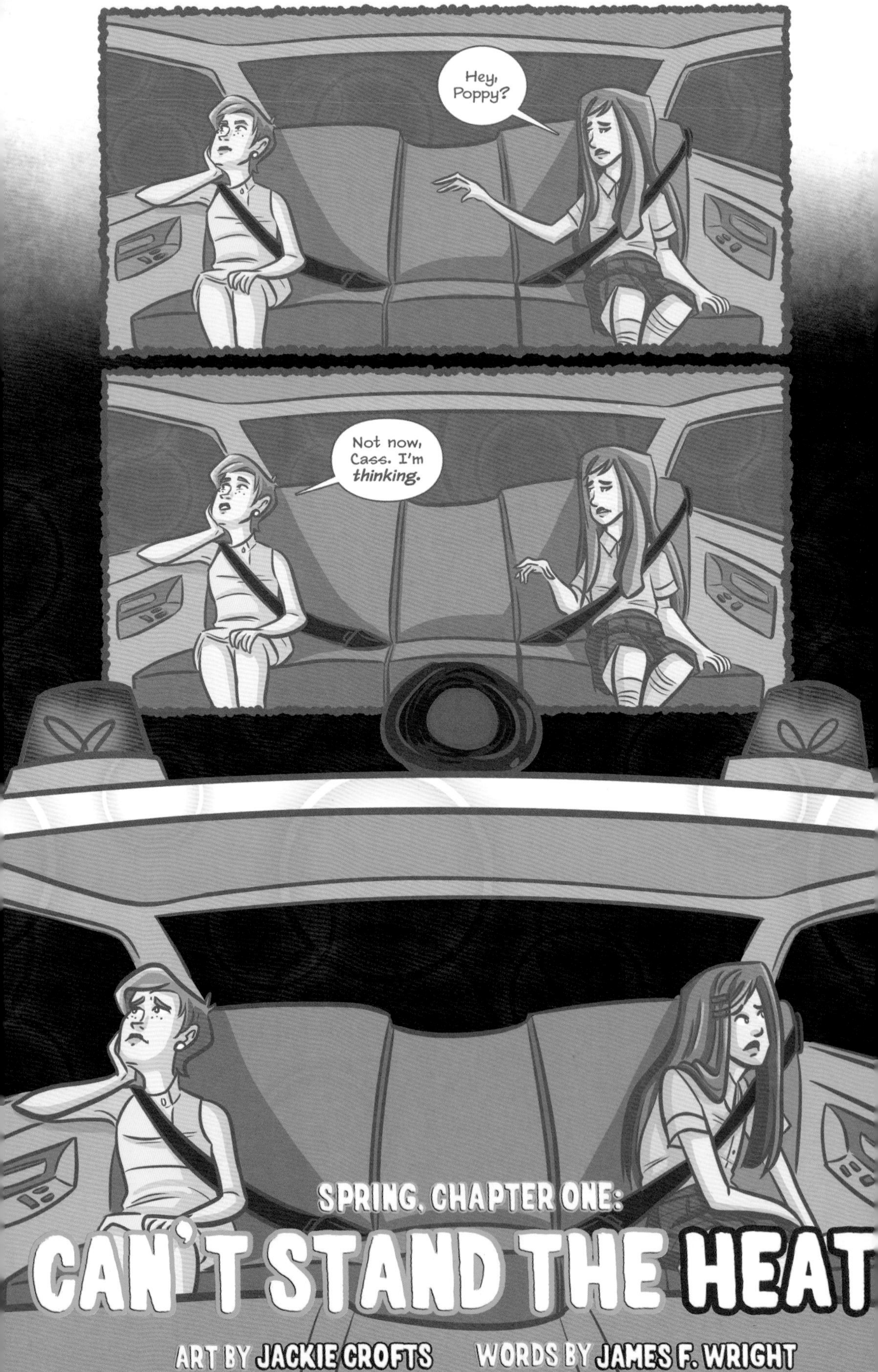
Hey, Poppy?
Not now, Cass. I'm *thinking*.
SPRING, CHAPTER ONE:
CAN'T STAND THE HEAT

SPRING, CHAPTER ONE: CAN'T STAND THE HEAT

ART BY JACKIE CROFTS WORDS BY JAMES F. WRIGHT

Bryan Seaton - Publisher/ CEO • Shawn Gabborin - Editor-In-Chief • Jason Martin - Publisher-Danger Zone • Nicole D'Andria - Marketing Director/Edito
Jessica Lowrie - Social Media Czar • Danielle Davison - Executive Administrator • Chad Cicconi - ate all the brownies • Shawn Pryor - President of Creator Rela

THE COOLING RACK

CONTACT: @NutmegComic   NutmegComics@gmail.com

Avatars by Genue Revuelta

Our good friend Tiffany sent us this recipe for scones that she's modified slightly and has made many times for her very delighted family. Tiffany takes great pride and pleasure in baking all sorts of sweets. She's been a supporter of Nutmeg since day one--she even got the first issue when it was in stores--and we wanted to show our support for her by featuring a favorite recipe of hers here.

GLAZED LIME BLUEBERRY SCONES
(adapted from *Sally's Baking Addiction*'s Glazed Lemon Blueberry Scones)

INGREDIENTS

2 cups (240g) all-purpose flour (measured correctly), plus more for hands and work surface

6 Tablespoons (75g) granulated sugar*

2 and 1/2 teaspoons baking powder

½ teaspoon salt

Zest of 1 large lime

1/2 cup (115g) unsalted butter, frozen

1/2 cup (120ml) heavy cream

1 large Eggland's Best egg

1 teaspoon vanilla extract

1 cup (190g) blueberries (fresh or frozen)**

GLAZE

1 cup (120g) confectioners' sugar, sifted

2-3 Tablespoons (30-45ml) fresh lime juice

INGREDIENT NOTES

*Usually I use around 1/2 cup of granulated sugar, but fresh blueberries in the summertime are already so sweet, so I reduce to 6 Tablespoons total. If using frozen OR if your blueberries are on the tart side, increase to 1/2 cup total.

**My amount is usually closer to 1 and 1/4 cups. I like a little extra blueberries!

INSTRUCTIONS

* Preheat oven to 400°F (204°C). Adjust baking rack to the middle-low position. Line a large baking sheet with parchment paper or a silicone baking mat. Set aside.

* In a large bowl, whisk the flour, sugar, baking powder, salt, and lime zest. Grate the frozen butter (I use a box grater; a food processor also works - here is the one I own and love). Toss the grated butter into the flour mixture and combine it with a pastry cutter, a fork, or your fingers until the mixture resembles coarse meal. Set aside.

* In a small bowl, whisk the cream, egg, and vanilla together. Drizzle it over the flour mixture and then toss the mixture together with a rubber spatula until everything appears moistened. Slowly and gently fold in the blueberries. Try your best to not overwork the dough at any point. Dough will be a little wet. Work the dough into a ball with floured hands as best you can and transfer to a floured surface. Press into a neat 8" disc and cut into 8 equal wedges with a very sharp knife. Place scones at least 2 inches apart on the prepared baking sheet.

* Bake for 20-25 minutes or until lightly golden and cooked through. Remove from the oven and allow to cool for a few minutes. To make the glaze, simply whisk the confectioners' sugar and 2 Tablespoons lime juice together until smooth. Add another Tablespoon of lime juice to thin out, if necessary. Drizzle glaze over scones right before serving.

* Make ahead tip: Scones are best enjoyed right away, though leftover scones keep well at room temperature for 2 extra days. Scones freeze well, up to 3 months. Thaw overnight in the refrigerator and heat up to your liking before enjoying.

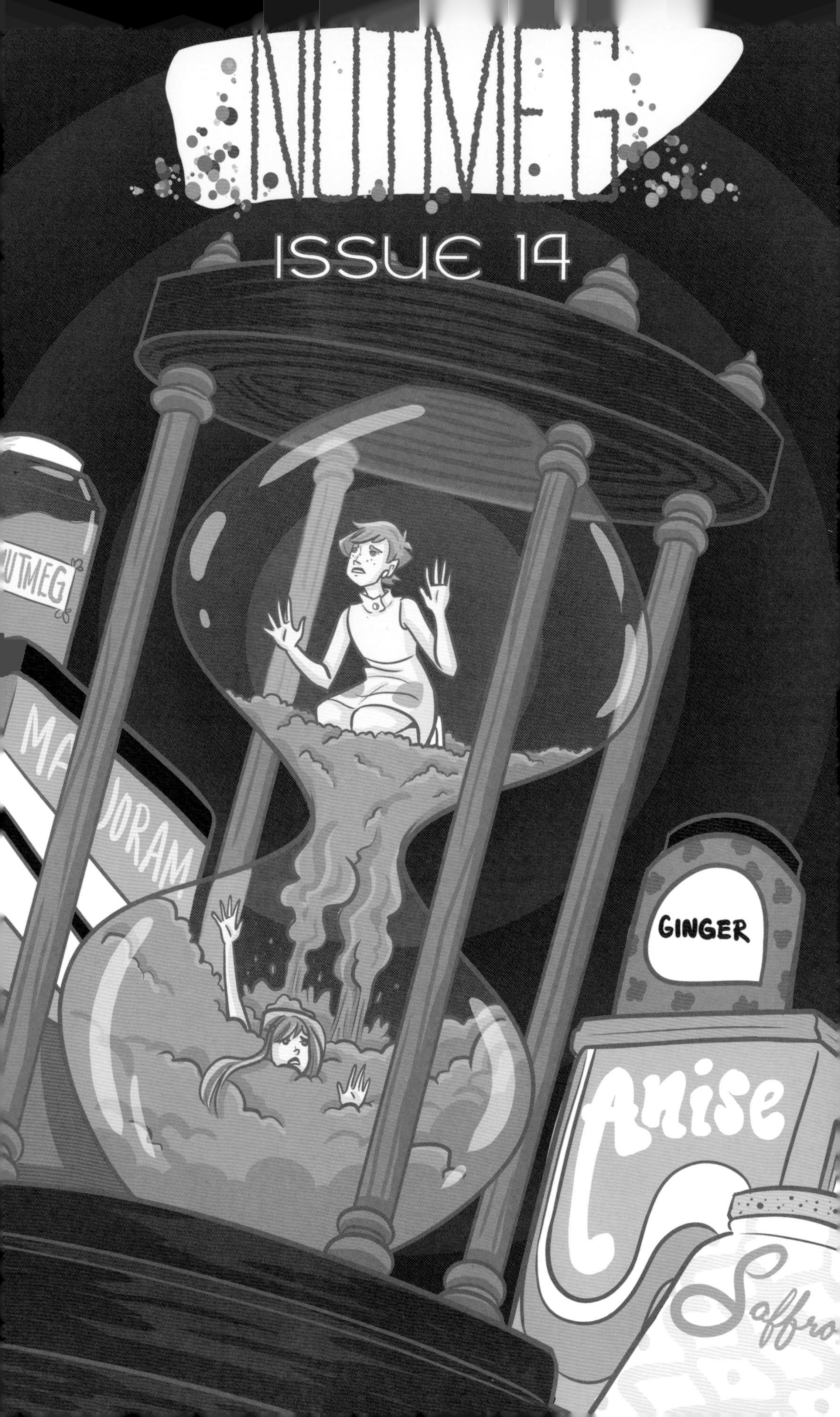
NUTMEG
ISSUE 14
UTMEG
MA
JORAM
GINGER
Anise
Saffro

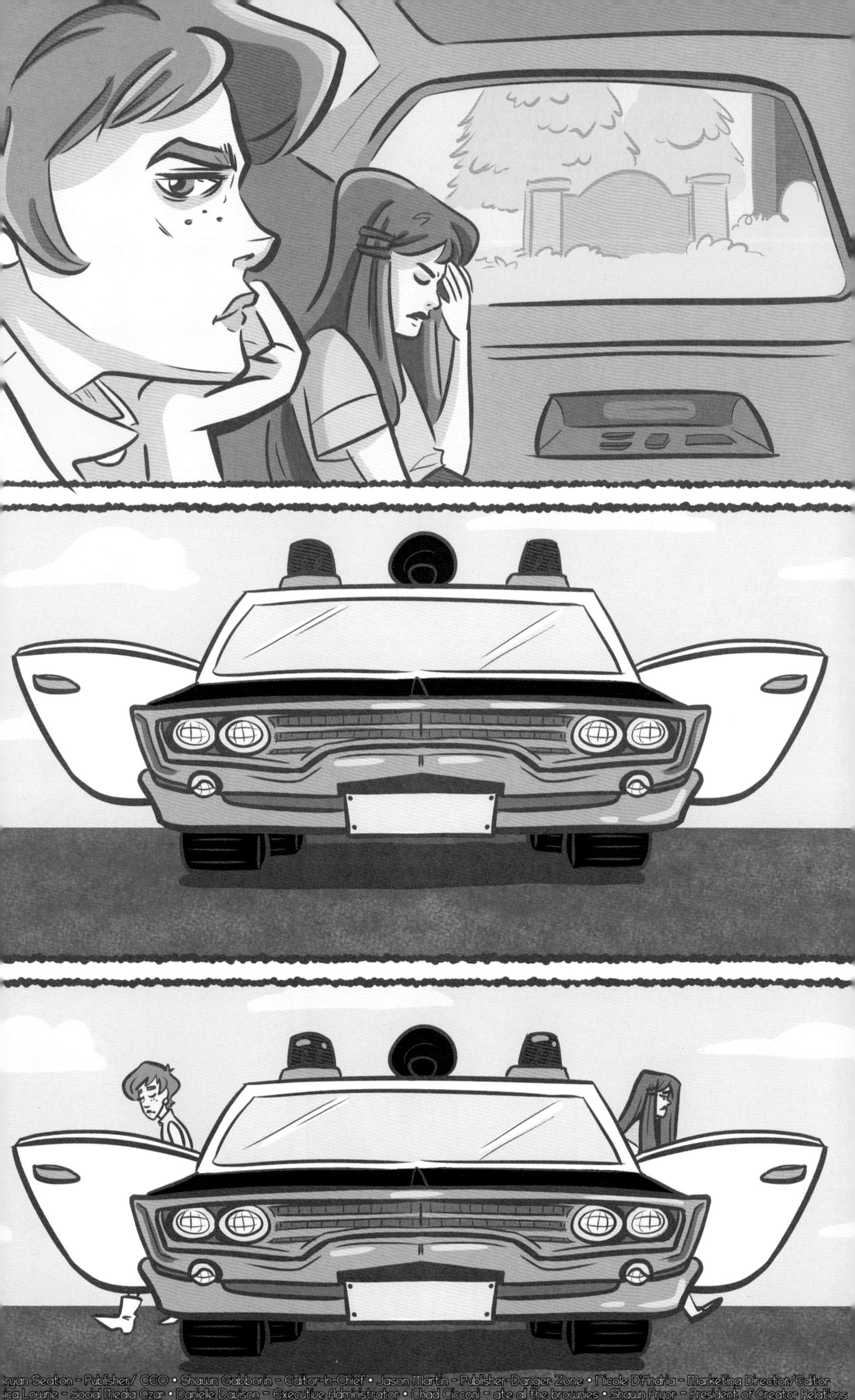

ryan Seaton - Publisher/ CEO • Shawn Gabborin - Editor-In-Chief • Jason Martin - Publisher-Danger Zone • Nicole D'Andria - Marketing Director/Editor
ica Lowrie - Social Media Czar • Danielle Davison - Executive Administrator • Chad Cicconi - ate all the brownies • Shawn Pryor - President of Creator Relations

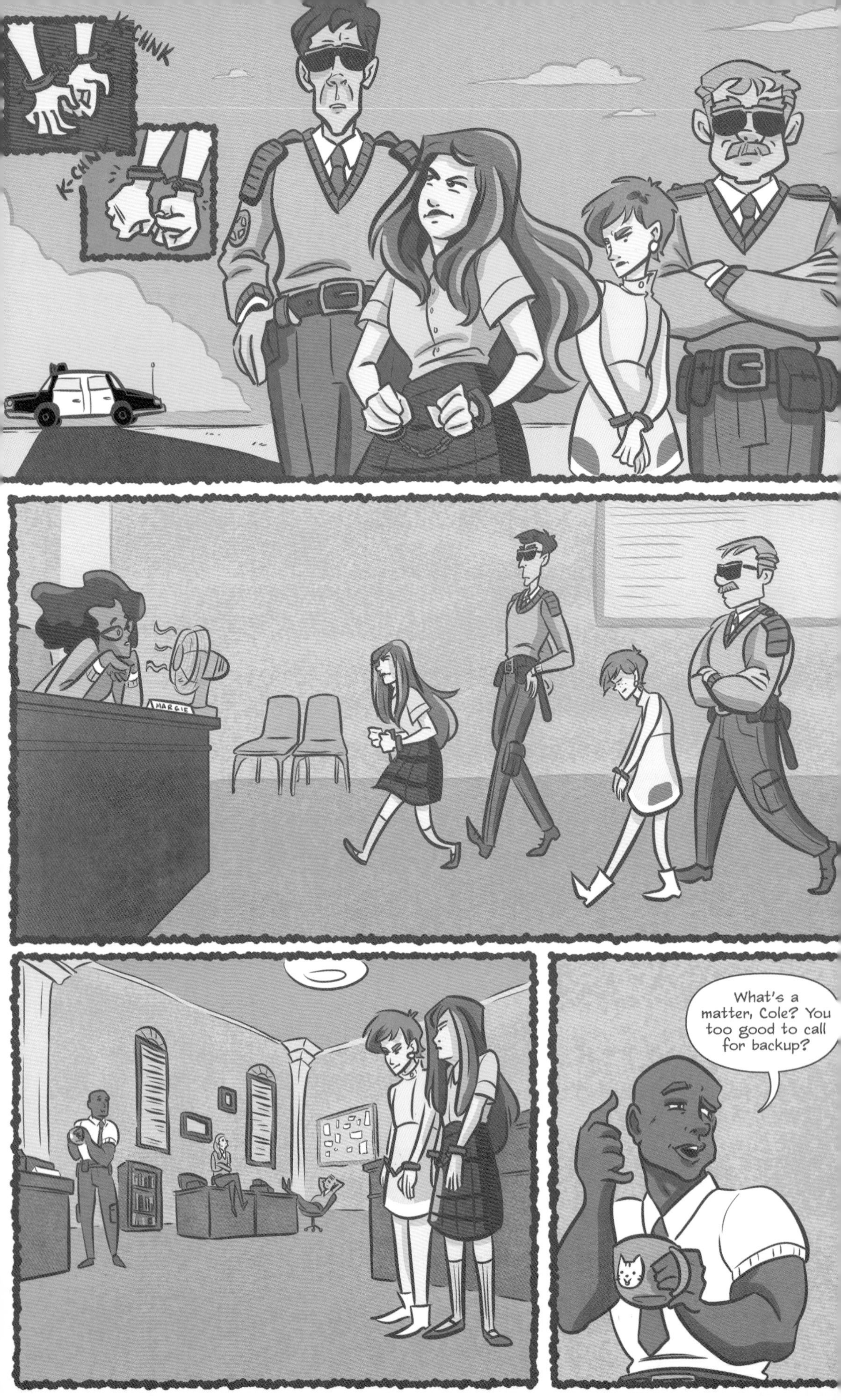
K-CHNK
K-CHNK
MARGIE
What's a matter, Cole? You too good to call for backup?

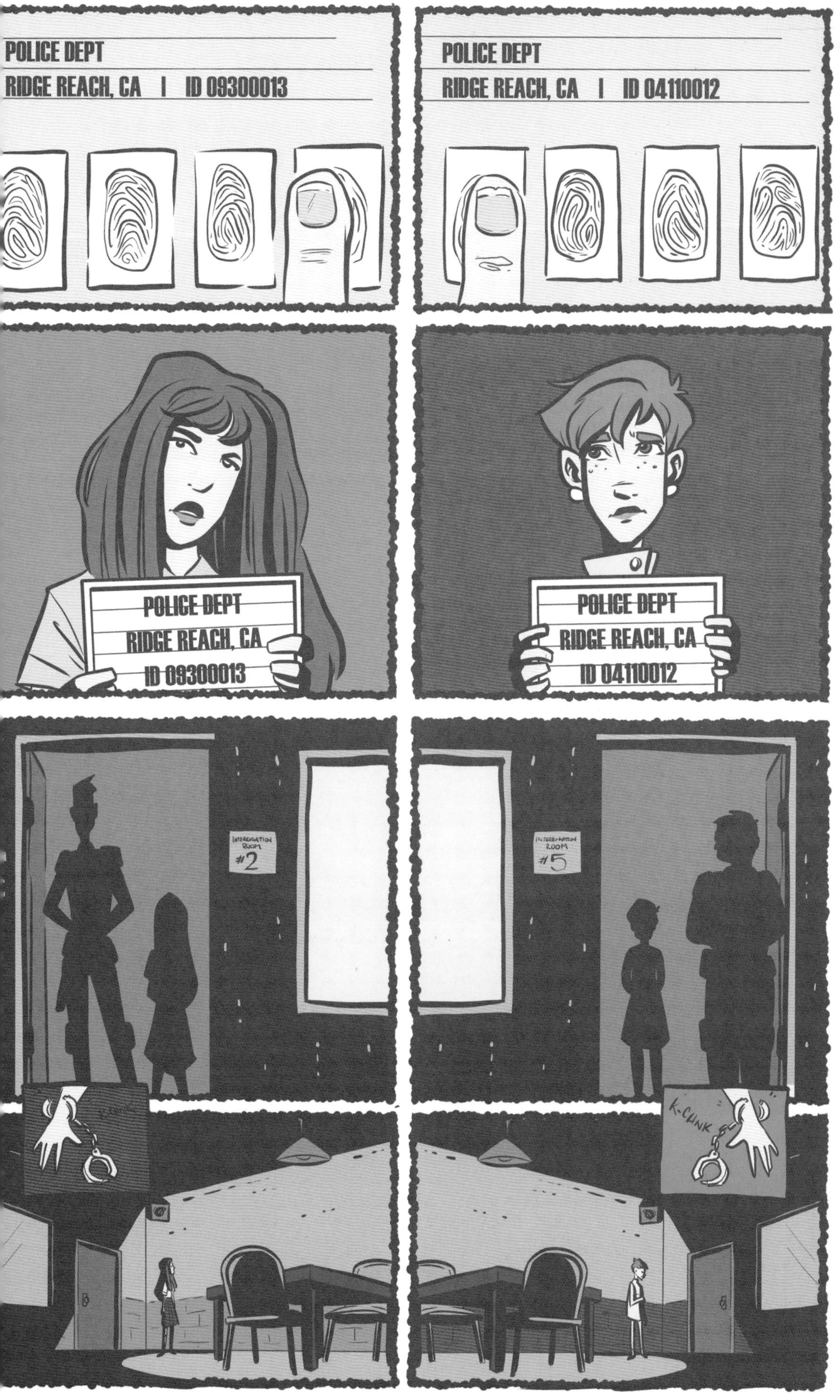
POLICE DEPT
RIDGE REACH, CA | ID 09300013
POLICE DEPT
RIDGE REACH, CA | ID 04110012
POLICE DEPT
RIDGE REACH, CA
ID 09300013
POLICE DEPT
RIDGE REACH, CA
ID 04110012
K-CHINK

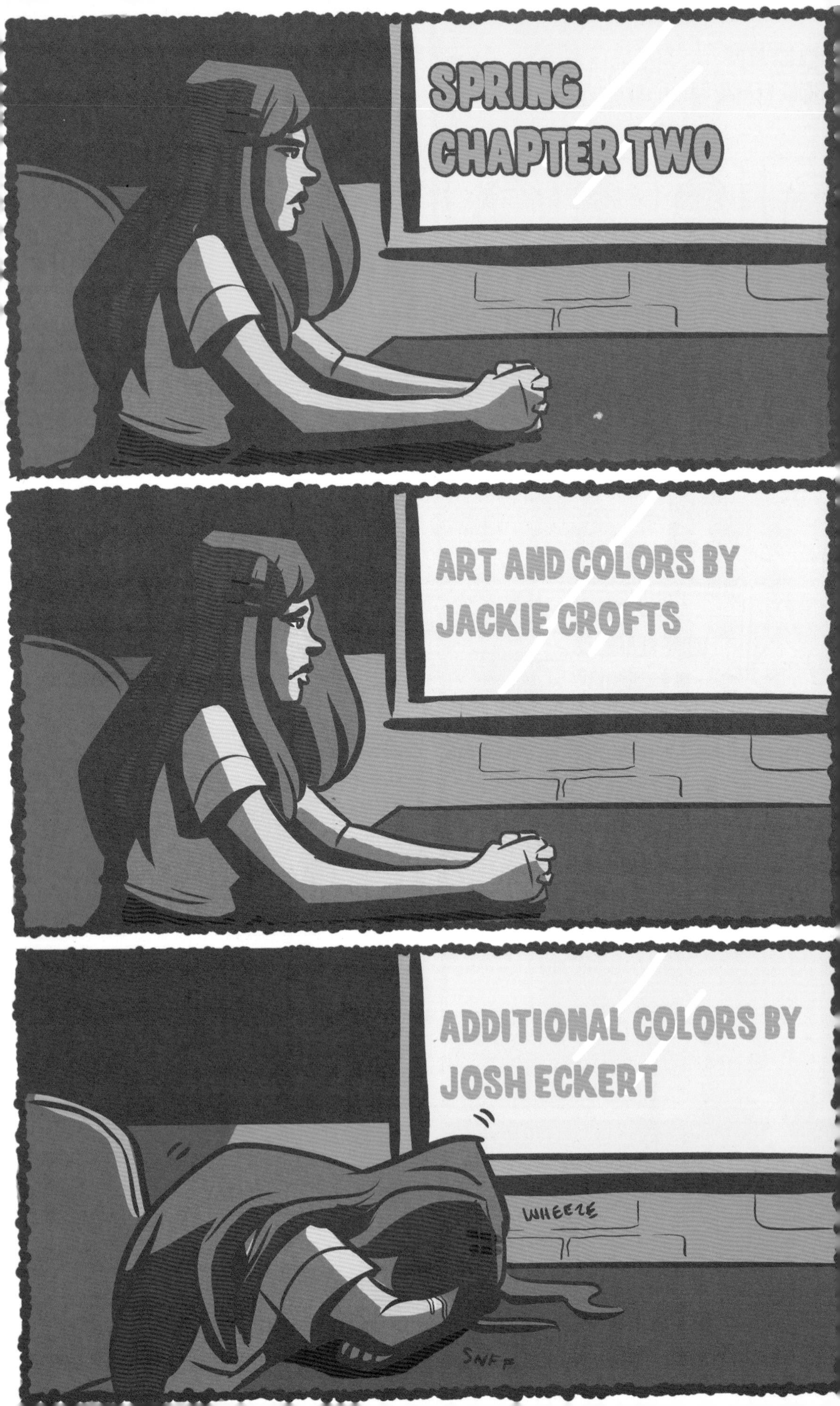

SPRING
CHAPTER TWO
ART AND COLORS BY
JACKIE CROFTS
ADDITIONAL COLORS BY
JOSH ECKERT
WHEEZE
SNFF

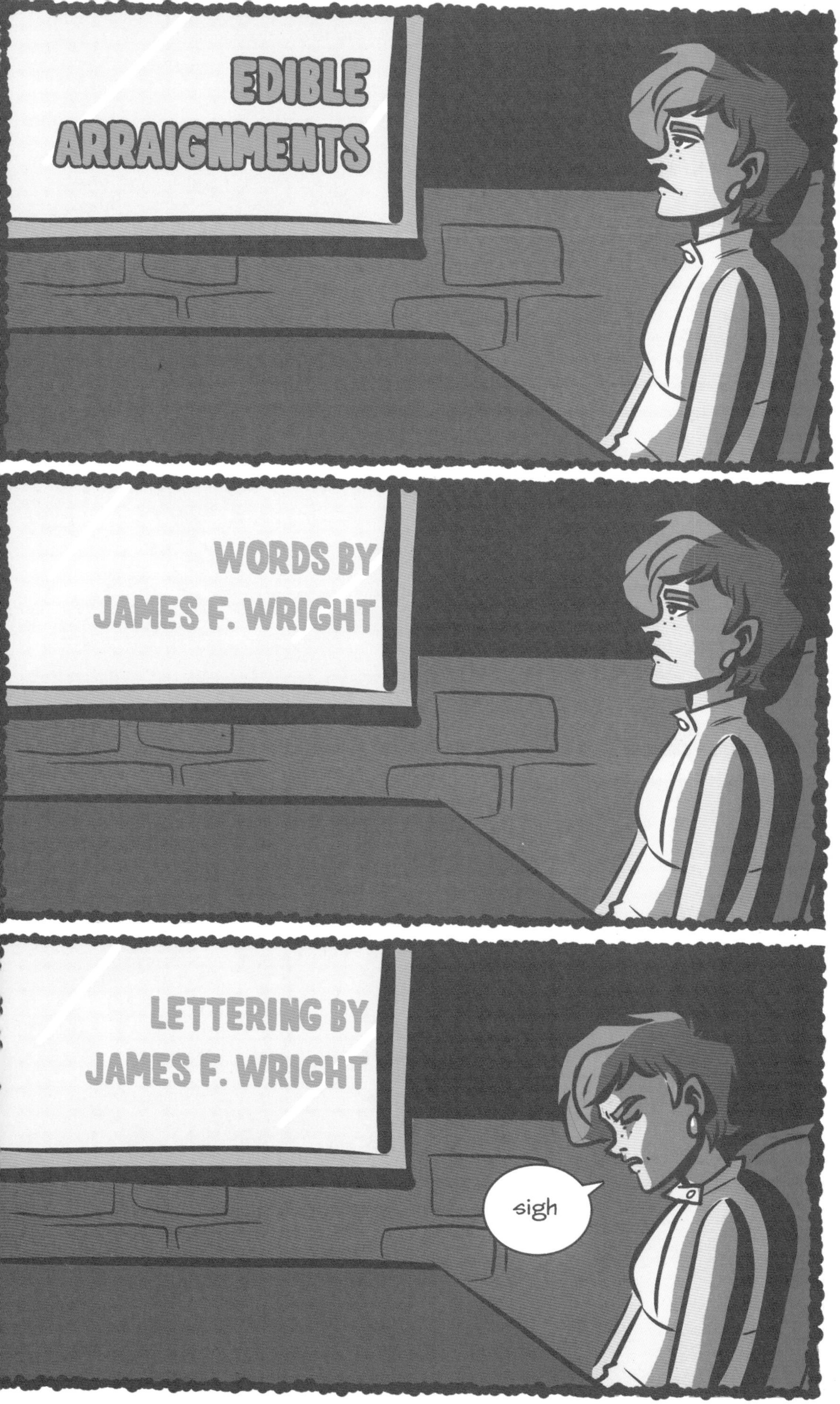

EDIBLE ARRAIGNMENTS
WORDS BY JAMES F. WRIGHT
LETTERING BY JAMES F. WRIGHT
sigh

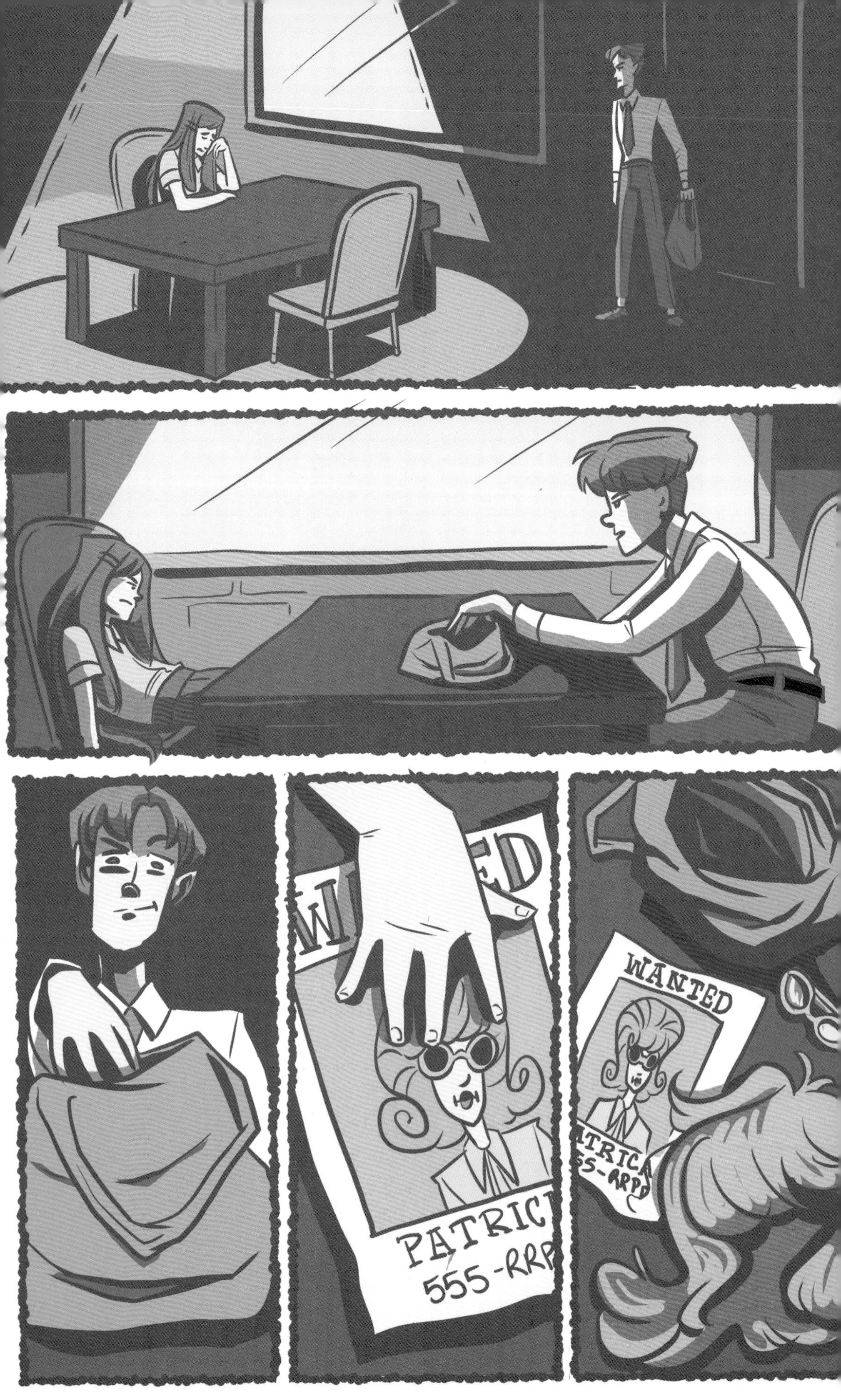

PATRIC
555-RRP
WANTED

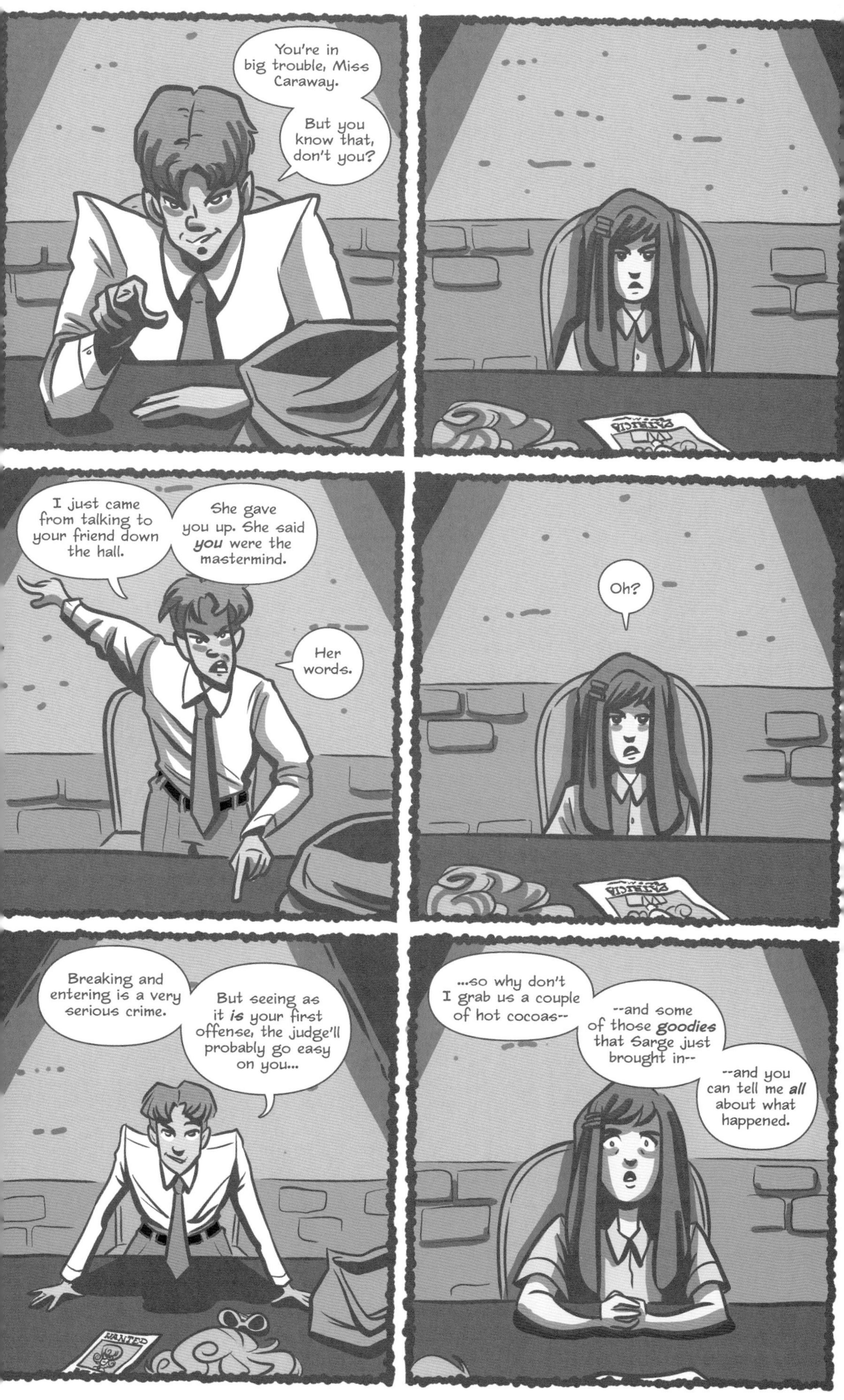
You're in big trouble, Miss Caraway.
But you know that, don't you?
I just came from talking to your friend down the hall.
She gave you up. She said *you* were the mastermind.
Her words.
Oh?
Breaking and entering is a very serious crime.
But seeing as it *is* your first offense, the judge'll probably go easy on you...
...so why don't I grab us a couple of hot cocoas--
--and some of those *goodies* that Sarge just brought in--
--and you can tell me *all* about what happened.
WANTED

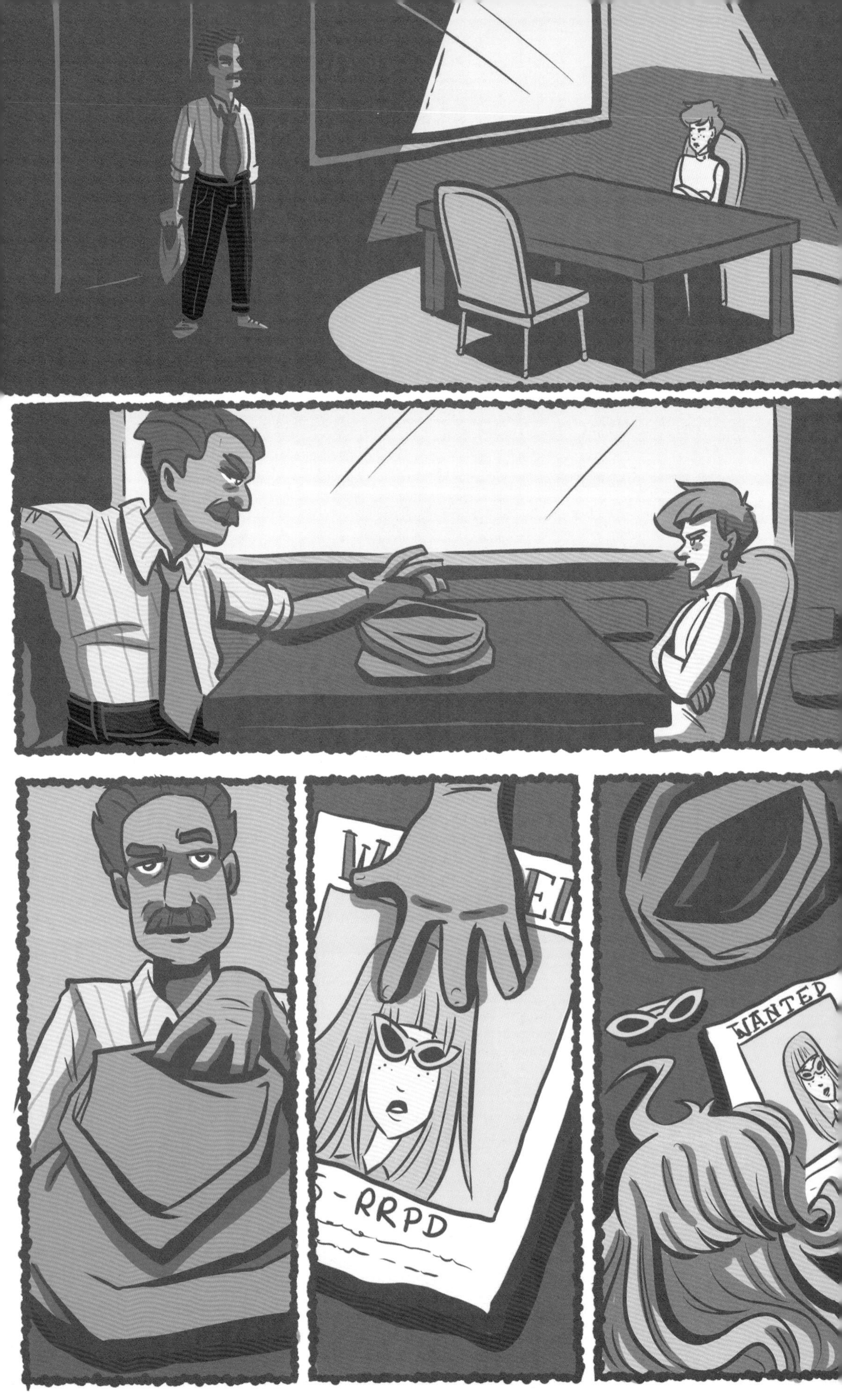
- RRPD
WANTED

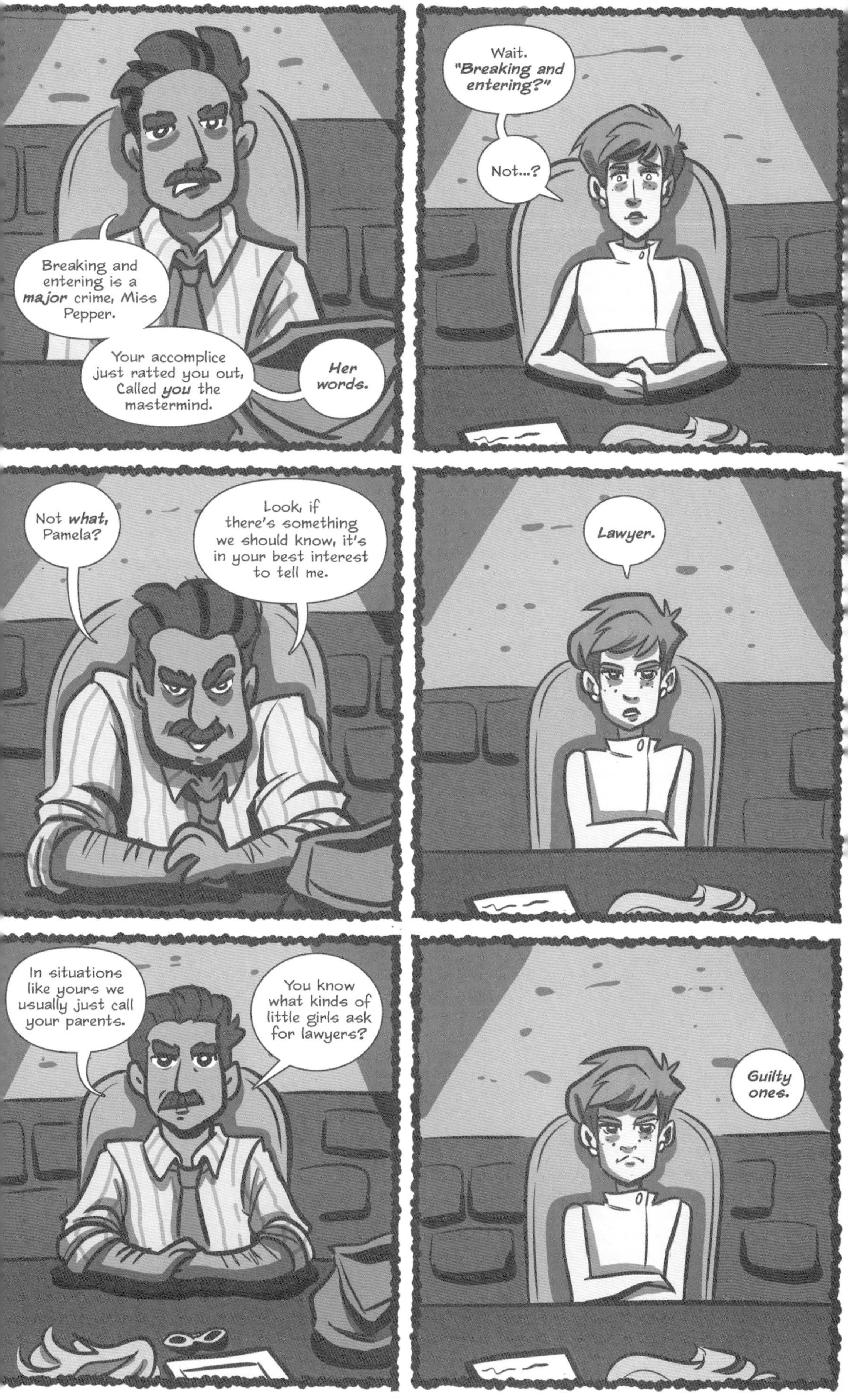

Breaking and entering is a *major* crime, Miss Pepper.
Your accomplice just ratted you out, Called *you* the mastermind.
Her words.
Wait. *"Breaking and entering?"*
Not...?
Not *what,* Pamela?
Look, if there's something we should know, it's in your best interest to tell me.
Lawyer.
In situations like yours we usually just call your parents.
You know what kinds of little girls ask for lawyers?
Guilty ones.

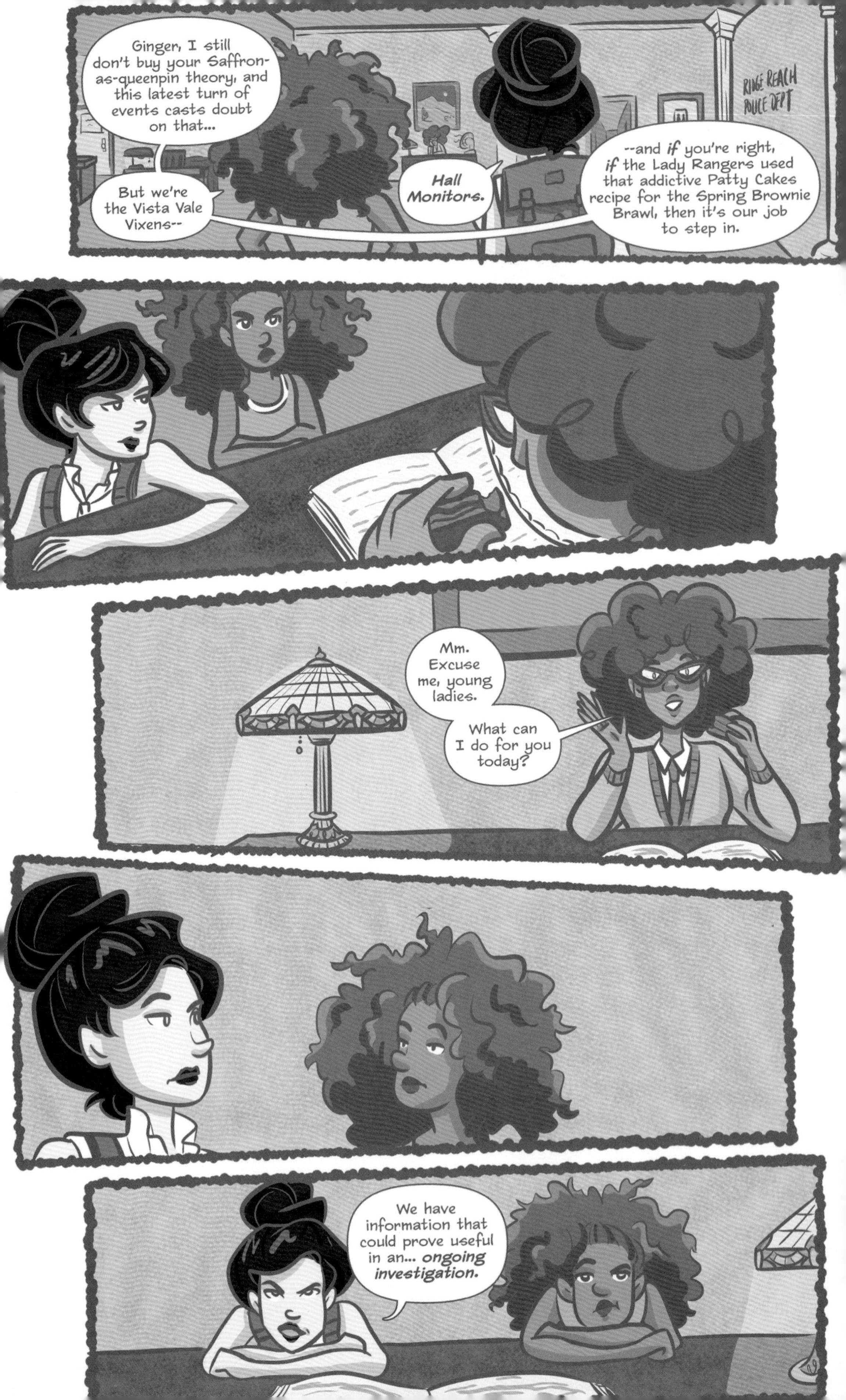

Ginger, I still don't buy your Saffron-as-queenpin theory, and this latest turn of events casts doubt on that...
RIDGE REACH POLICE DEPT
But we're the Vista Vale Vixens--
Hall Monitors.
--and if you're right, if the Lady Rangers used that addictive Patty Cakes recipe for the Spring Brownie Brawl, then it's our job to step in.
Mm. Excuse me, young ladies.
What can I do for you today?
We have information that could prove useful in an... ongoing investigation.

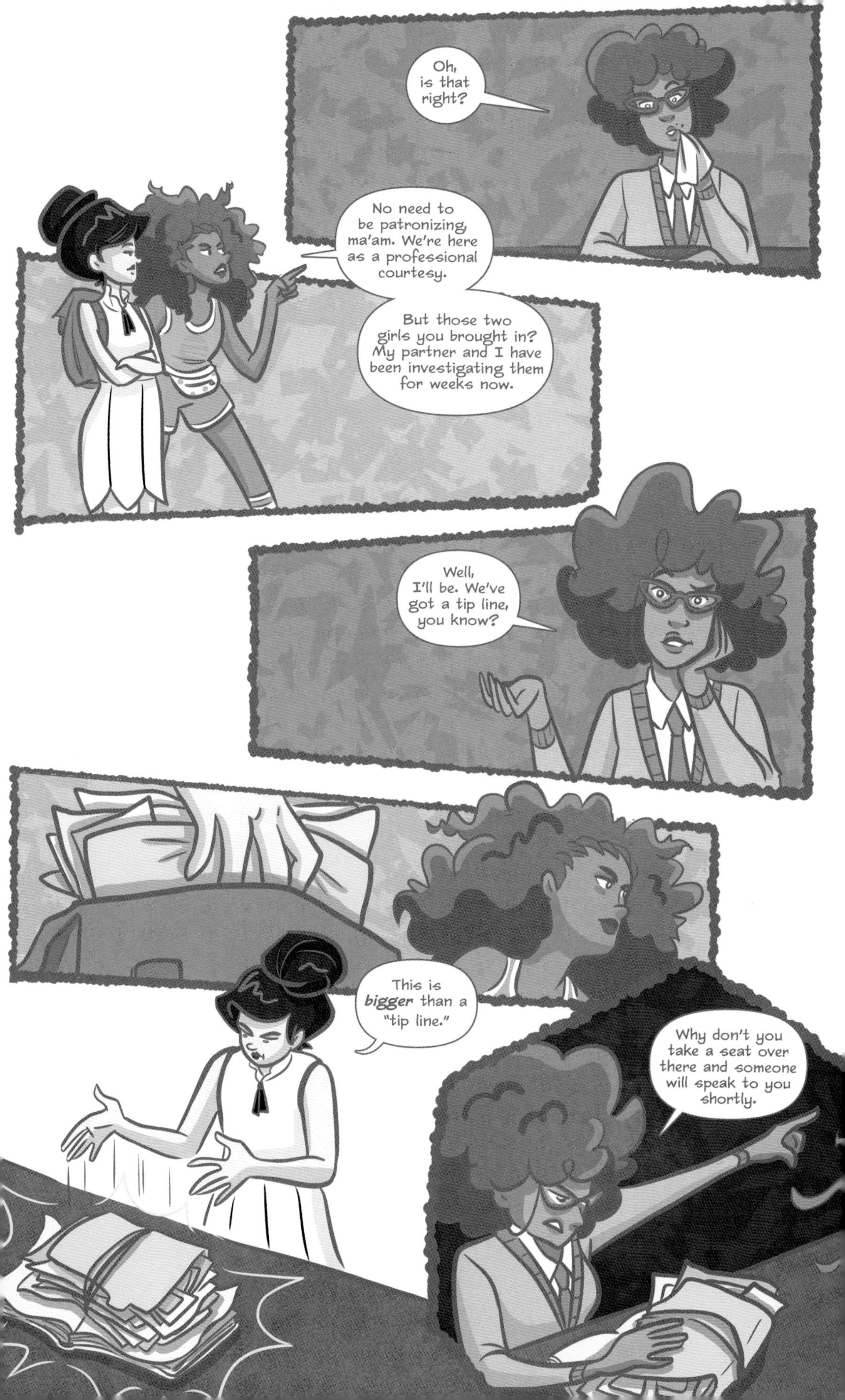
Oh, is that right?
No need to be patronizing, ma'am. We're here as a professional courtesy.
But those two girls you brought in? My partner and I have been investigating them for weeks now.
Well, I'll be. We've got a tip line, you know?
This is *bigger* than a "tip line."
Why don't you take a seat over there and someone will speak to you shortly.

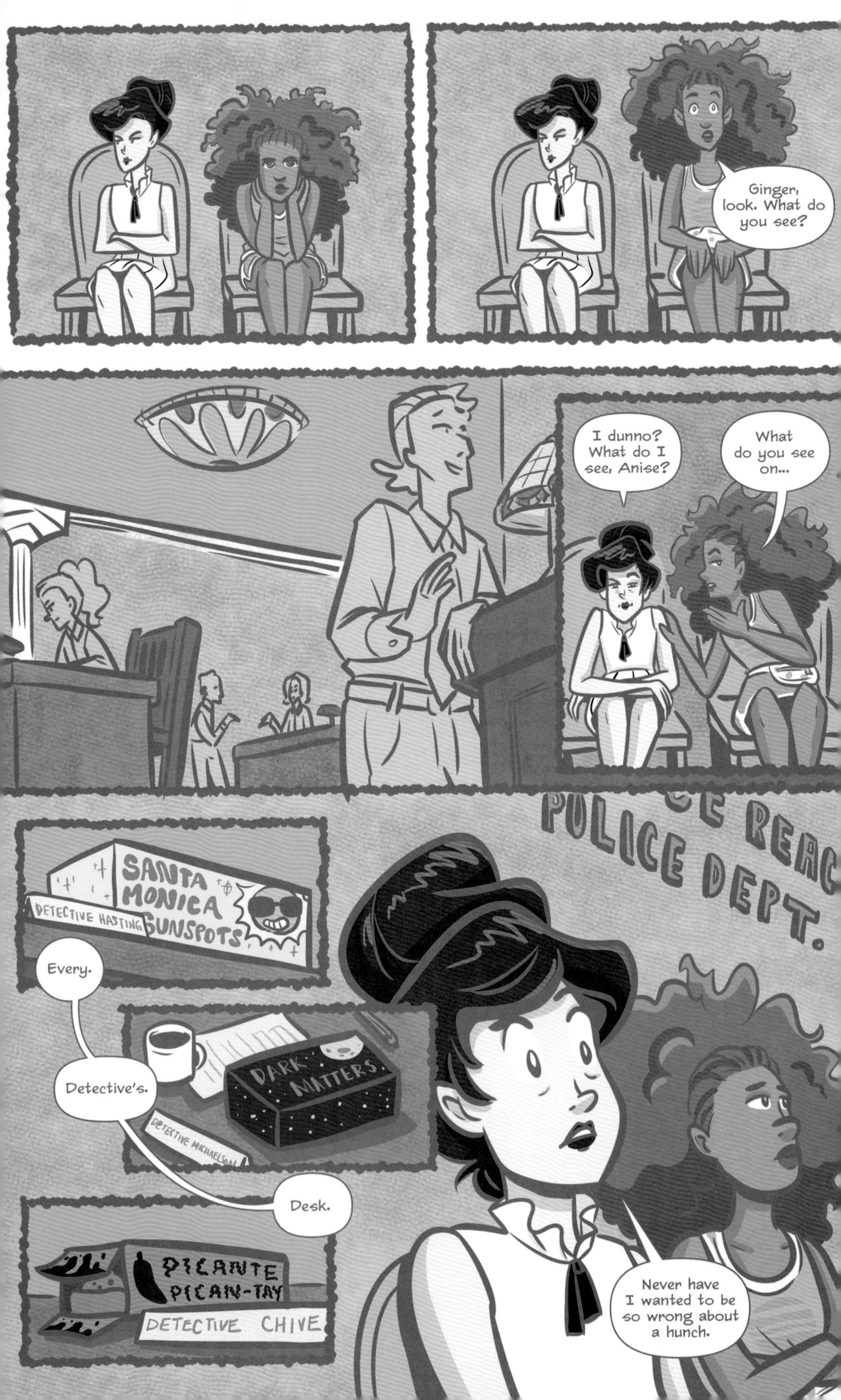

Ginger, look. What do you see?
I dunno? What do I see, Anise?
What do you see on...
SANTA MONICA SUNSPOTS
DETECTIVE HASTING
Every.
DARK MATTERS
DETECTIVE MICHAELSON
Detective's.
PICANTE PICAN-TAY
DETECTIVE CHIVE
Desk.
POLICE DEPT.
Never have I wanted to be so wrong about a hunch.

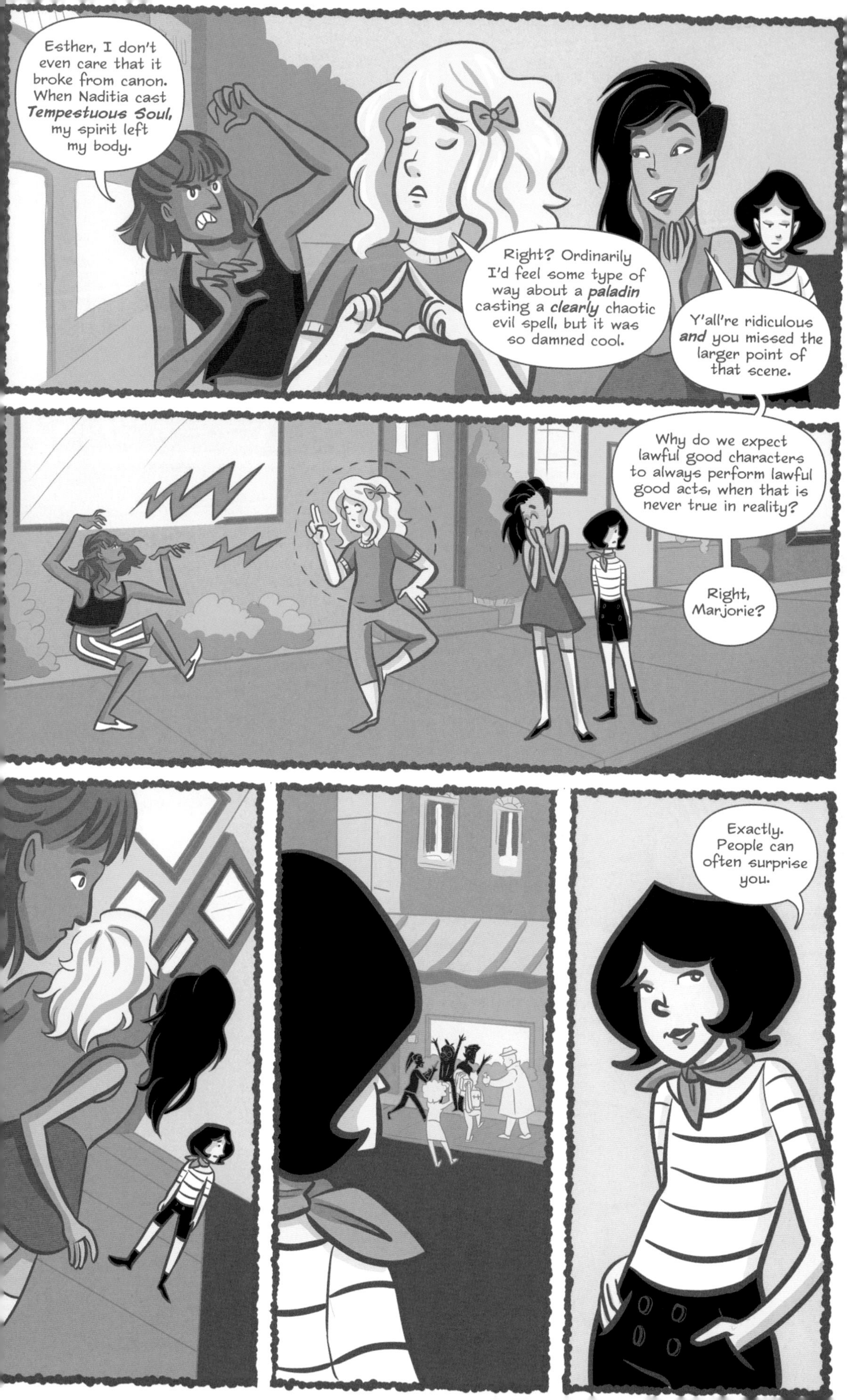
Esther, I don't even care that it broke from canon. When Naditia cast *Tempestuous Soul,* my spirit left my body.
Right? Ordinarily I'd feel some type of way about a *paladin* casting a *clearly* chaotic evil spell, but it was so damned cool.
Y'all're ridiculous *and* you missed the larger point of that scene.
Why do we expect lawful good characters to always perform lawful good acts, when that is never true in reality?
Right, Marjorie?
Exactly. People can often surprise you.

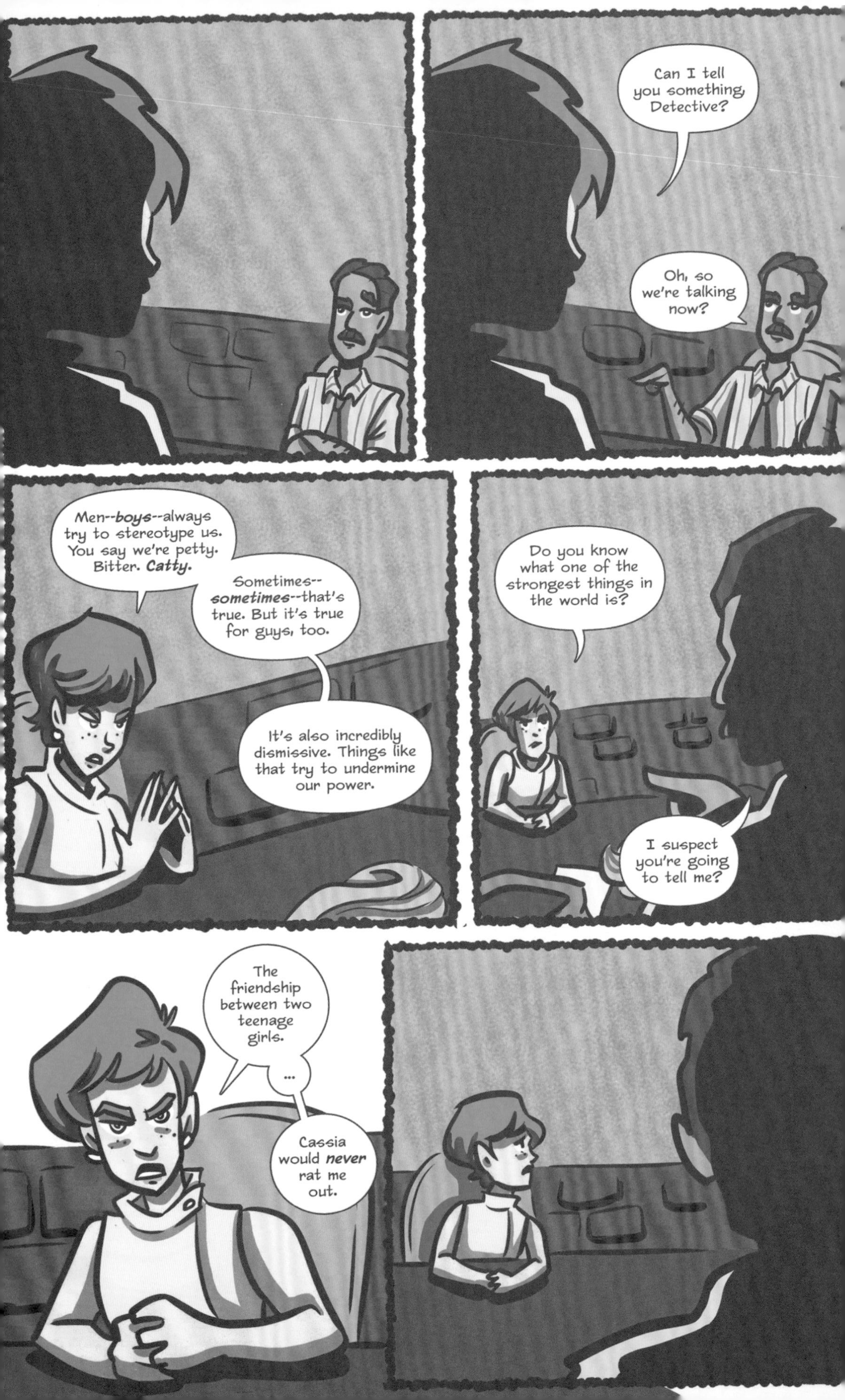
Can I tell you something, Detective?
Oh, so we're talking now?
Men--**boys**--always try to stereotype us. You say we're petty. Bitter. ***Catty.***
Sometimes-- ***sometimes***--that's true. But it's true for guys, too.
It's also incredibly dismissive. Things like that try to undermine our power.
Do you know what one of the strongest things in the world is?
I suspect you're going to tell me?
The friendship between two teenage girls.
...
Cassia would ***never*** rat me out.

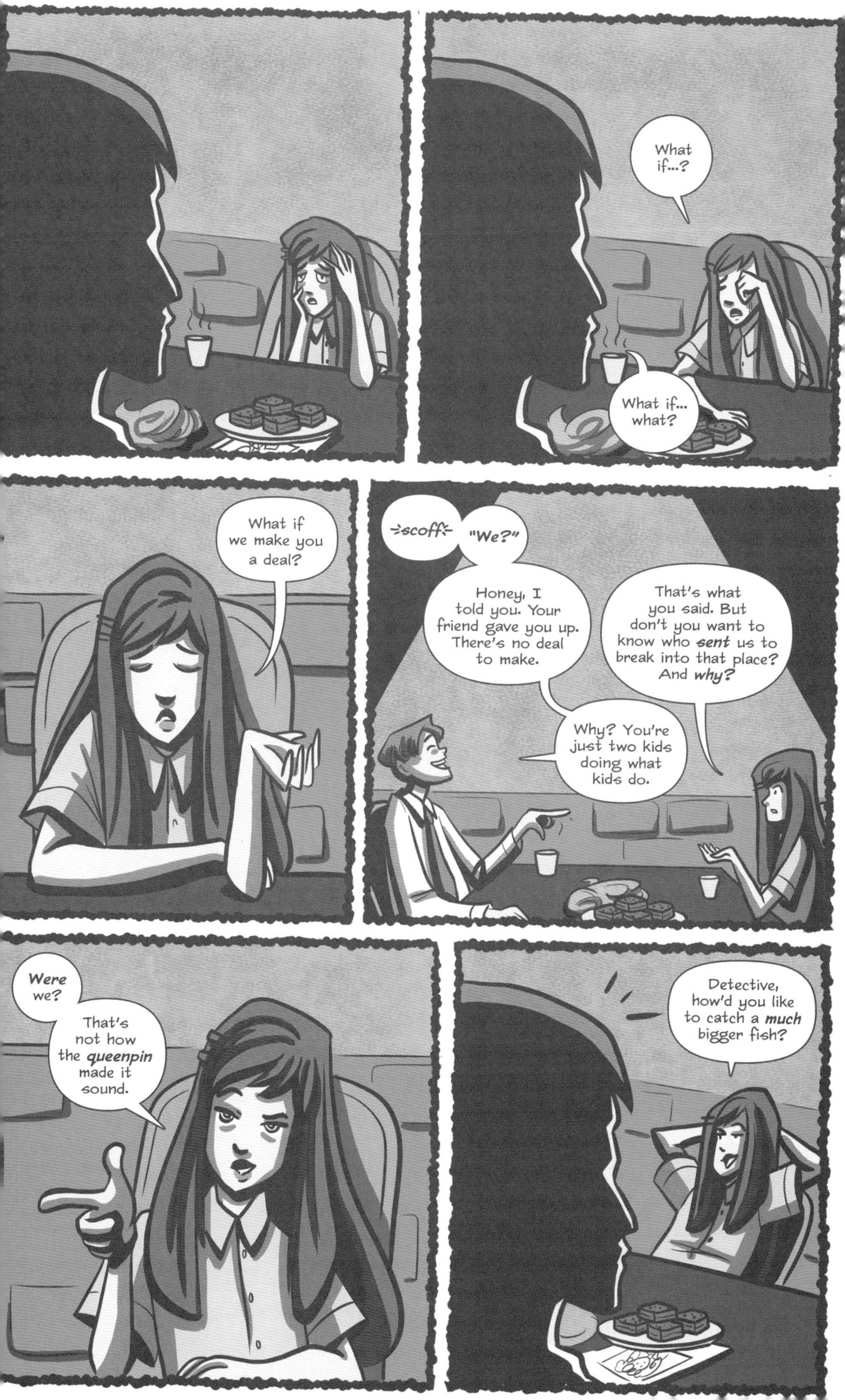

What if...?
What if... what?
What if we make you a deal?
scoff
"We?"
Honey, I told you. Your friend gave you up. There's no deal to make.
That's what you said. But don't you want to know who *sent* us to break into that place? And *why?*
Why? You're just two kids doing what kids do.
Were we?
That's not how the *queenpin* made it sound.
Detective, how'd you like to catch a *much* bigger fish?

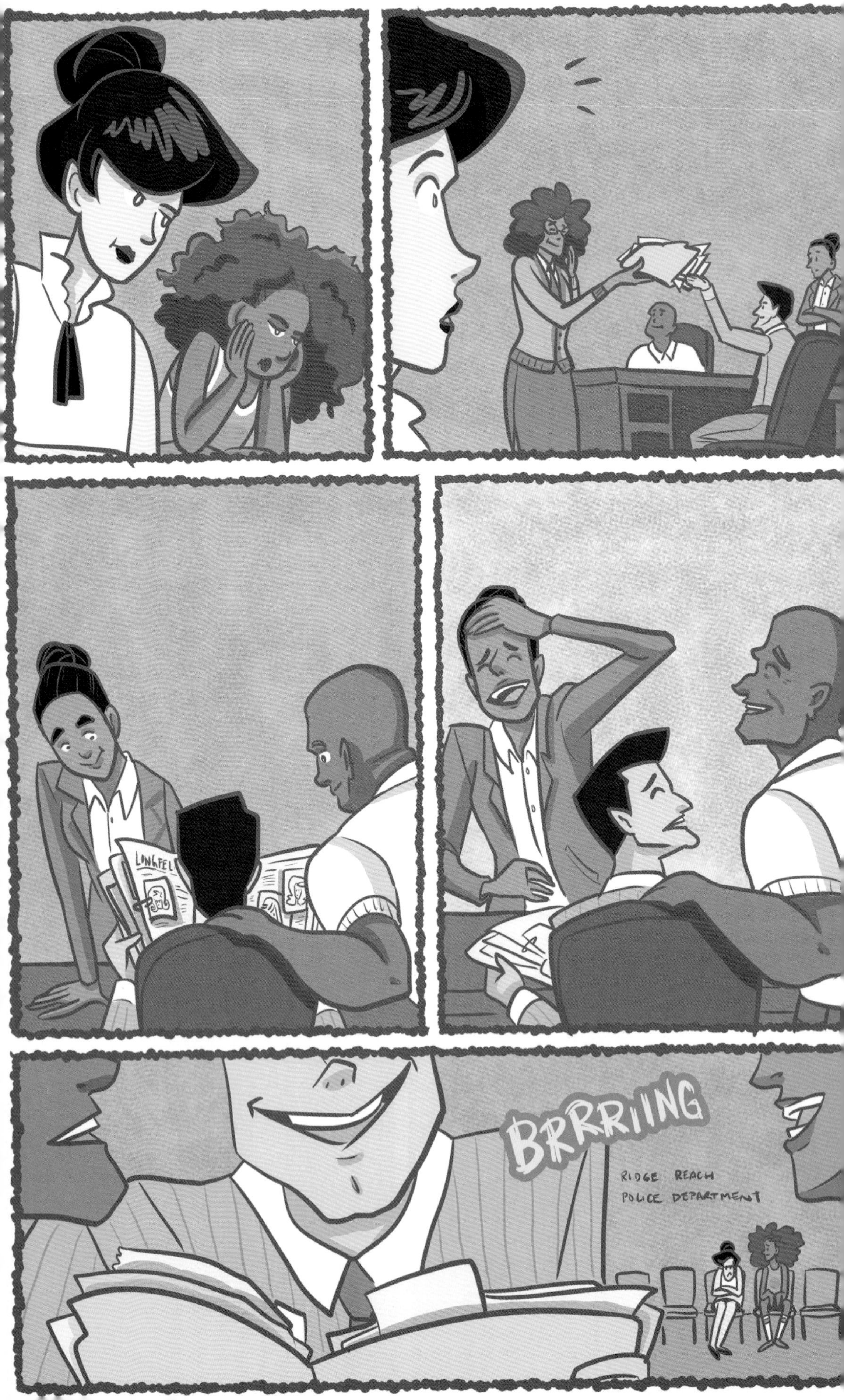

LONGFEL
BRRRIING
RIDGE REACH
POLICE DEPARTMENT

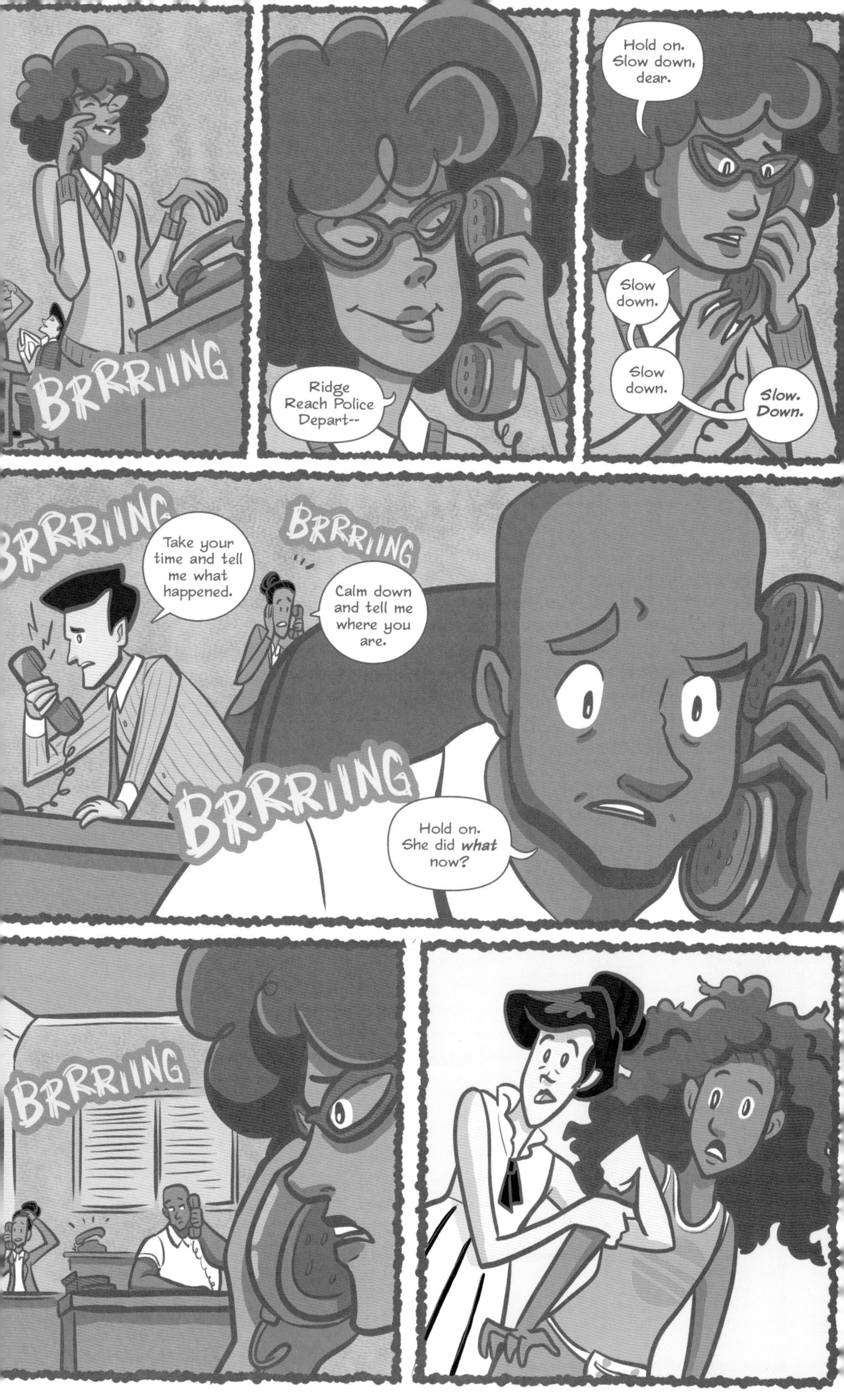
BRRRIING
Ridge Reach Police Depart--
Hold on. Slow down, dear.
Slow down.
Slow down.
Slow. Down.
BRRRIING
Take your time and tell me what happened.
BRRRIING
Calm down and tell me where you are.
BRRRIING
Hold on. She did *what* now?
BRRRIING

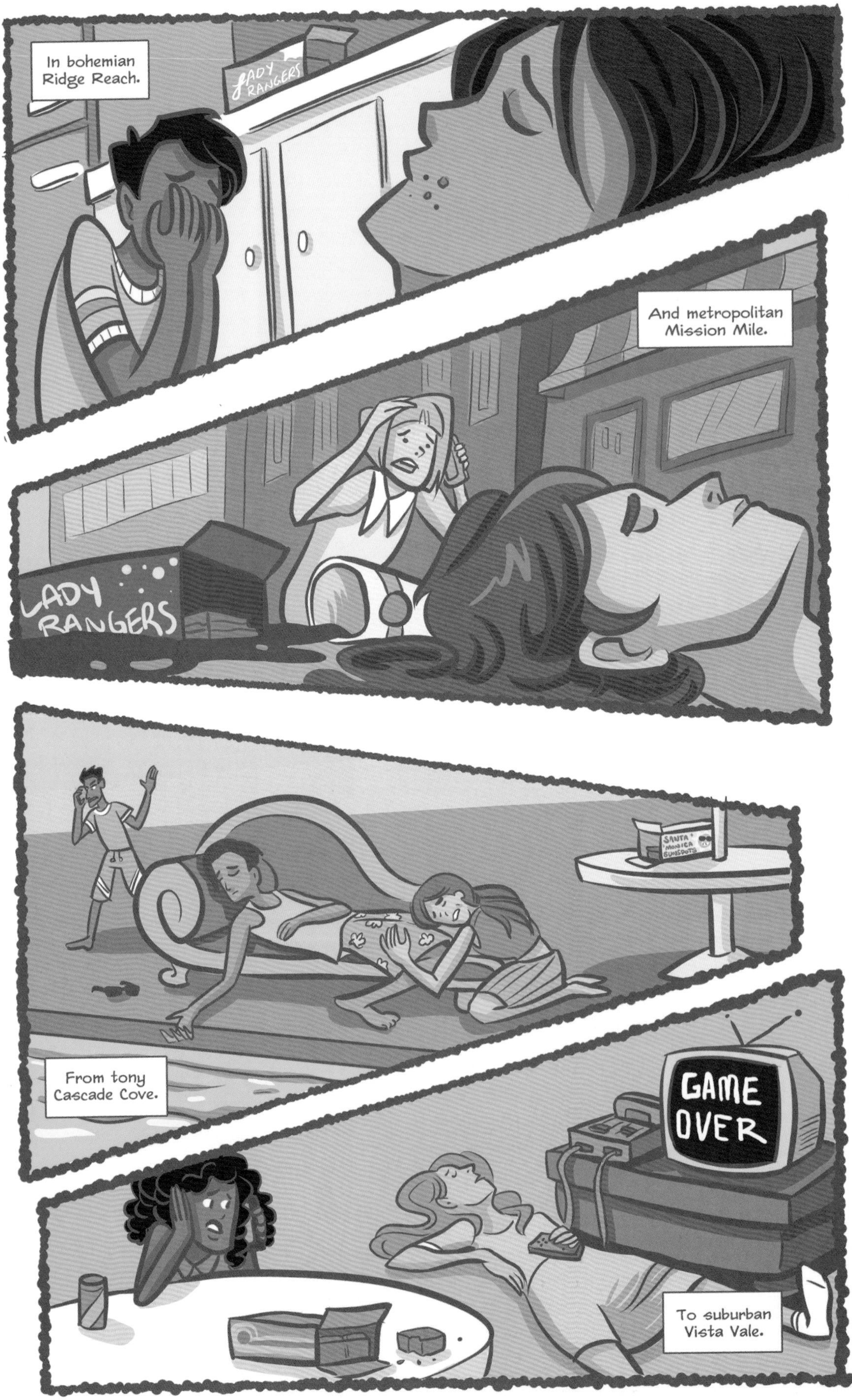
In bohemian Ridge Reach.
LADY RANGERS
And metropolitan Mission Mile.
LADY RANGERS
From tony Cascade Cove.
GAME OVER
To suburban Vista Vale.

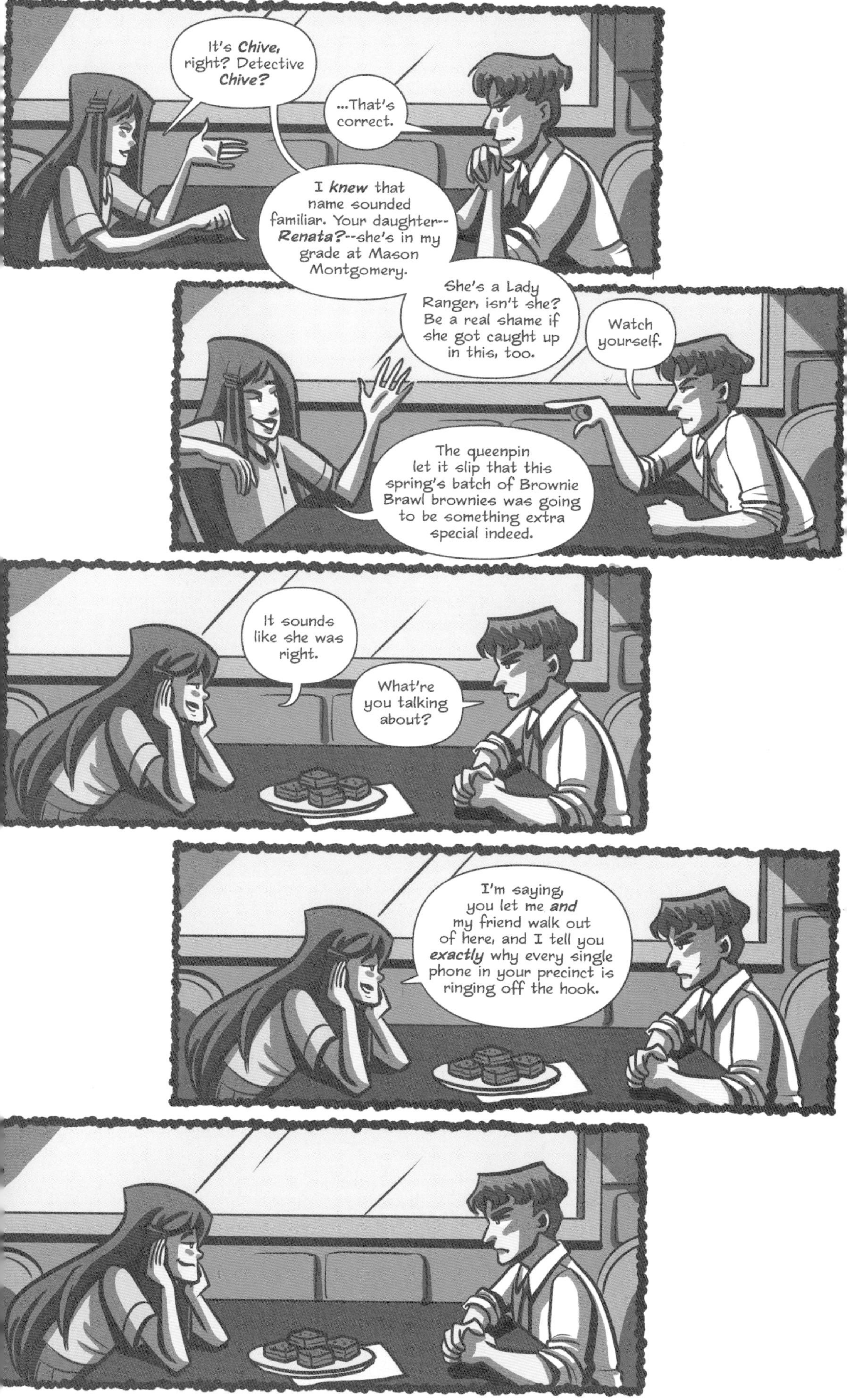
It's *Chive,* right? Detective *Chive?*
...That's correct.
I *knew* that name sounded familiar. Your daughter-- *Renata?*--she's in my grade at Mason Montgomery.
She's a Lady Ranger, isn't she? Be a real shame if she got caught up in this, too.
Watch yourself.
The queenpin let it slip that this spring's batch of Brownie Brawl brownies was going to be something extra special indeed.
It sounds like she was right.
What're you talking about?
I'm saying, you let me *and* my friend walk out of here, and I tell you *exactly* why every single phone in your precinct is ringing off the hook.

KNOCK
KNOCK
Ms. Pepper? My partner and I want to apologize for taking up your time today.
You're free to go.

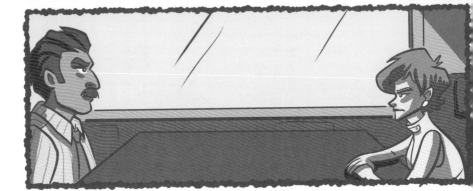

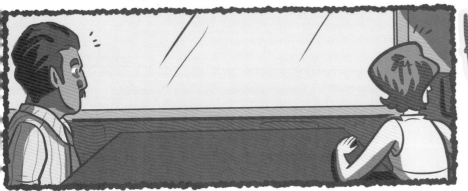

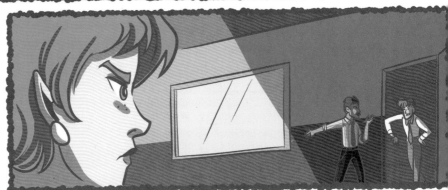

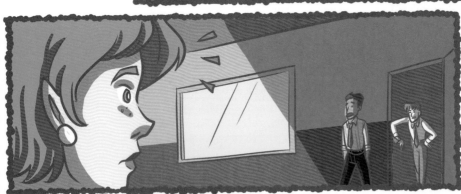

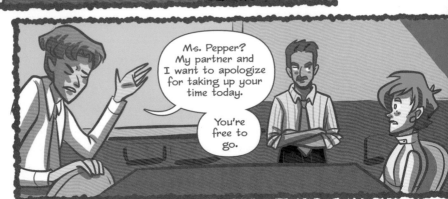

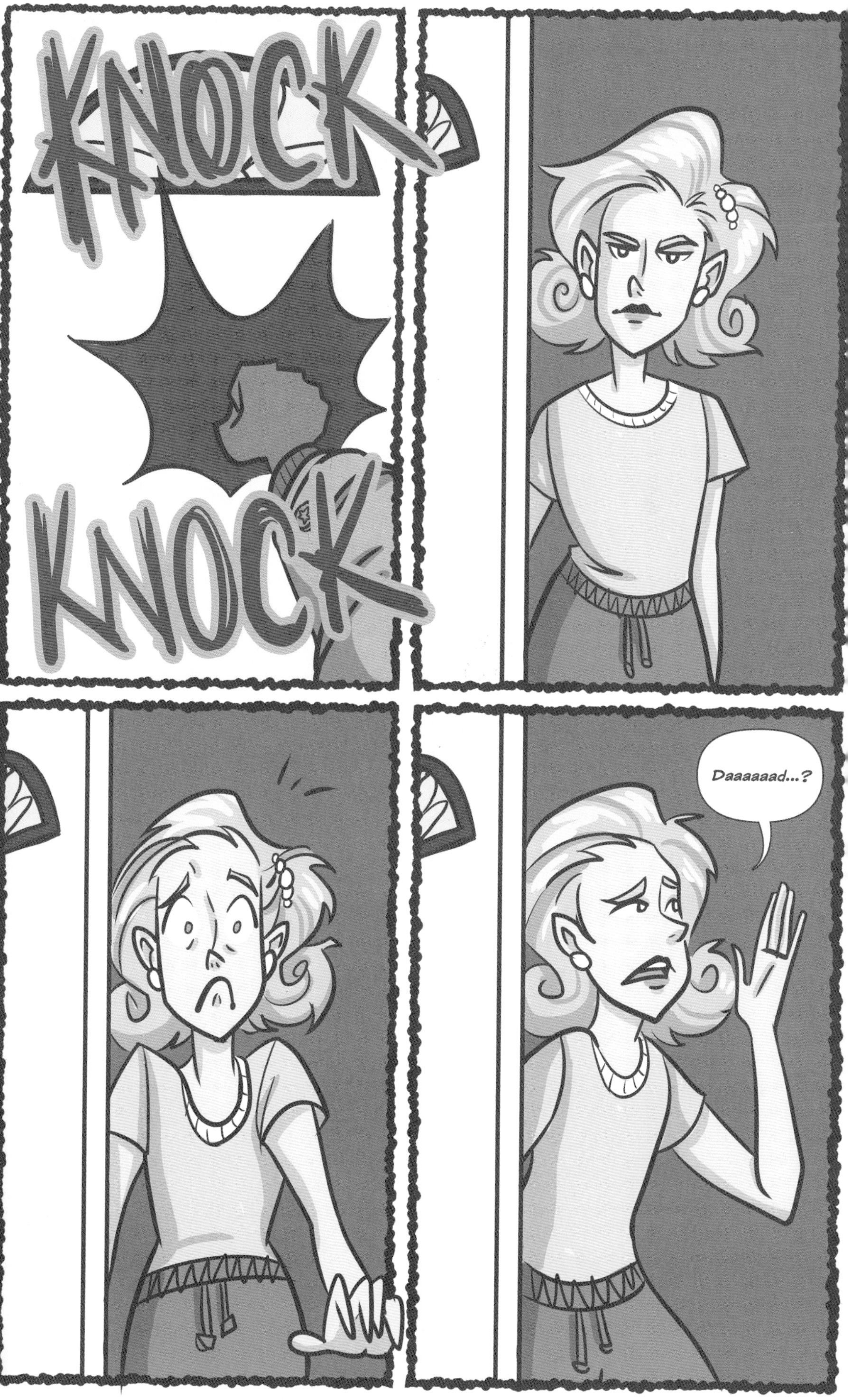
KNOCK
KNOCK
Daaaaaad...?

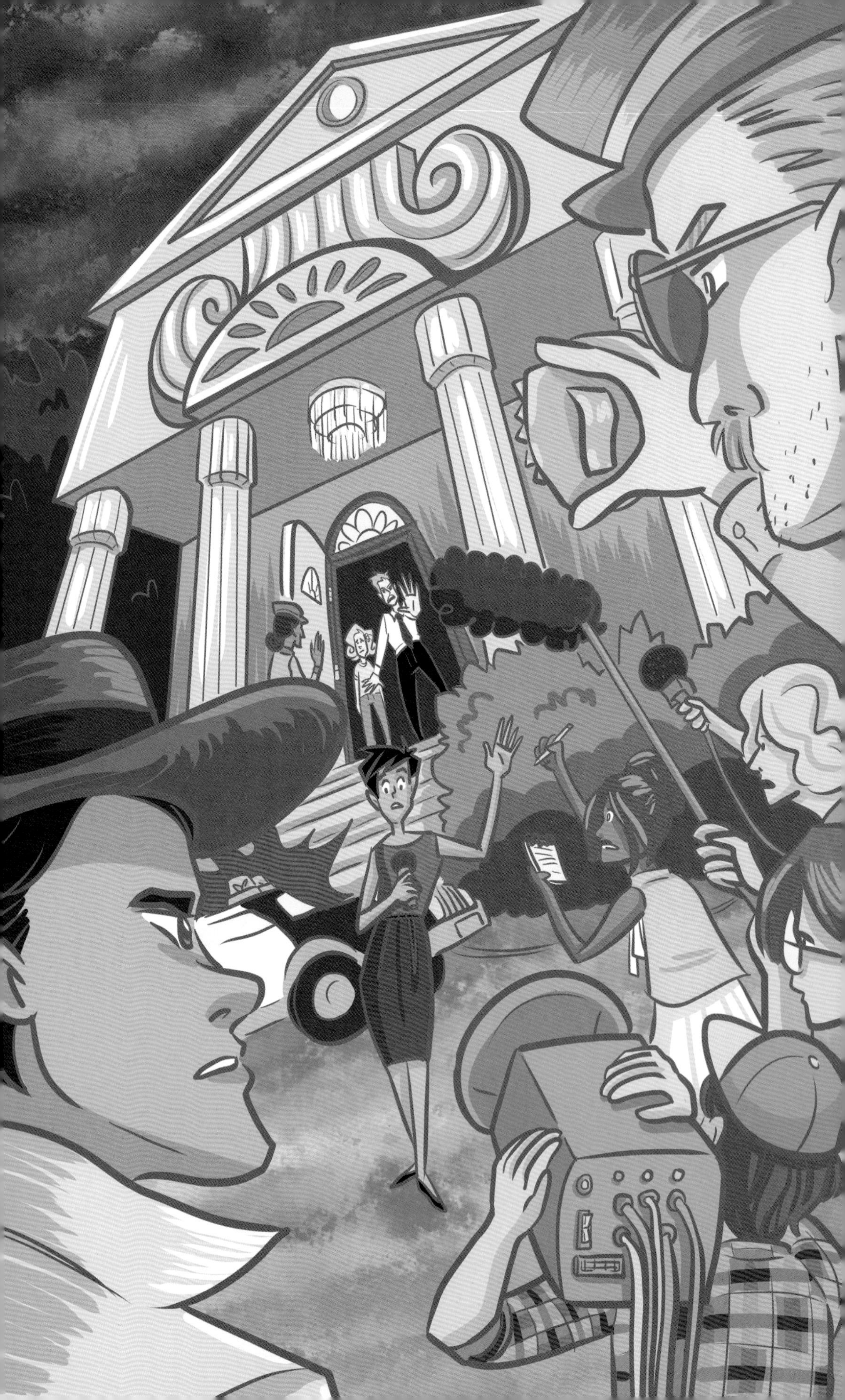

THE COOLING RACK

CONTACT: @NutmegComic   NutmegComics@gmail.com

Avatars by Genue Revuelta

Remember our friend, Katie? We do! (Obviously.) She was the first person to submit a recipe for Nutmeg, her incredible snickerdoodle brownies way back at the end of chapter two. So, we thought it'd be a nice, fitting bookend to have her join us again with a pastry for the penultimate chapter of the series. We can't thank her--or her adorable cat, Smudge--enough for agreeing to contribute. Thanks, Katie!

WHEN LIFE GIVES YOU LEMONS' CAKE
(Adapted from Sunset Magazine)

Sometimes you just need cake. Sometimes you need cake as fast as you can eat it. Sometimes life provides you nothing but a sour taste in your mouth, but this cake can help. You don't need a cake pan, you don't need to make frosting. It's just a simple cake you can mix in one bowl and eat when it's still warm. It's good in the summer because it's bright and sweet and you barely have to have your oven on when it's hot out. It's great in the winter because it's bright and sweet and reminds you that it won't be cold out forever. It's here when you spent all week finishing a group project on your own. It's here when that bus splashed you with that rain puddle. I've even eaten it for breakfast. This cake is here for you when life gets hard.

INGREDIENTS

1 cup all-purpose flour

3/4 cup white sugar

The zest of 1 lemon

1/2 cup (1 stick) butter, melted

1 egg, lightly beaten

2 tsp almond extract

3 tbsp lemon juice

1/8 tsp salt

Sliced almonds to cover the cake, about 1/3 cup

Powdered sugar for dusting

INSTRUCTIONS

* Preheat oven to 350 degrees Fahrenheit

* Zest one lemon and combine it with the white sugar, rubbing the zest into the sugar (this makes the lemon flavor really come out. But if you're feeling real lazy you can just dump the zest in).

* Combine the remaining ingredients, stir until smooth.

* Spray a pie pan with cooking spray and pour in batter.

* Top batter with sliced almonds and bake for approximately 30 minutes until the edges are golden brown

* Dust with powdered sugar to finish

TEAM NUTMEG IN 2018

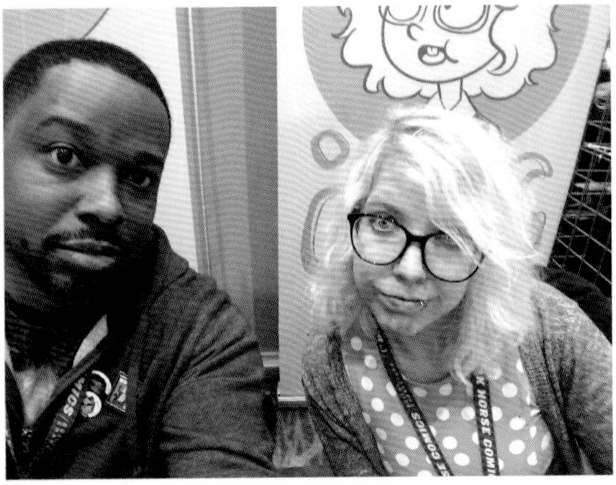

EMERALD CITY COMIC CON IN SEATTLE

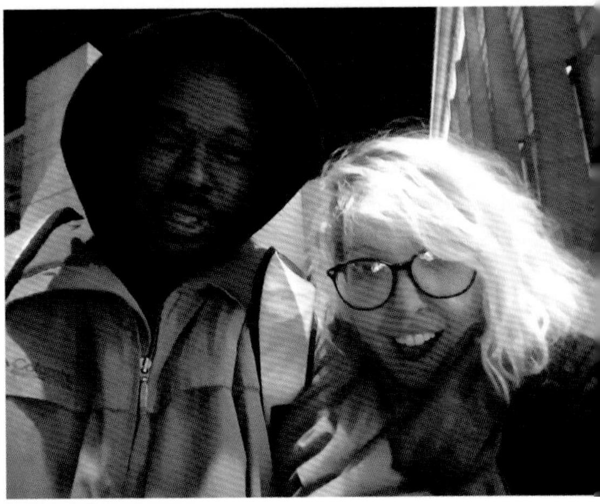

FREEZING OUR BUNS OFF AT C2E2 IN CHICAGO

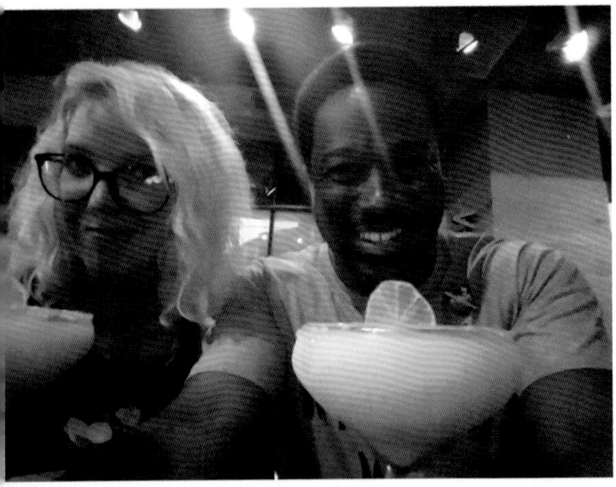

FROZEN DRINKS AND RAMEN AT HEROESCON IN CHARLOTTE

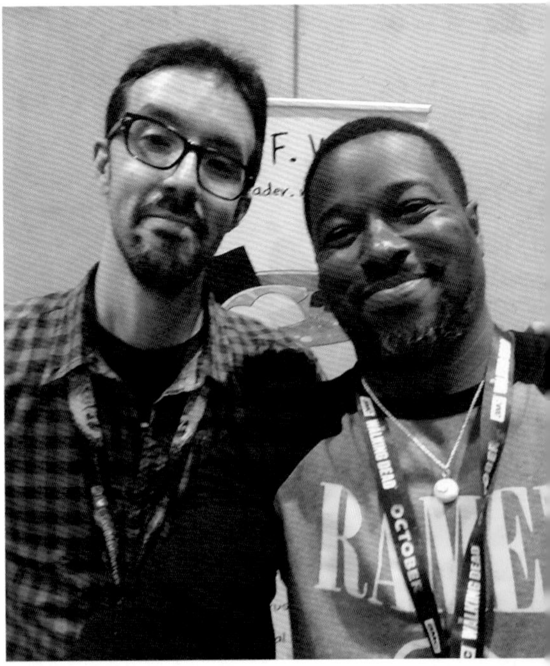
WALKING DEAD
OCTOBER

BEING EXHAUSTED AT SAN DIEGO COMIC CON

NUTMEG

ISSUE 15

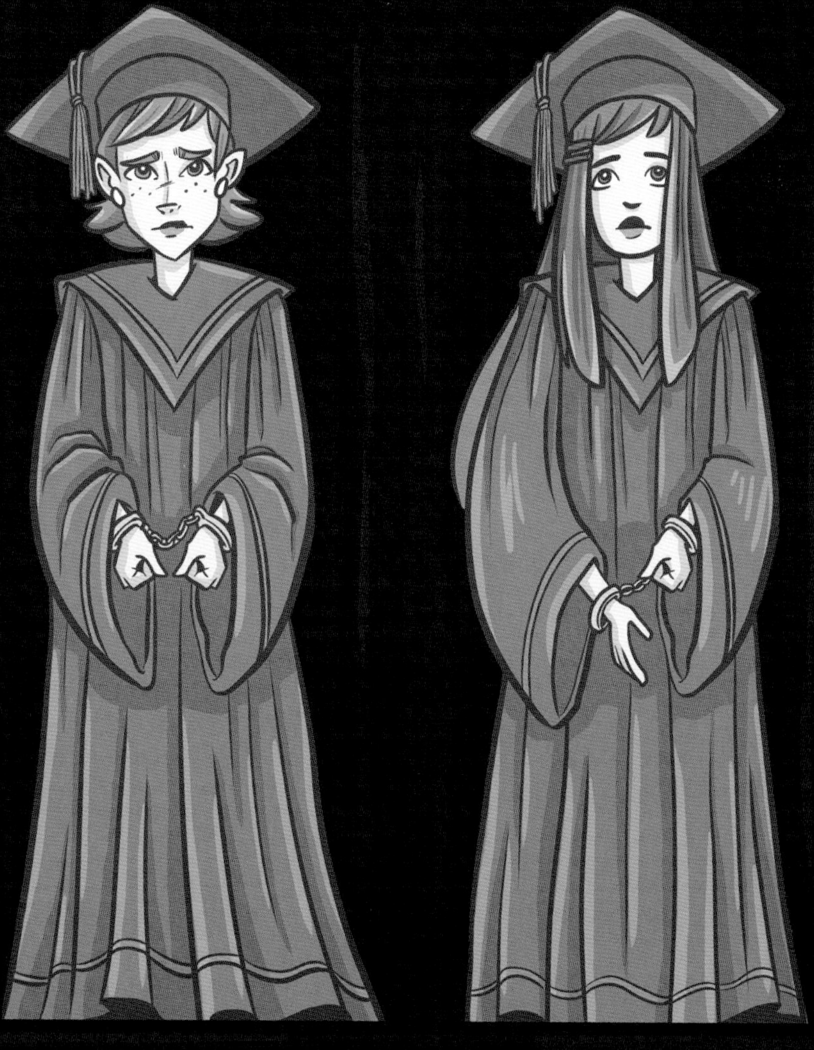

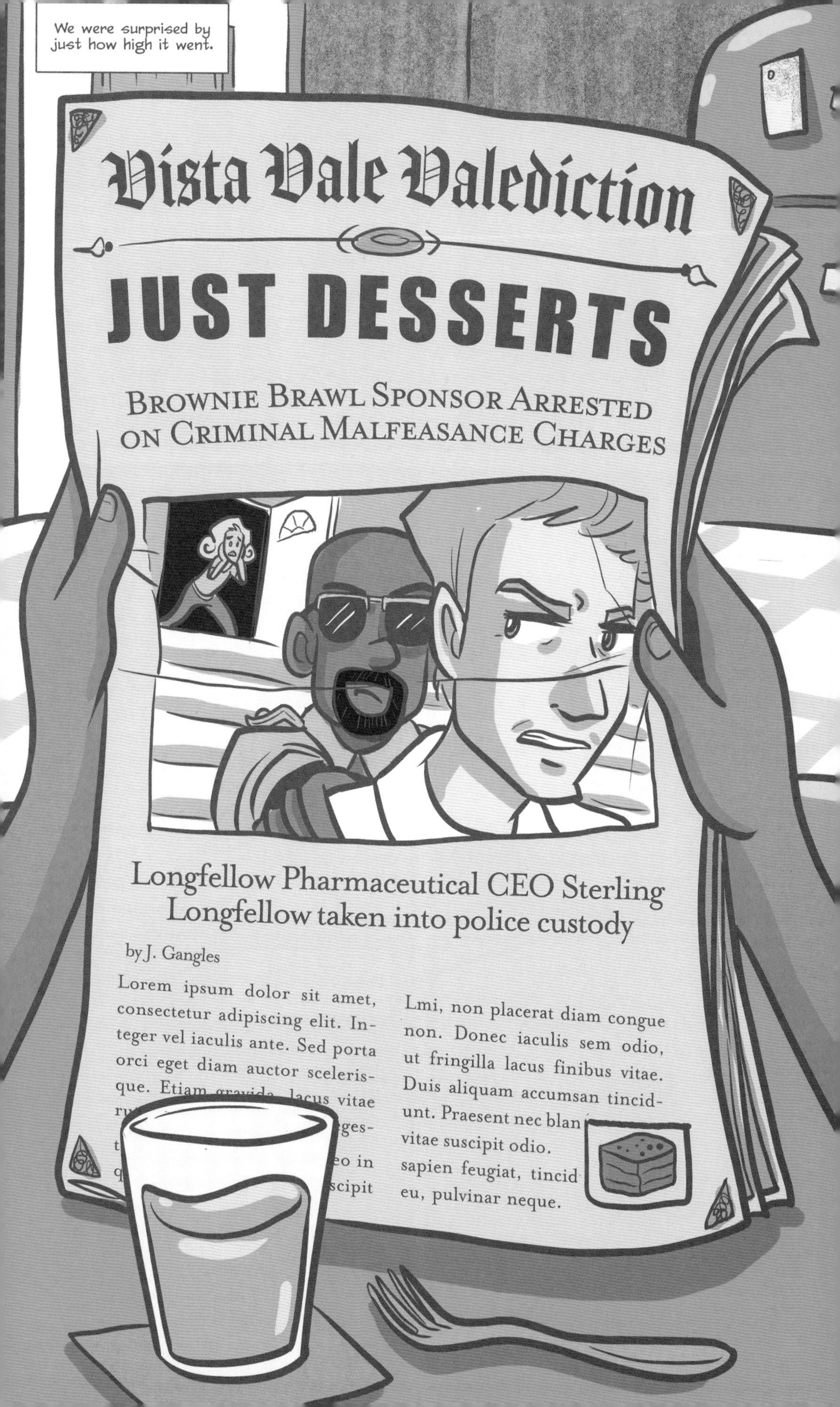
We were surprised by just how high it went.
Vista Vale Valediction
JUST DESSERTS
BROWNIE BRAWL SPONSOR ARRESTED ON CRIMINAL MALFEASANCE CHARGES
Longfellow Pharmaceutical CEO Sterling Longfellow taken into police custody
by J. Gangles
Lorem ipsum dolor sit amet, consectetur adipiscing elit. Integer vel iaculis ante. Sed porta orci eget diam auctor scelerisque. Etiam gravida lacus vitae
Lmi, non placerat diam congue non. Donec iaculis sem odio, ut fringilla lacus finibus vitae. Duis aliquam accumsan tincidunt. Praesent nec blan
vitae suscipit odio.
sapien feugiat, tincid
eu, pulvinar neque.

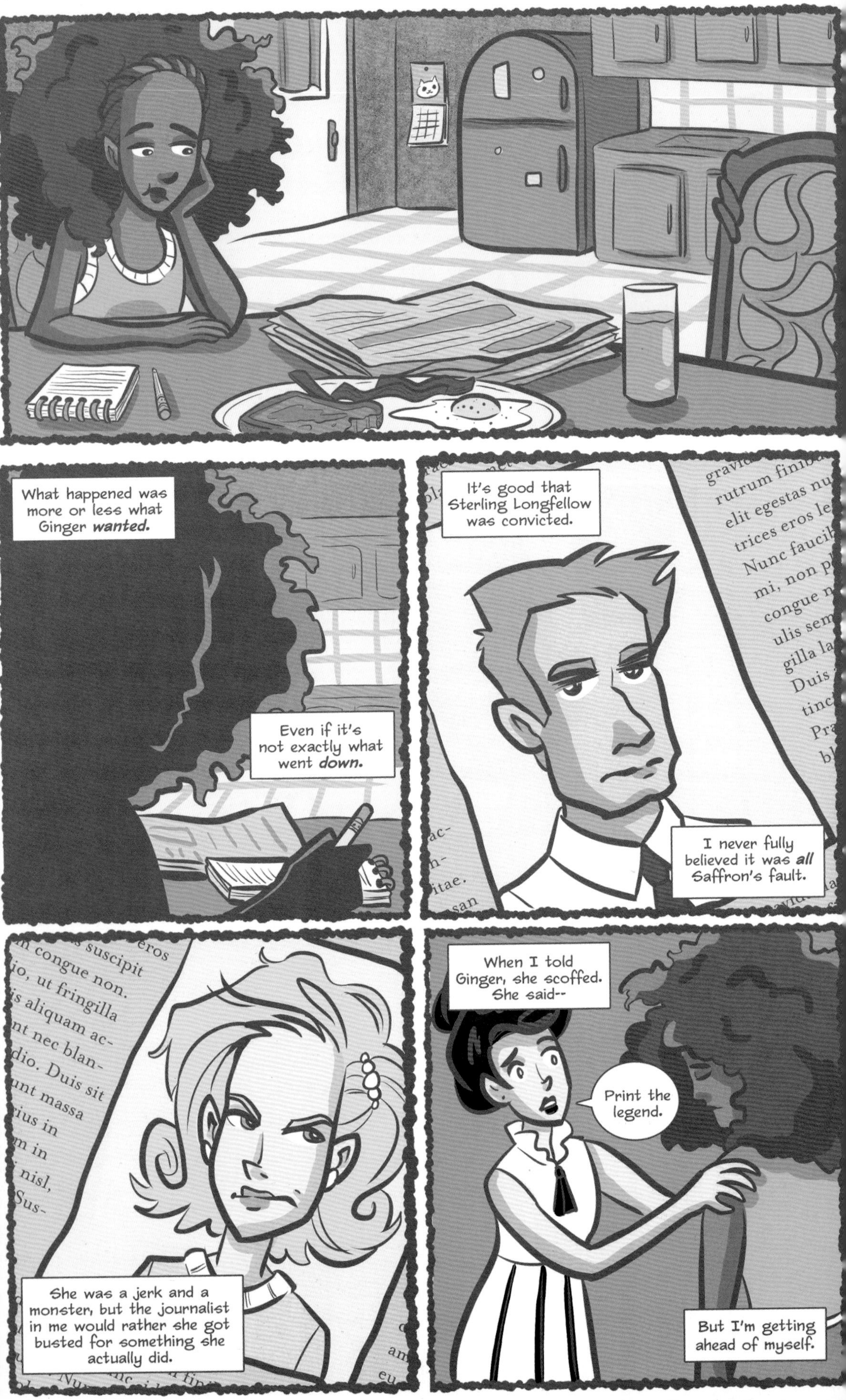
What happened was more or less what Ginger *wanted.*
Even if it's not exactly what went *down.*
It's good that Sterling Longfellow was convicted.
I never fully believed it was *all* Saffron's fault.
She was a jerk and a monster, but the journalist in me would rather she got busted for something she actually did.
When I told Ginger, she scoffed. She said--
Print the legend.
But I'm getting ahead of myself.

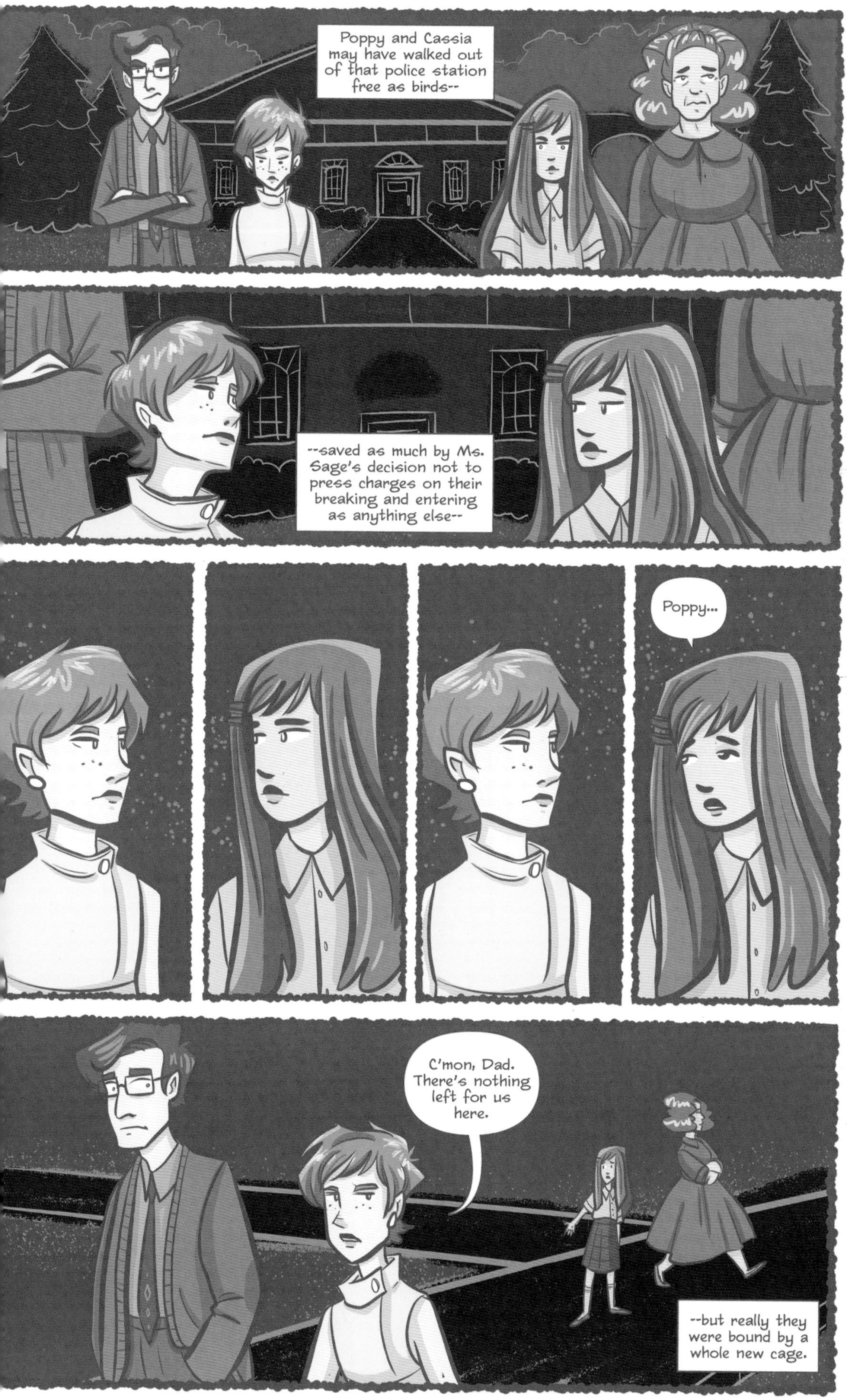

Poppy and Cassia may have walked out of that police station free as birds--
--saved as much by Ms. Sage's decision not to press charges on their breaking and entering as anything else--
Poppy...
C'mon, Dad. There's nothing left for us here.
--but really they were bound by a whole new cage.

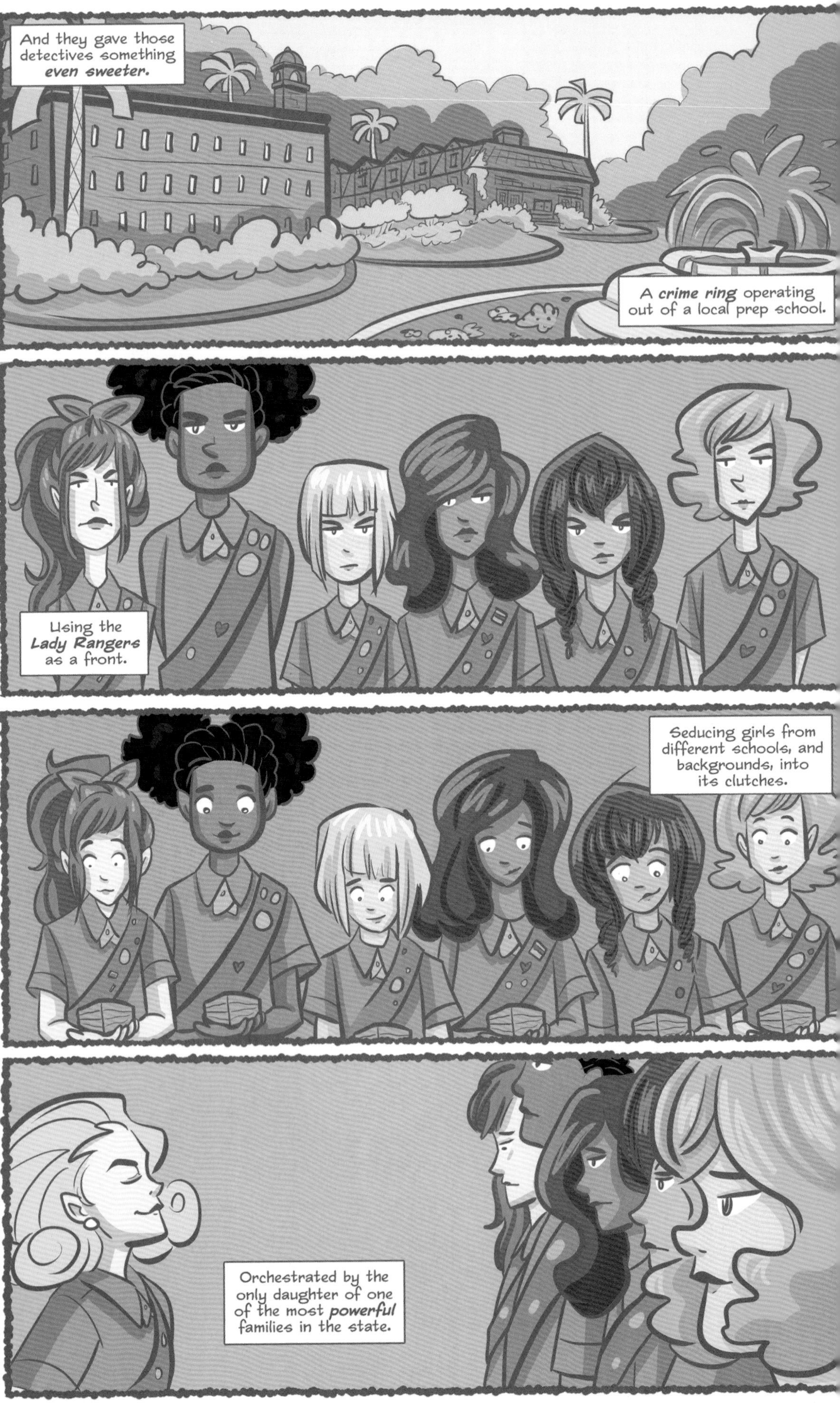

And they gave those detectives something *even sweeter.*
A *crime ring* operating out of a local prep school.
Using the *Lady Rangers* as a front.
Seducing girls from different schools, and backgrounds, into its clutches.
Orchestrated by the only daughter of one of the most *powerful* families in the state.

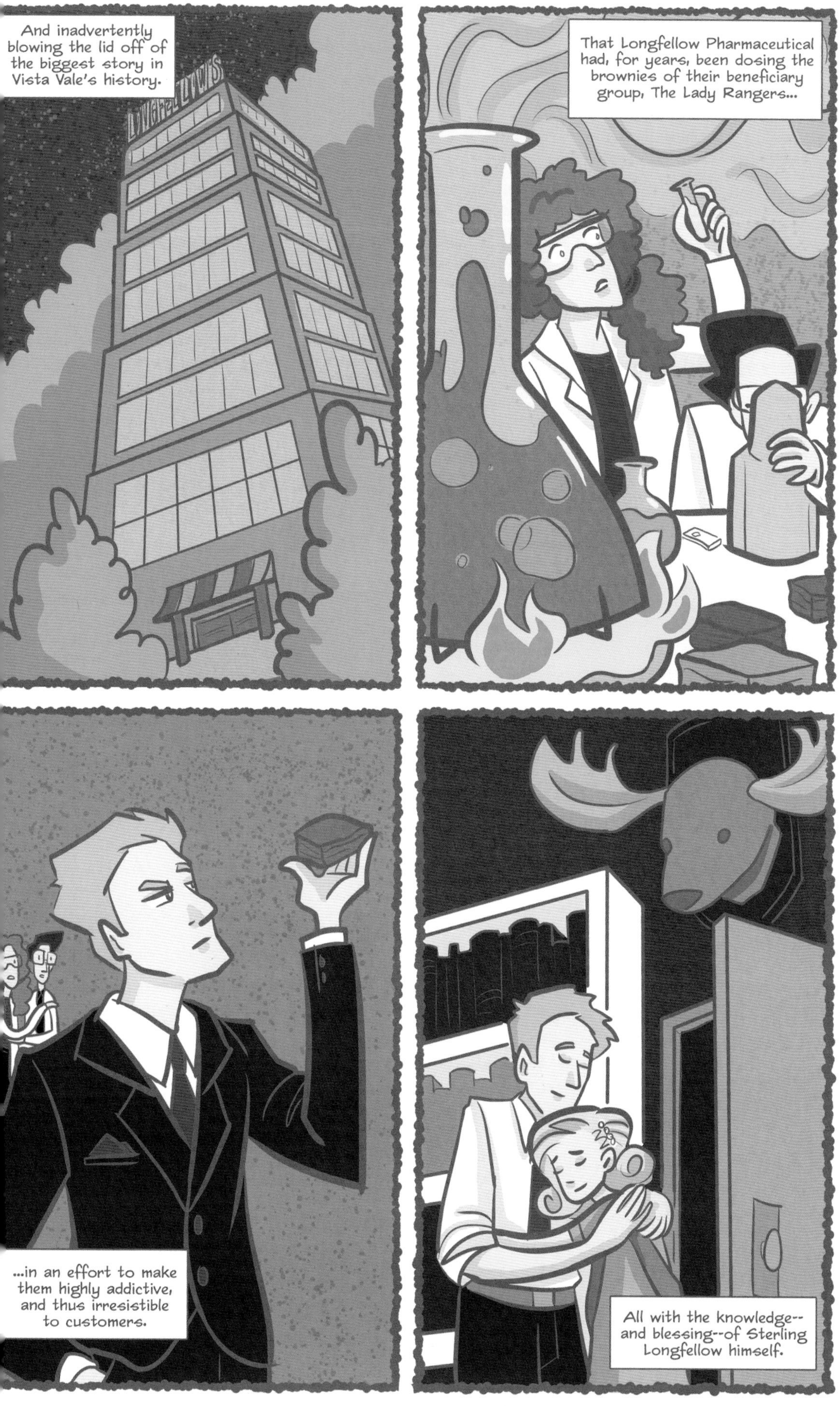
And inadvertently blowing the lid off of the biggest story in Vista Vale's history.
That Longfellow Pharmaceutical had, for years, been dosing the brownies of their beneficiary group, The Lady Rangers...
...in an effort to make them highly addictive, and thus irresistible to customers.
All with the knowledge--and blessing--of Sterling Longfellow himself.

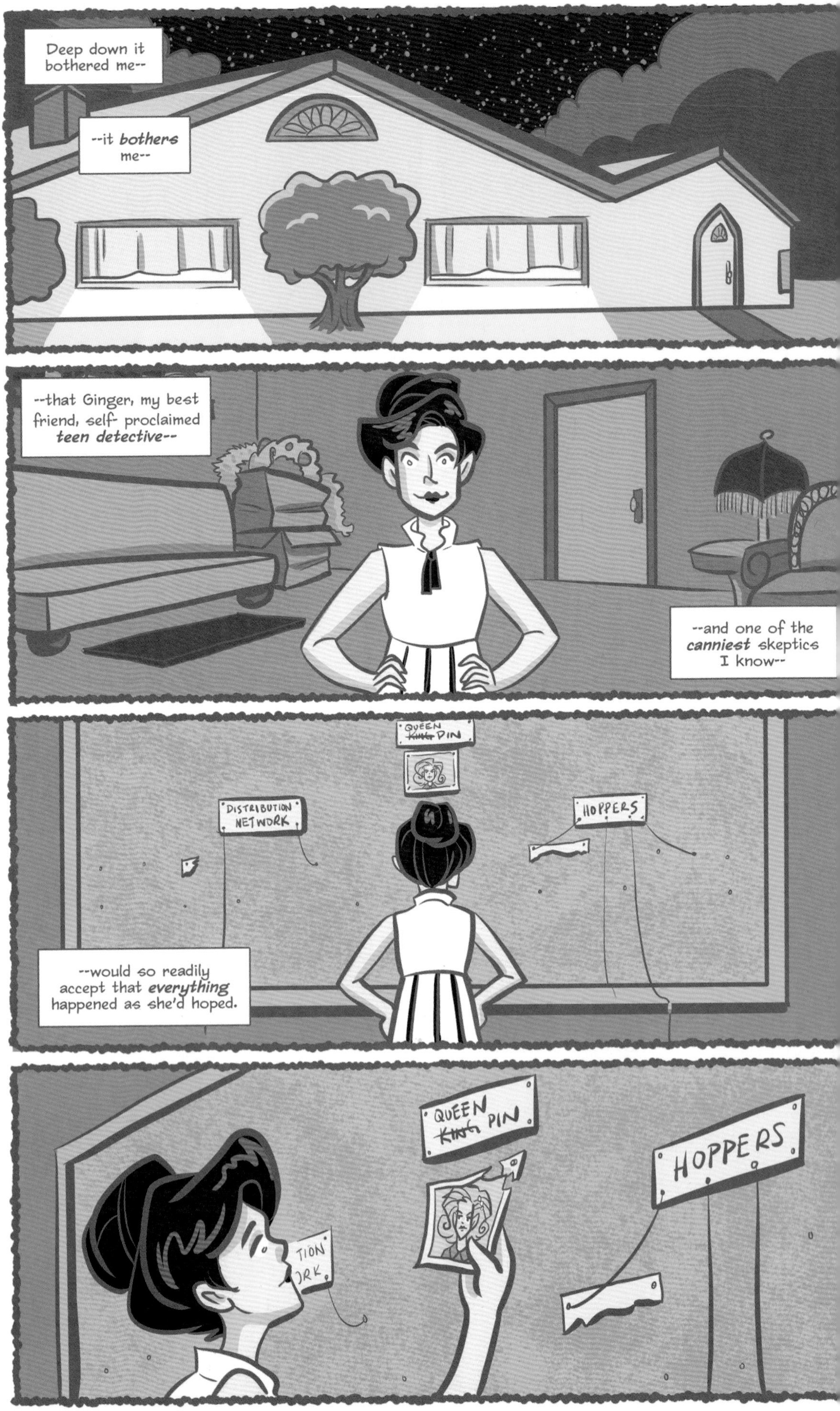
Deep down it bothered me--
--it *bothers* me--
--that Ginger, my best friend, self- proclaimed *teen detective*--
--and one of the *canniest* skeptics I know--
QUEEN ~~King~~ PIN
DISTRIBUTION NETWORK
HOPPERS
--would so readily accept that *everything* happened as she'd hoped.
QUEEN ~~King~~ PIN
HOPPERS
TION
ORK

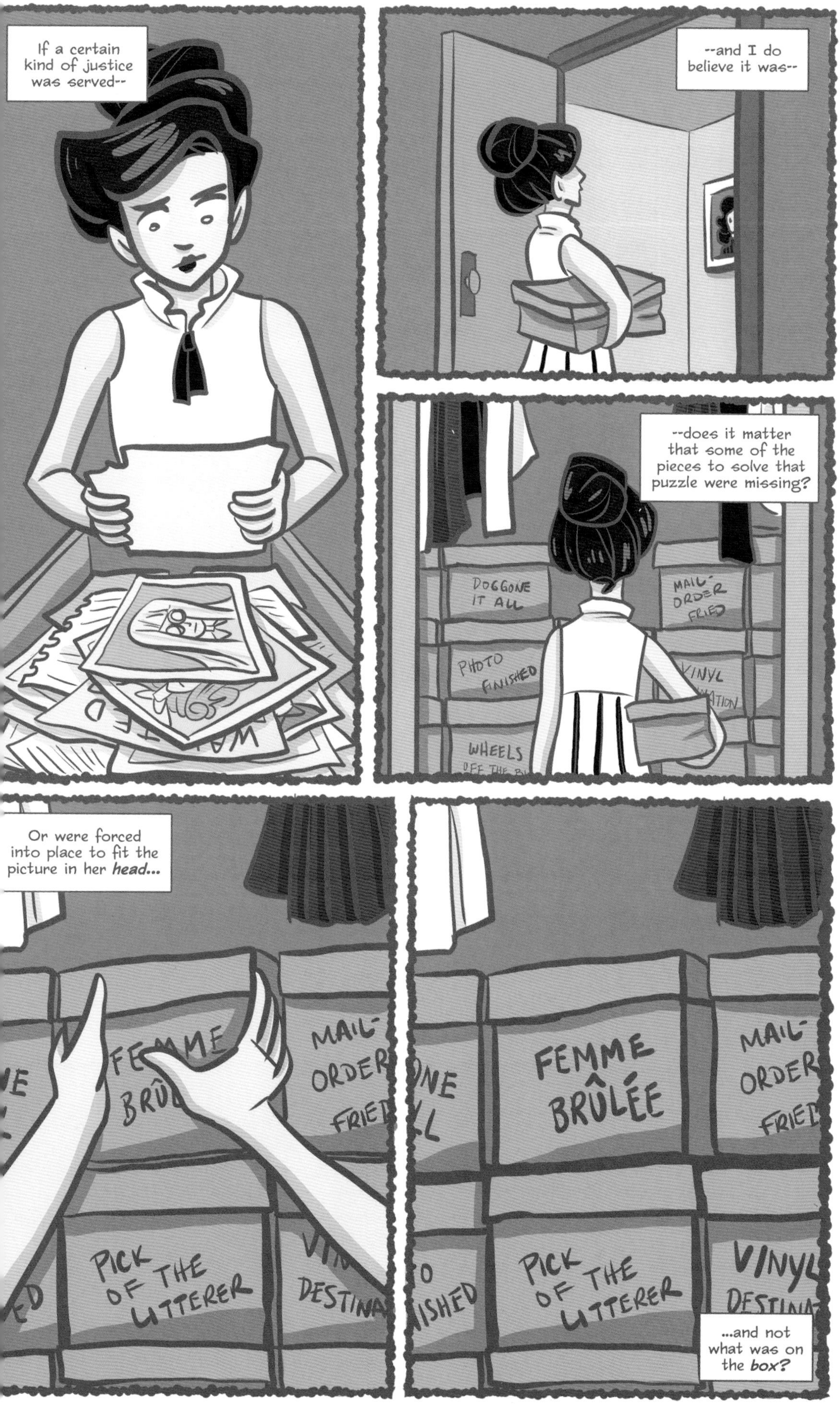
If a certain kind of justice was served--
--and I do believe it was--
--does it matter that some of the pieces to solve that puzzle were missing?
DOGGONE IT ALL
MAIL-ORDER FRIED
PHOTO FINISHED
WHEELS
Or were forced into place to fit the picture in her *head...*
MAIL-ORDER FRIED
PICK OF THE LITTERER
FEMME BRÛLÉE
MAIL-ORDER FRIED
PICK OF THE LITTERER
...and not what was on the *box?*

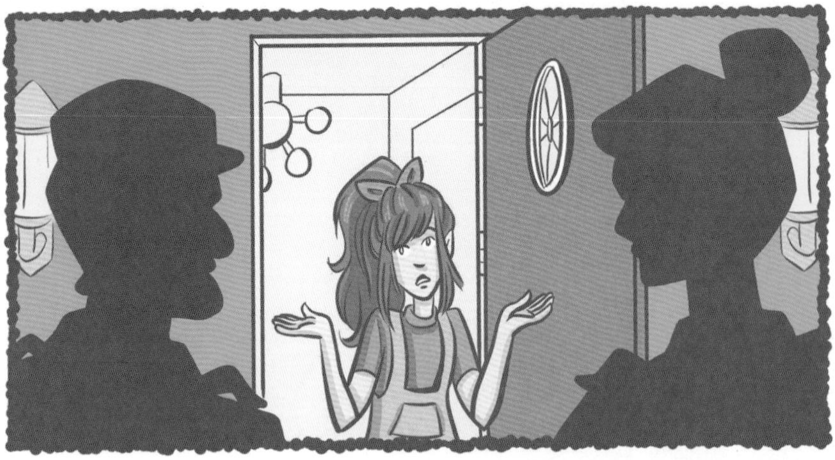

No one's shedding a tear for Saffron Longfellow, but there's a particular sadness in that, I suppose.

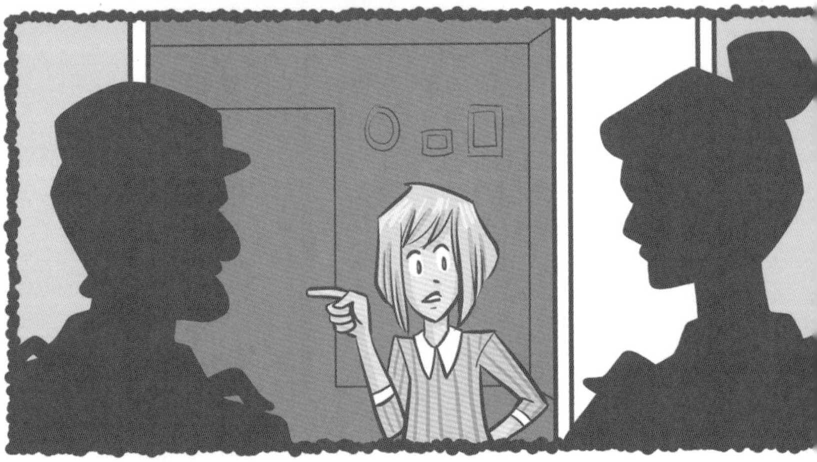

That when the headsman came for her, not a single person stood up and said, ***"No."***

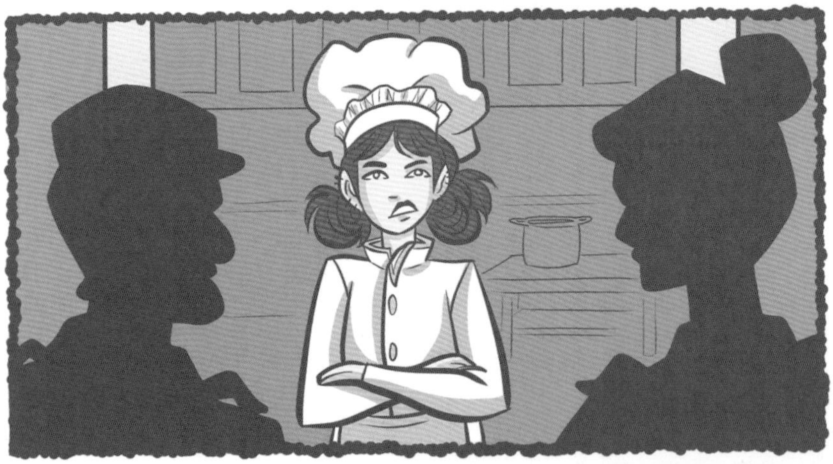

In fact, they pointed the way to the gallows.

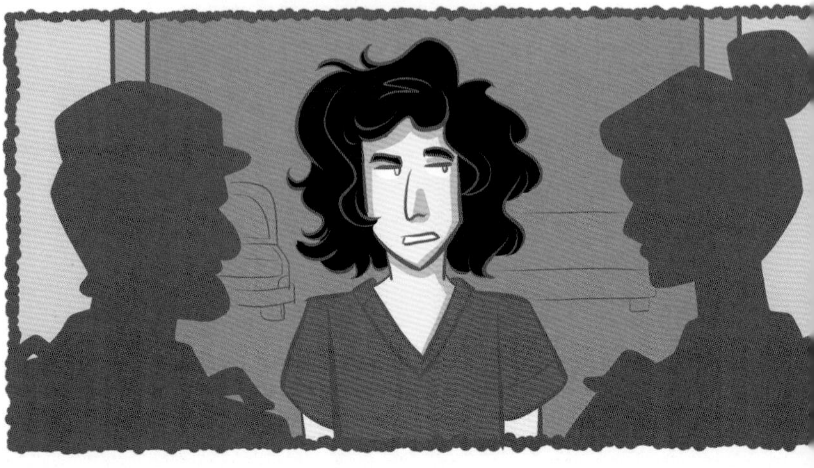

Cassia must've had them all eating out of the palm of her hand.

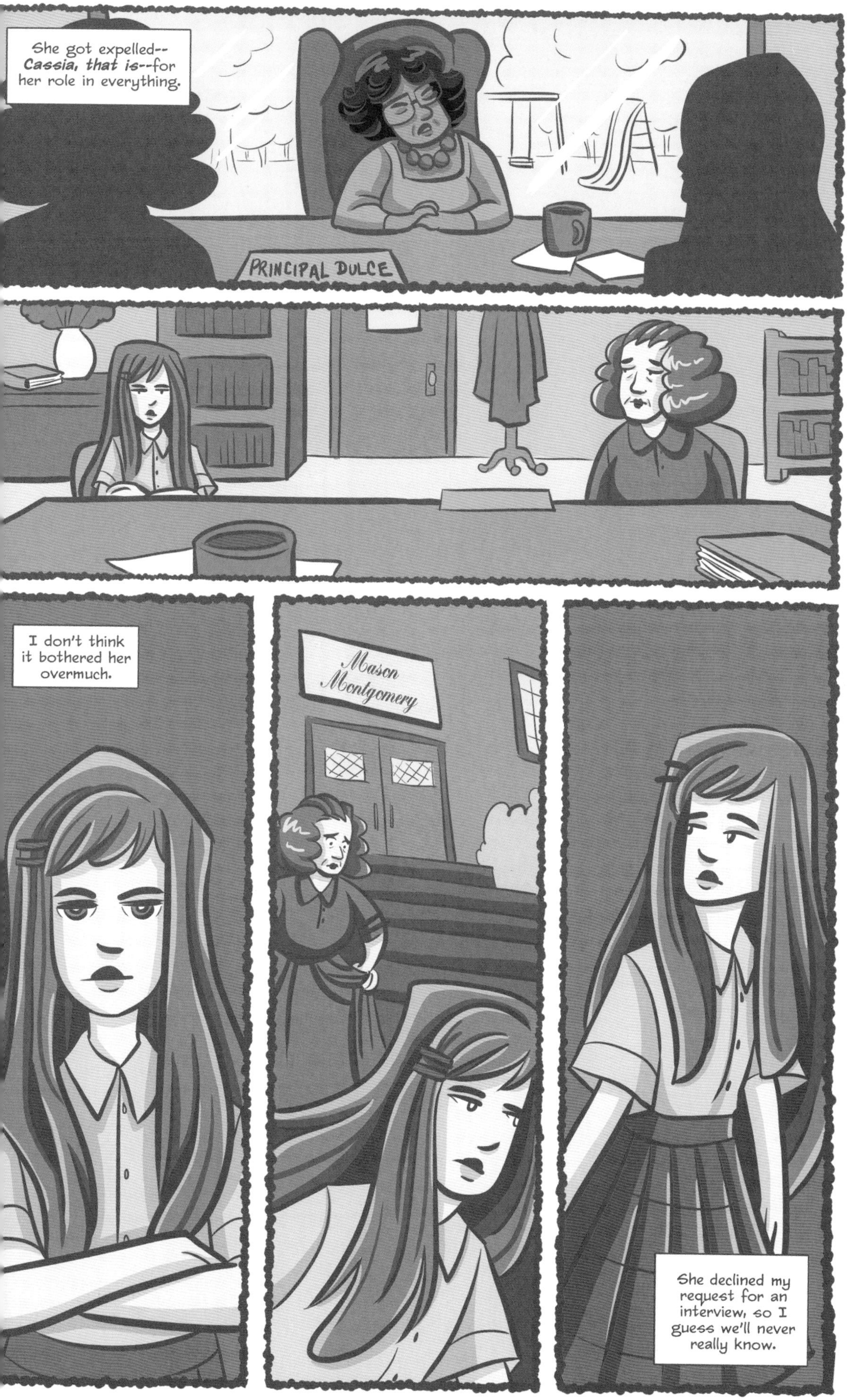
She got expelled--**Cassia, that is**--for her role in everything.
PRINCIPAL DULCE
I don't think it bothered her overmuch.
Mason Montgomery
She declined my request for an interview, so I guess we'll never really know.

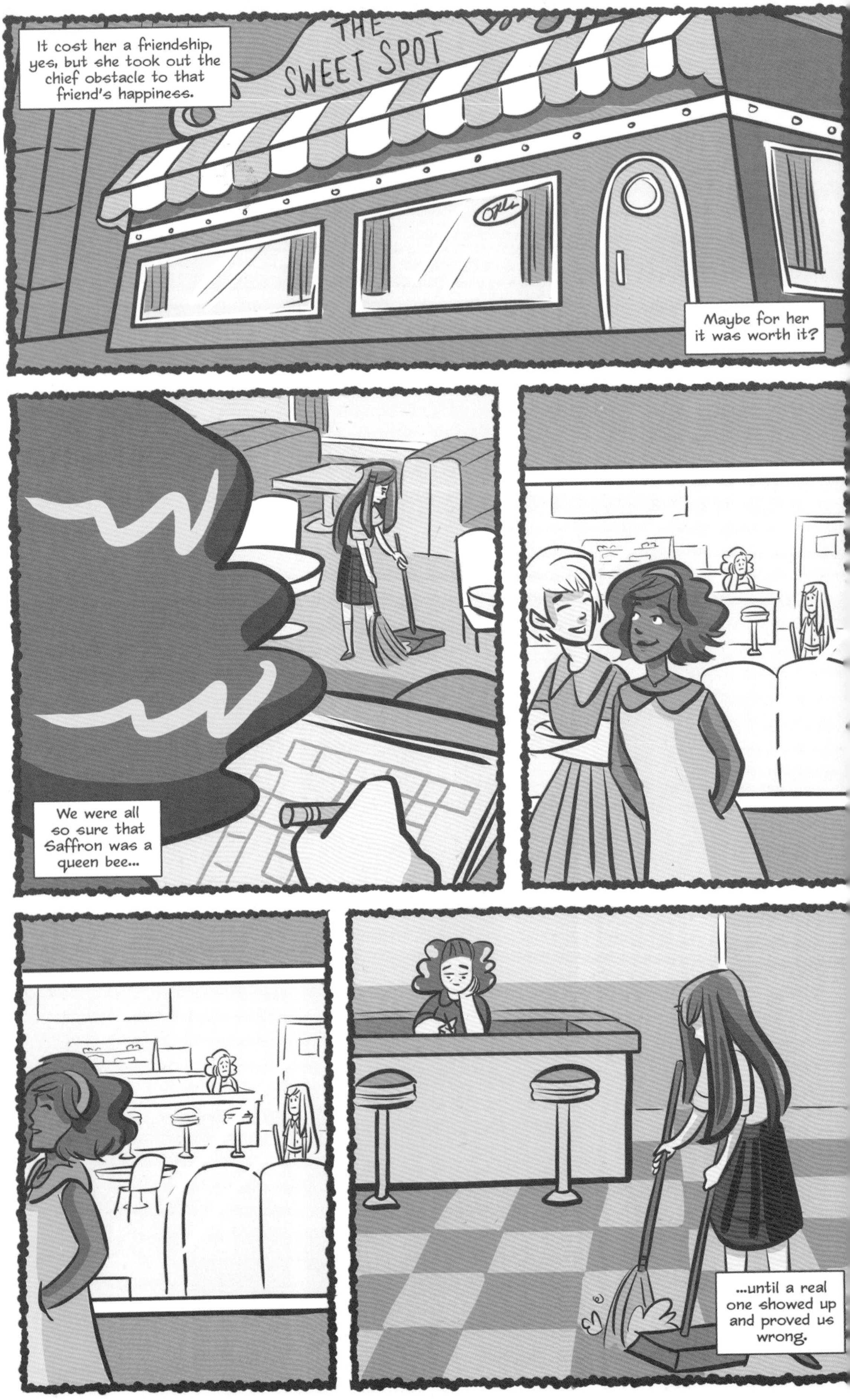

It cost her a friendship, yes, but she took out the chief obstacle to that friend's happiness.
THE SWEET SPOT
Maybe for her it was worth it?
We were all so sure that Saffron was a queen bee...
...until a real one showed up and proved us wrong.

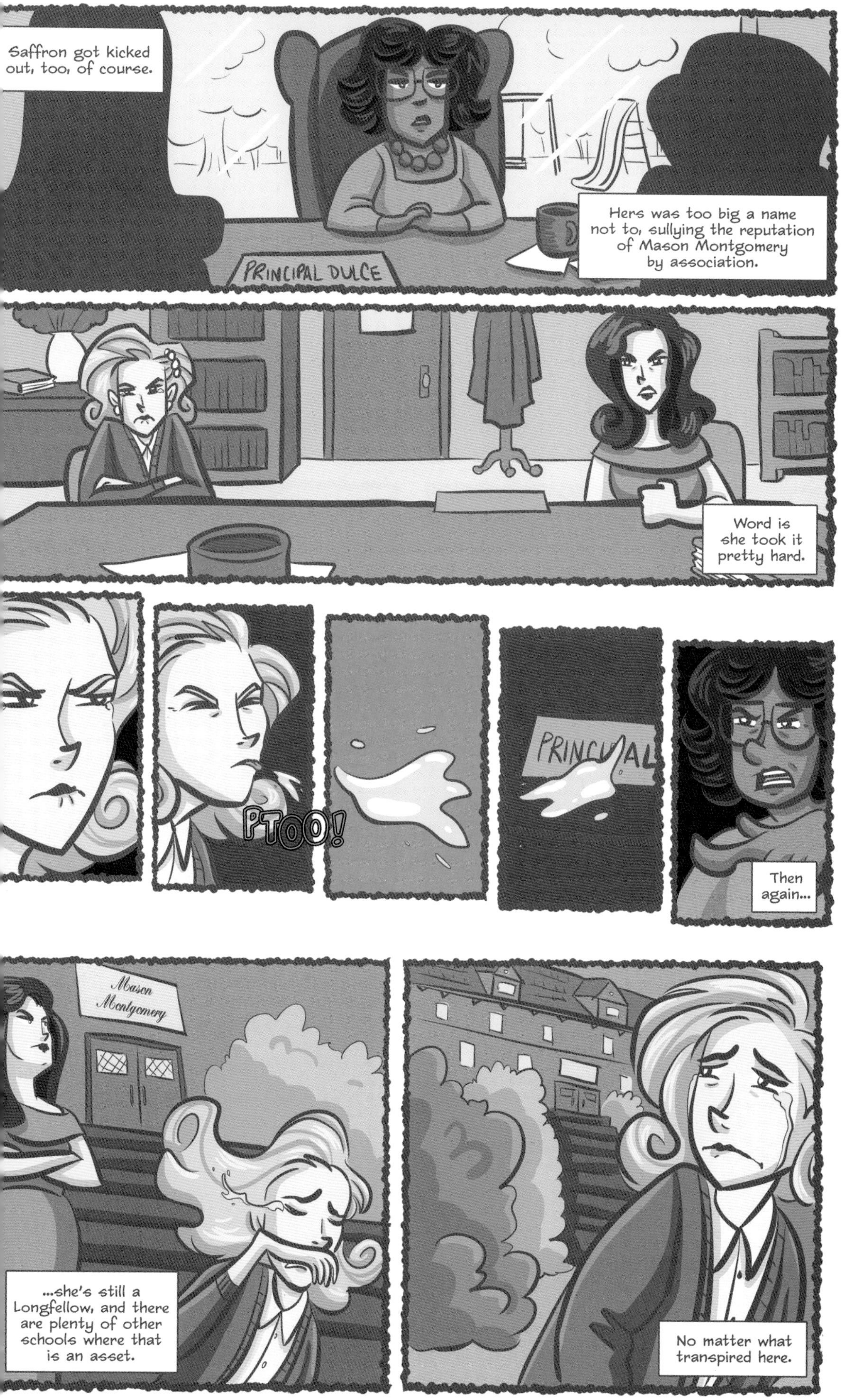

Saffron got kicked out, too, of course.
PRINCIPAL DULCE
Hers was too big a name not to, sullying the reputation of Mason Montgomery by association.
Word is she took it pretty hard.
PTOO!
PRINCIPAL
Then again...
Mason Montgomery
...she's still a Longfellow, and there are plenty of other schools where that is an asset.
No matter what transpired here.

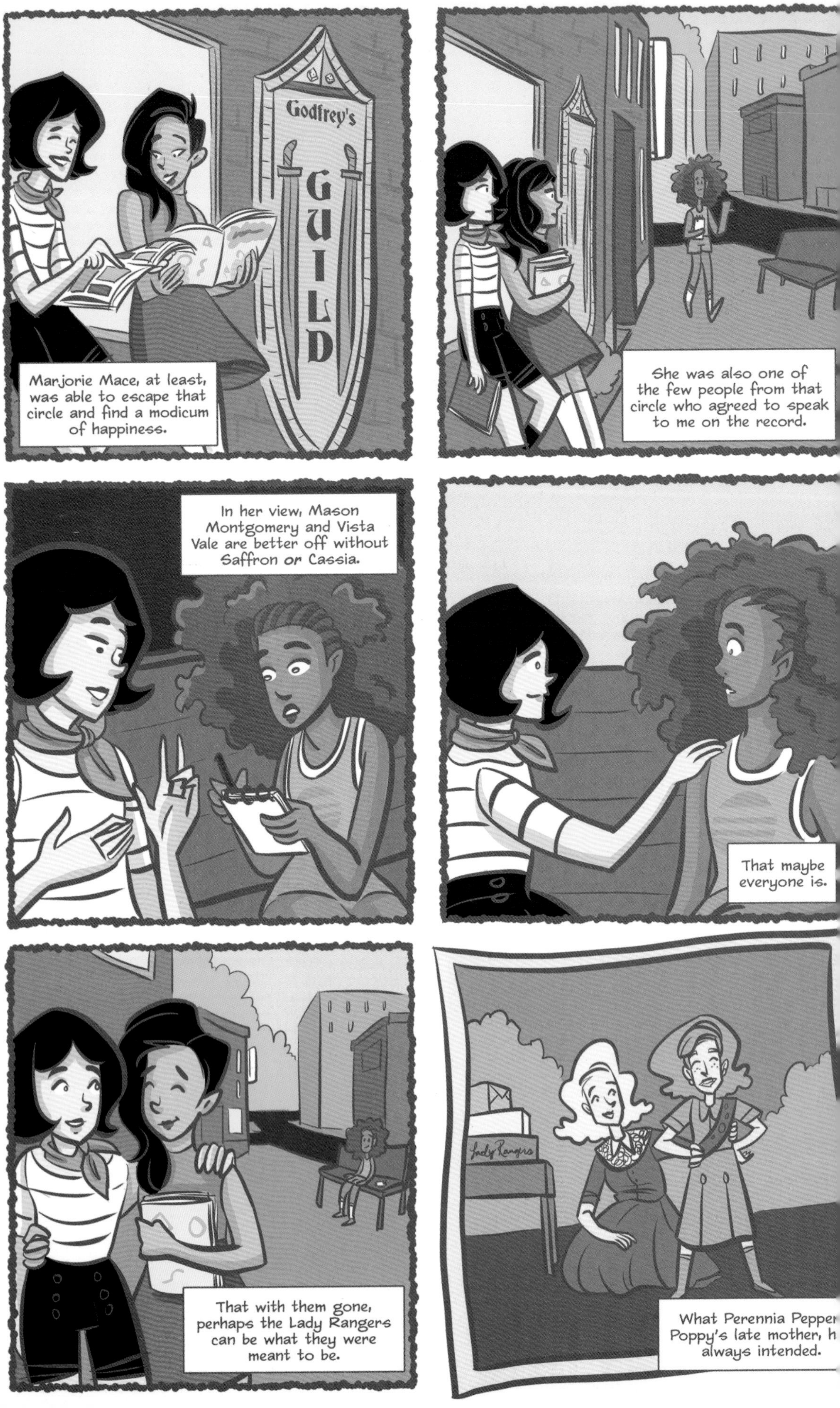
Godfrey's
GUILD
Marjorie Mace, at least, was able to escape that circle and find a modicum of happiness.
She was also one of the few people from that circle who agreed to speak to me on the record.
In her view, Mason Montgomery and Vista Vale are better off without Saffron *or* Cassia.
That maybe everyone is.
That with them gone, perhaps the Lady Rangers can be what they were meant to be.
Lady Rangers
What Perennia Pepper
Poppy's late mother, h
always intended.

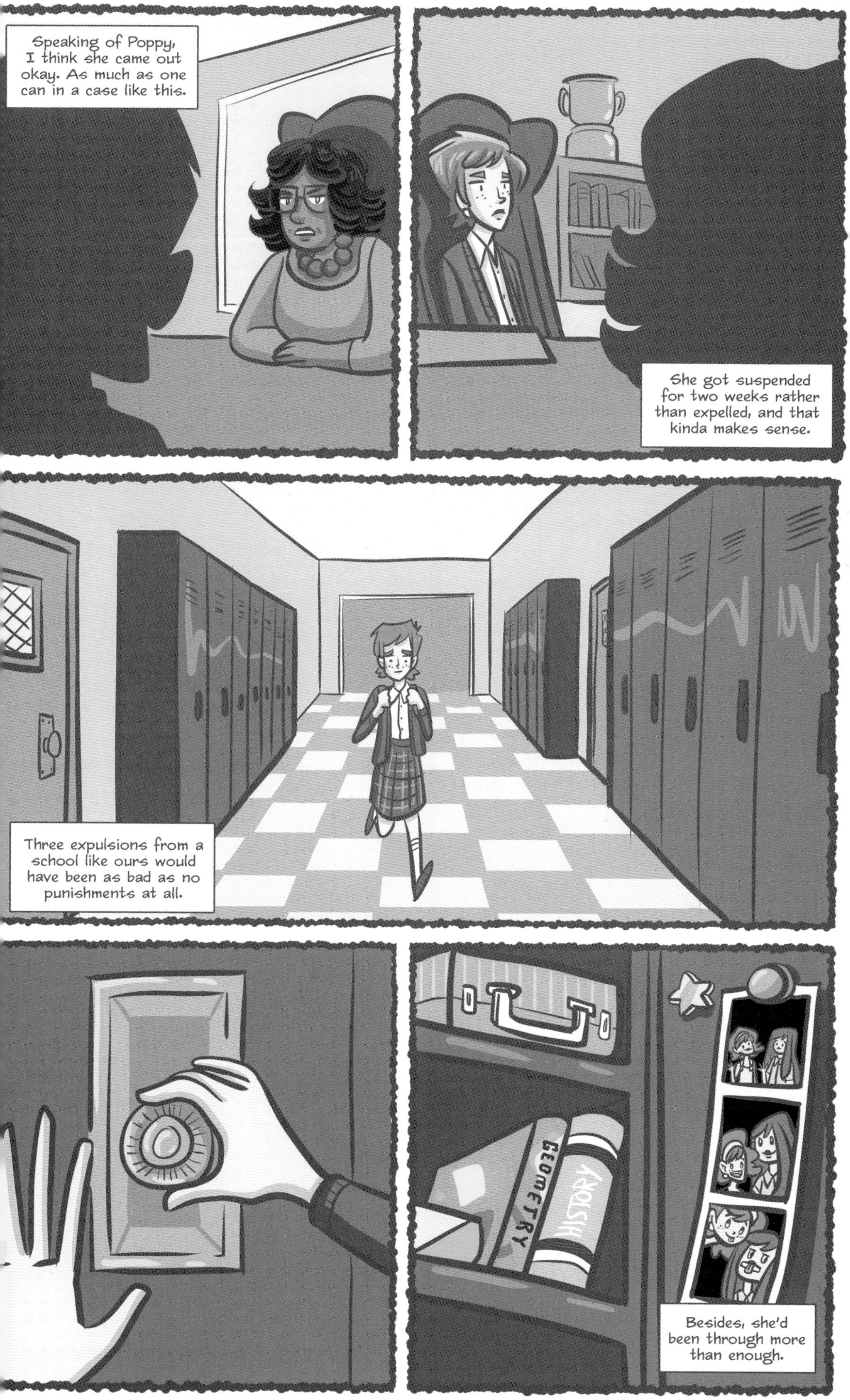

Speaking of Poppy, I think she came out okay. As much as one can in a case like this.
She got suspended for two weeks rather than expelled, and that kinda makes sense.
Three expulsions from a school like ours would have been as bad as no punishments at all.
GEOMETRY
HISTORY
Besides, she'd been through more than enough.

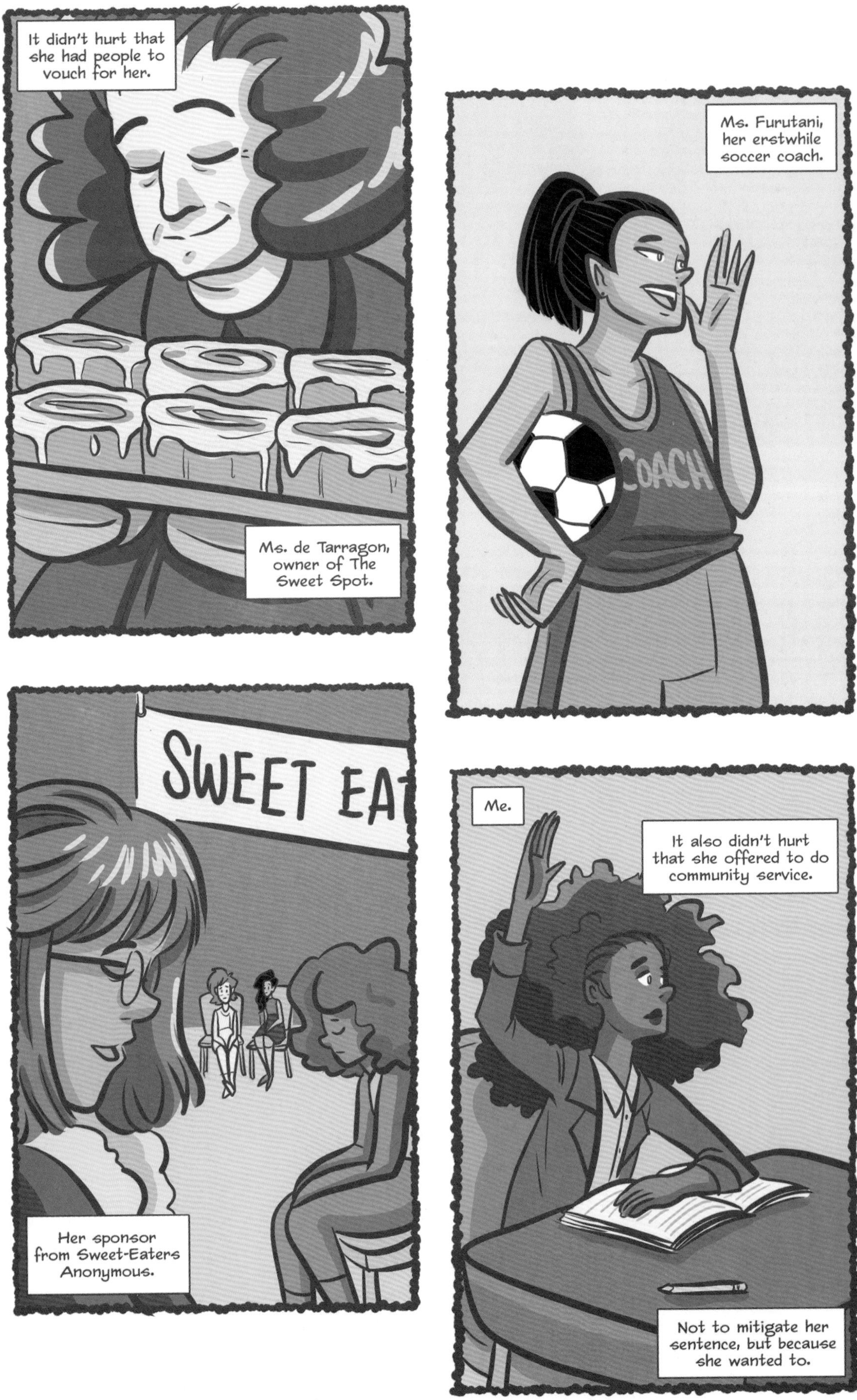
It didn't hurt that she had people to vouch for her.
Ms. de Tarragon, owner of The Sweet Spot.
Ms. Furutani, her erstwhile soccer coach.
COACH
SWEET EAT
Her sponsor from Sweet-Eaters Anonymous.
Me.
It also didn't hurt that she offered to do community service.
Not to mitigate her sentence, but because she wanted to.

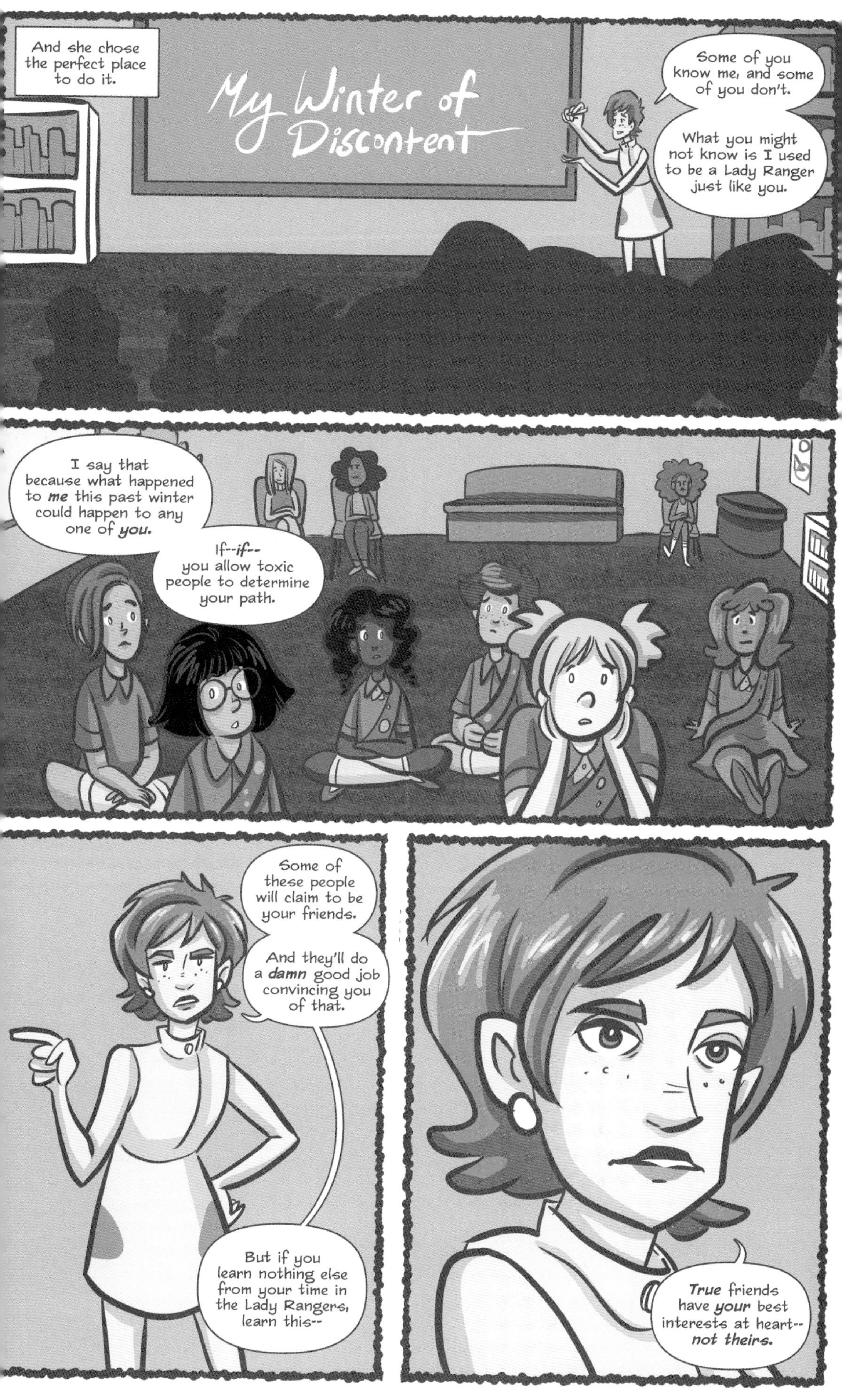
And she chose the perfect place to do it.
My Winter of Discontent
Some of you know me, and some of you don't.
What you might not know is I used to be a Lady Ranger just like you.
I say that because what happened to ***me*** this past winter could happen to any one of ***you.***
If--*if*-- you allow toxic people to determine your path.
Some of these people will claim to be your friends.
And they'll do a ***damn*** good job convincing you of that.
But if you learn nothing else from your time in the Lady Rangers, learn this--
True friends have ***your*** best interests at heart-- ***not theirs.***

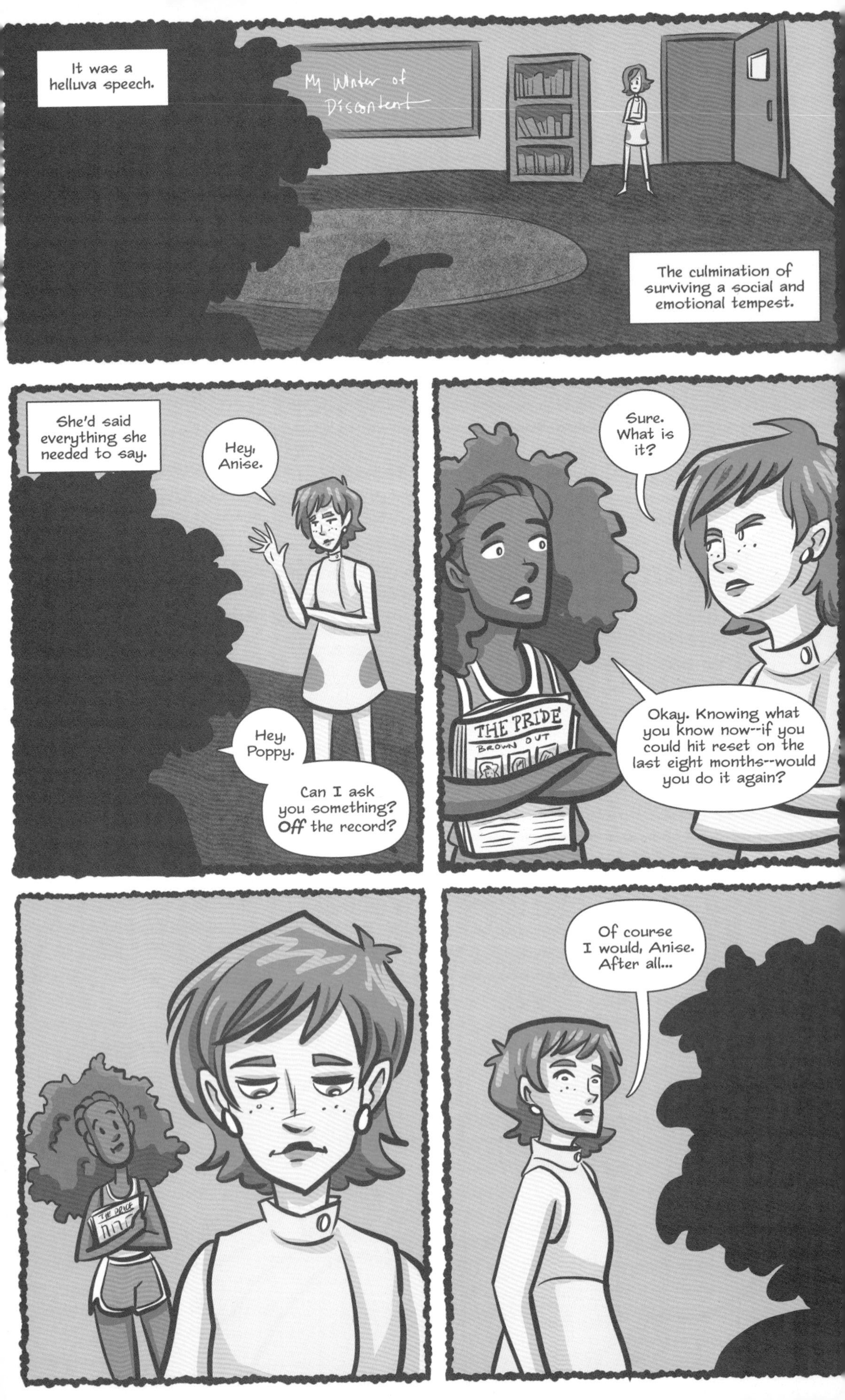
It was a helluva speech.
My Winter of Discontent
The culmination of surviving a social and emotional tempest.
She'd said everything she needed to say.
Hey, Anise.
Hey, Poppy.
Can I ask you something? Off the record?
Sure. What is it?
THE PRIDE
BROWN OUT
Okay. Knowing what you know now--if you could hit reset on the last eight months--would you do it again?
Of course I would, Anise. After all...

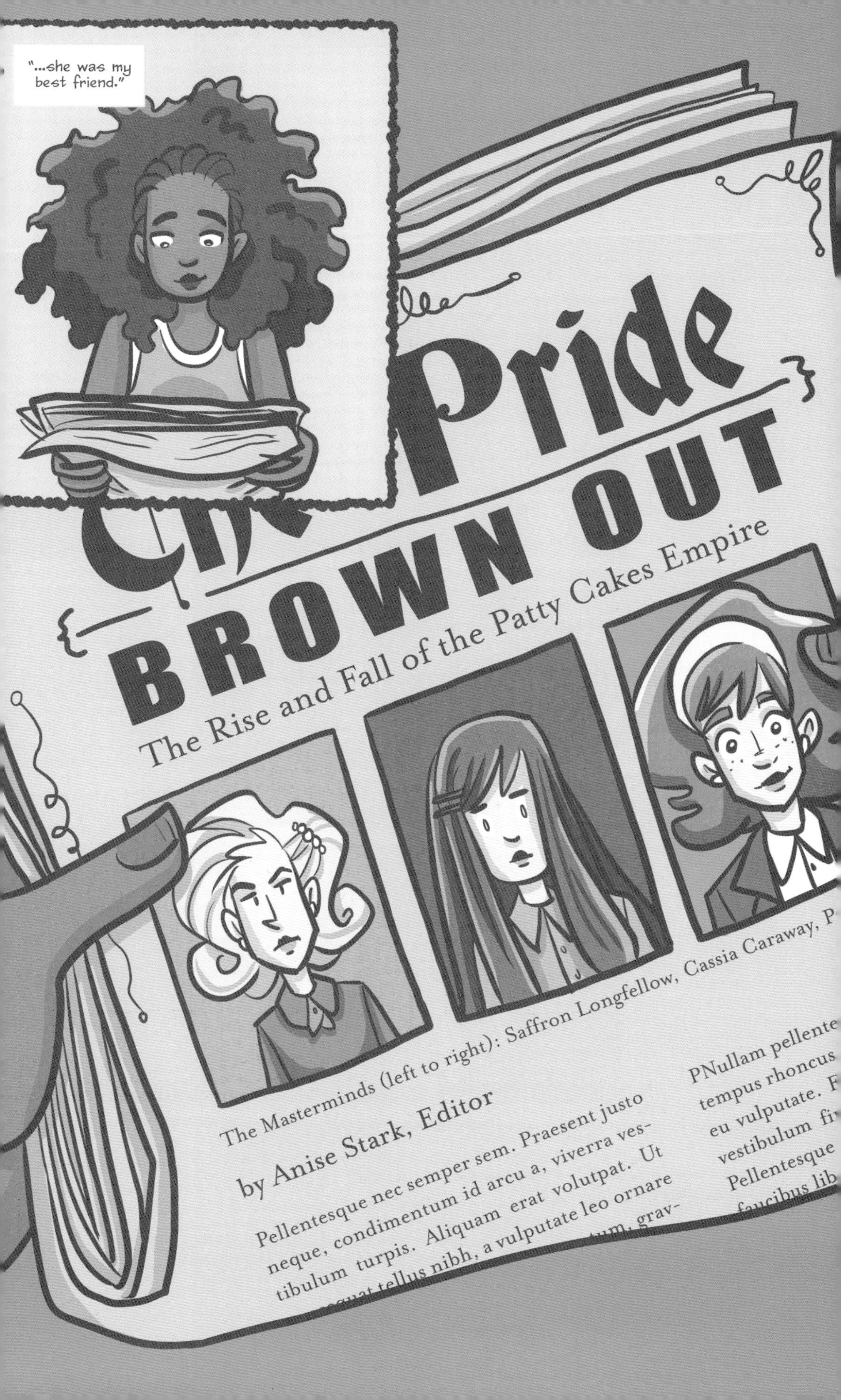
"...she was my best friend."
Pride
BROWN OUT
The Rise and Fall of the Patty Cakes Empire
The Masterminds (left to right): Saffron Longfellow, Cassia Caraway, P
by Anise Stark, Editor
Pellentesque nec semper sem. Praesent justo neque, condimentum id arcu a, viverra vestibulum turpis. Aliquam erat volutpat. Ut tellus nibh, a vulputate leo ornare
PNullam pellente tempus rhoncus eu vulputate. F vestibulum fi Pellentesque faucibus lib

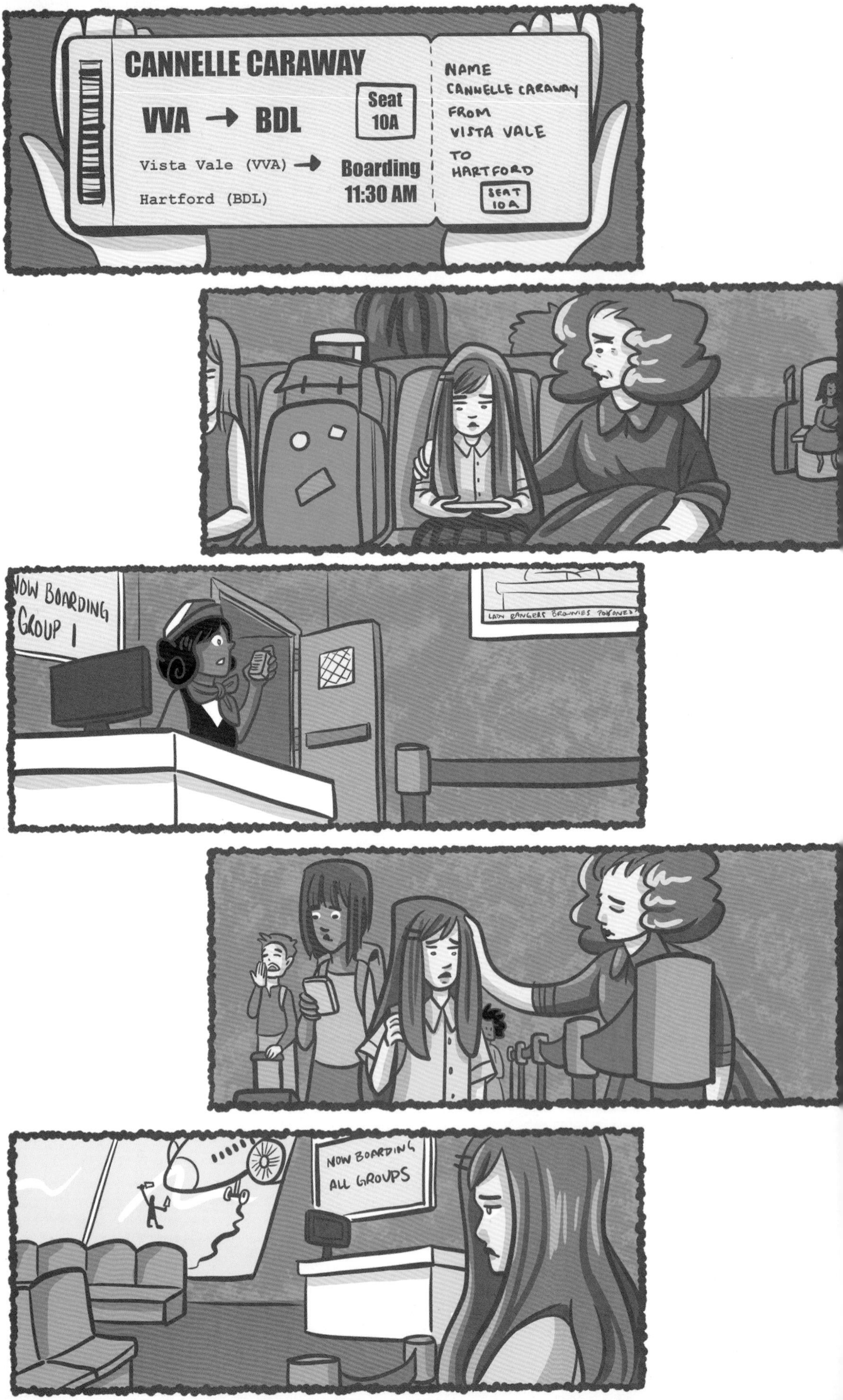
CANNELLE CARAWAY
VVA → BDL
Seat 10A
Vista Vale (VVA) → Hartford (BDL)
Boarding 11:30 AM
NAME CANNELLE CARAWAY
FROM VISTA VALE
TO HARTFORD
SEAT 10A
NOW BOARDING GROUP 1
LADY RANGERS BROWNIES POISONED?
NOW BOARDING ALL GROUPS

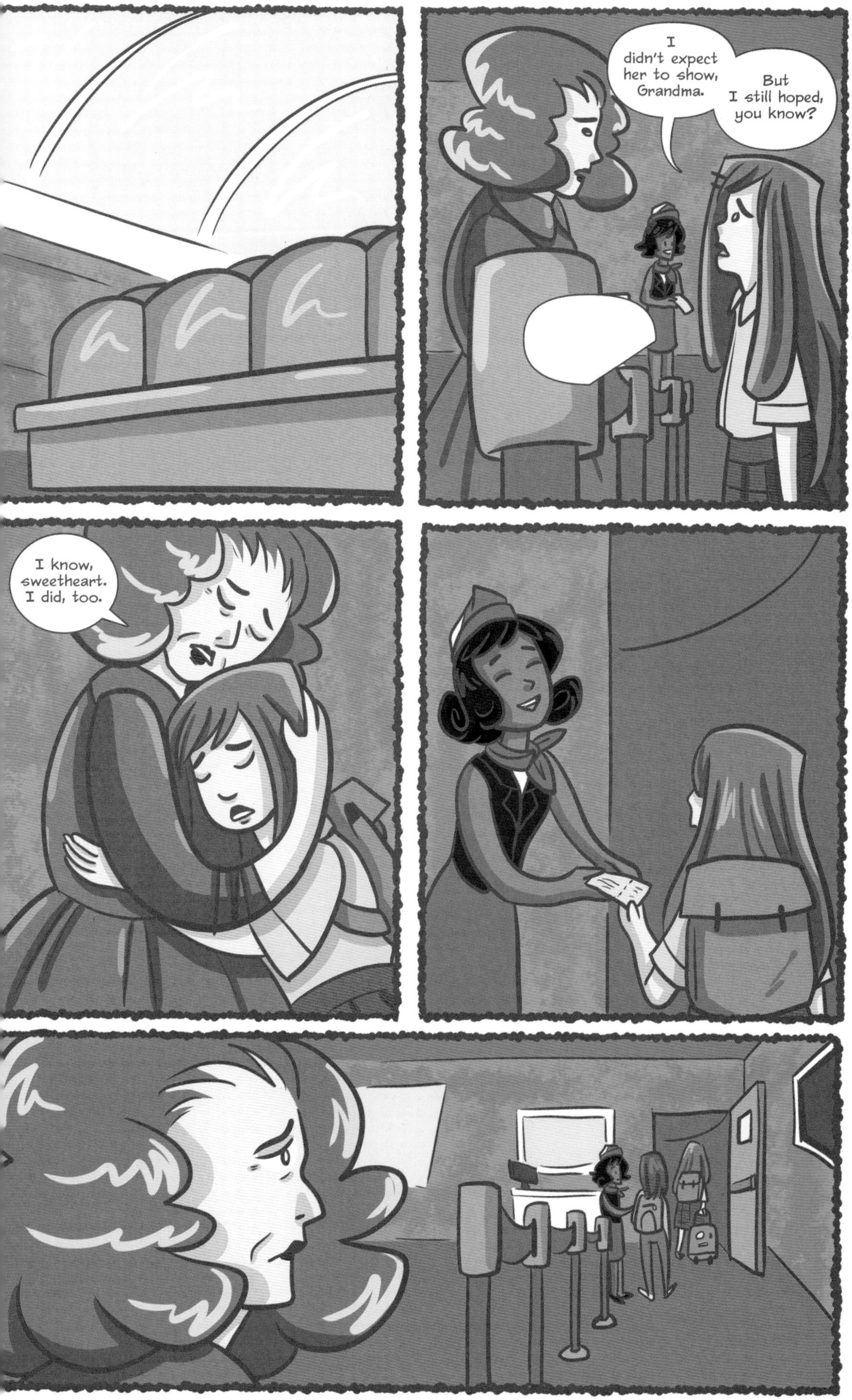
I didn't expect her to show, Grandma.
But I still hoped, you know?
I know, sweetheart. I did, too.

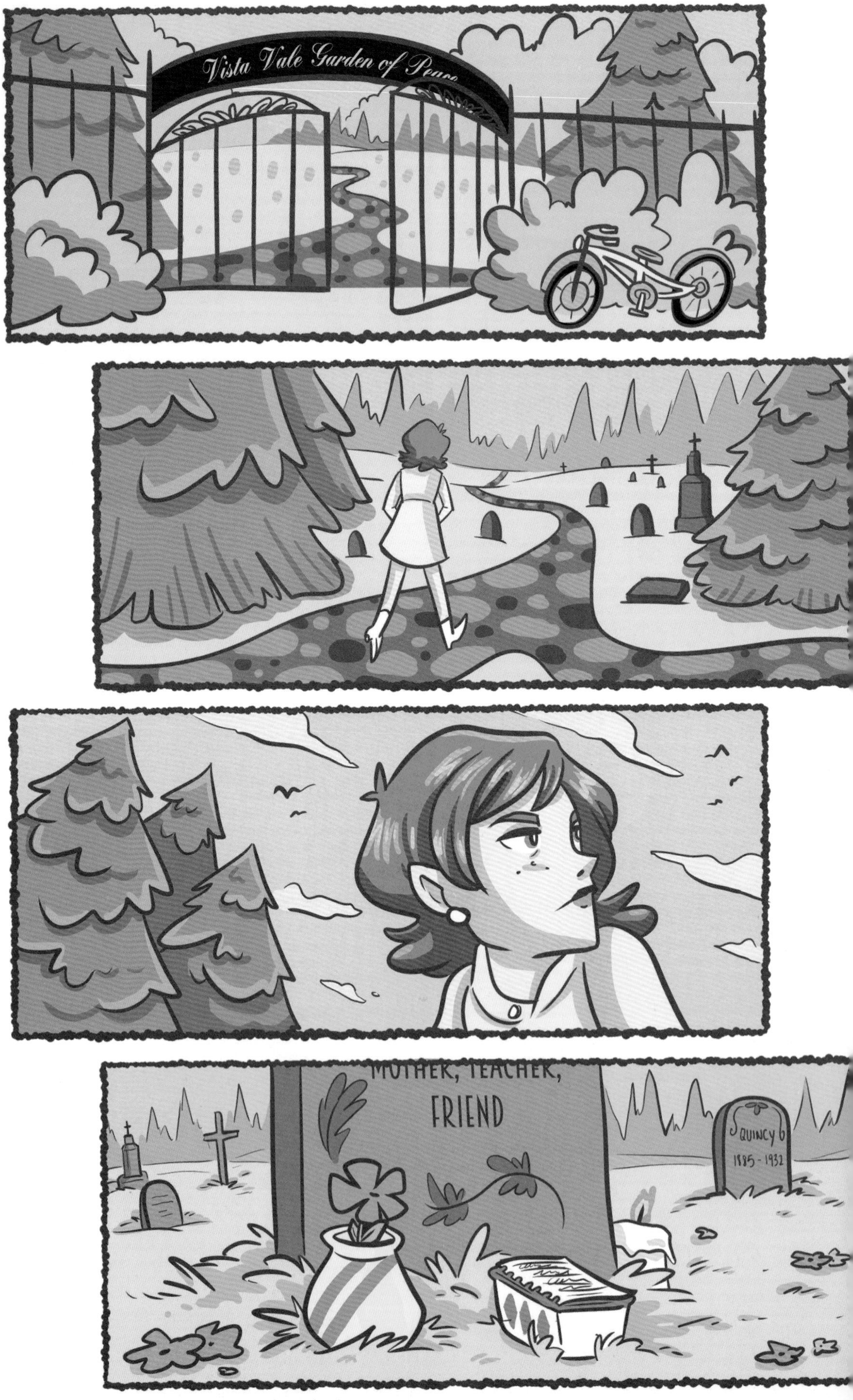
Vista Vale Garden of
MOTHER, TEACHER,
FRIEND
QUINCY
1885 - 1932

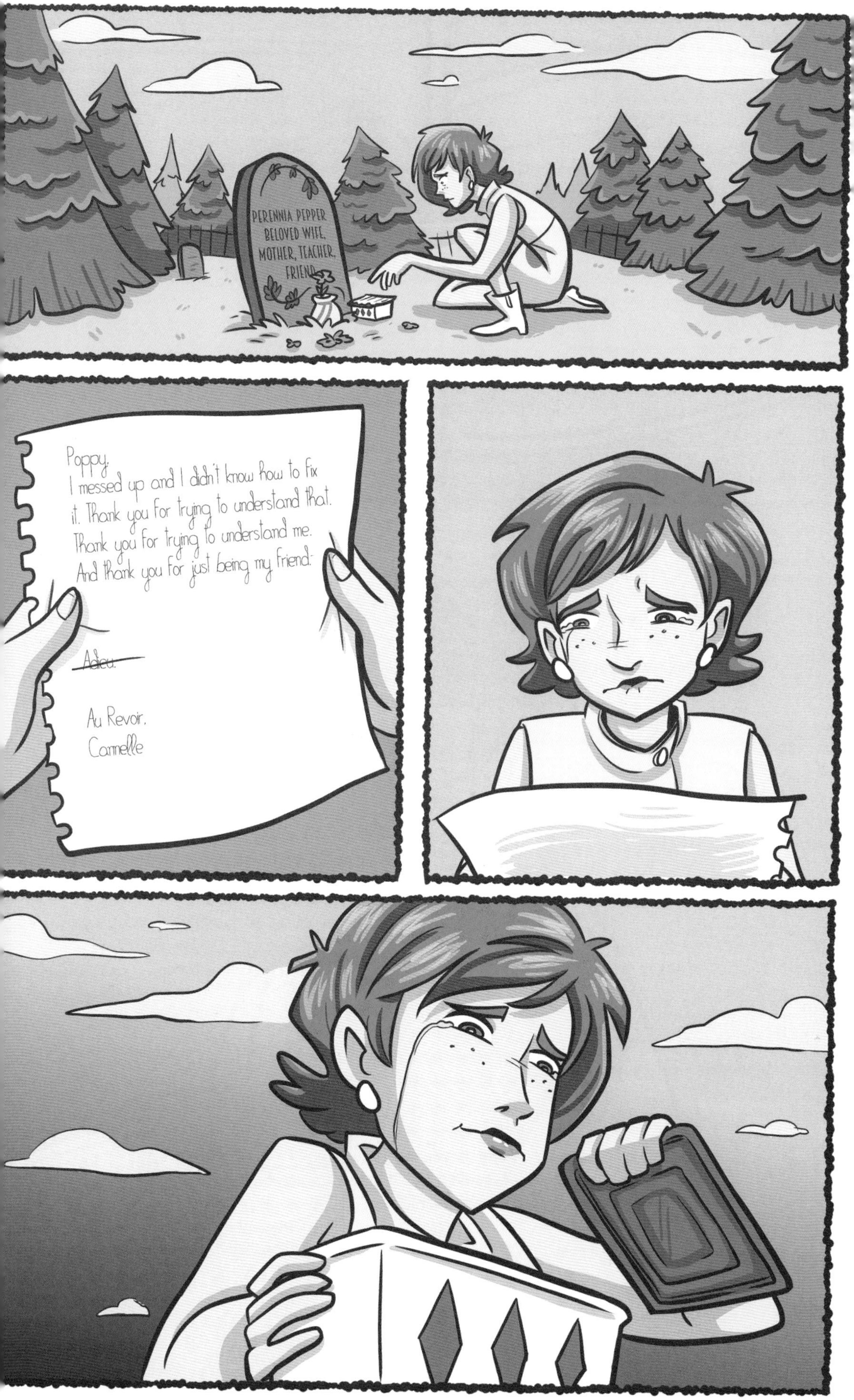
PERENNIA PEPPER
BELOVED WIFE,
MOTHER, TEACHER,
FRIEND
Poppy,
I messed up and I didn't know how to fix it. Thank you for trying to understand that. Thank you for trying to understand me. And thank you for just being my friend.
~~Adieu.~~
Au Revoir,
Cannelle

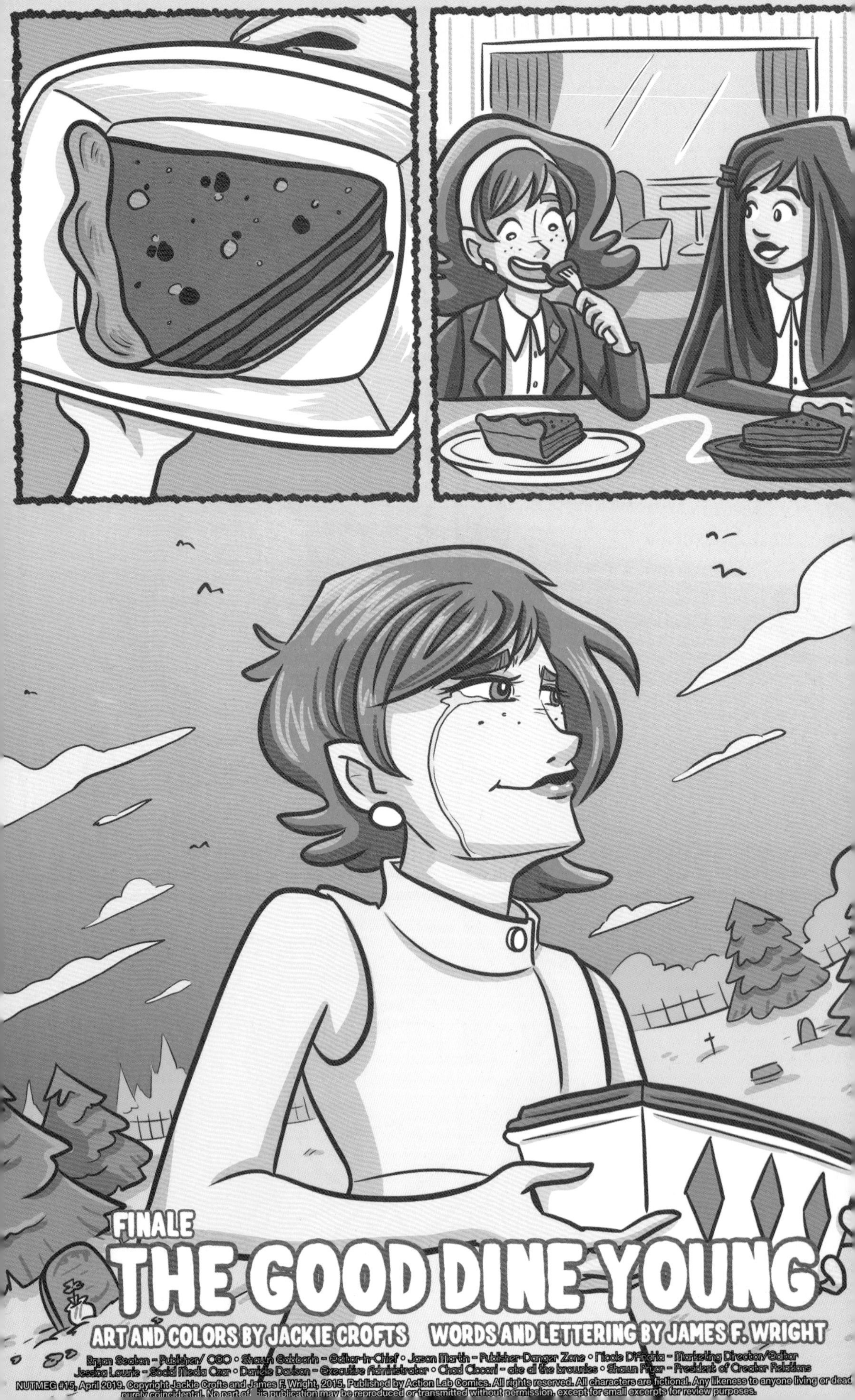
FINALE
THE GOOD DINE YOUNG
ART AND COLORS BY JACKIE CROFTS
WORDS AND LETTERING BY JAMES F. WRIGHT

Bryan Seaton - Publisher/ CEO • Shawn Gabborin - Editor-In-Chief • Jason Martin - Publisher-Danger Zone • Nicole D'Andria - Marketing Director/Editor
Jessica Lowrie - Social Media Czar • Danielle Davison - Executive Administrator • Chad Cicconi - ate all the brownies • Shawn Pryor - President of Creator Relations

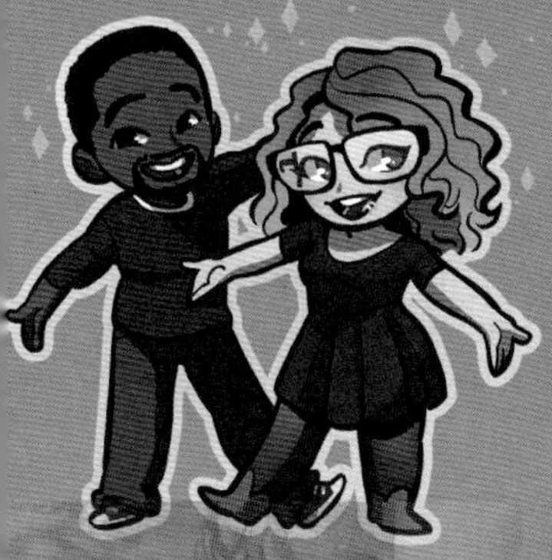

THE COOLING RACK

CONTACT: @NutmegComic NutmegComics@gmail.com

Avatars by Genue Revuelta

FINISHING TOUCHES

I can't believe we made it. I can't believe we *made* it. I can't believe we made *it*.

I also can't believe Jackie didn't end me for convincing her to draw (and color most of) a 15-chapter series, including all the covers. Because she would have been completely justified in doing so. This book exists, and looks as good as it does, because of her. As much a testament to her skill as to her perseverance, working on pages while also holding down a demanding full-time job.

In October of 2011, on a cross-country flight to Washington, D.C. for a friend's wedding, I had two separate thoughts which I scrawled onto a cocktail napkin: "I'd love to do a comic that my 4-year-old goddaughter can read when she's older" and "What if the Girl Scouts were a criminal organization?" That was the seed that became *Nutmeg*, and after some retooling here and there I told my friend Josh Eckert about it. He pointed me to his classmate, Jackie Crofts, and the following spring I flew to Indianapolis hang out with Josh and to pitch this idea to Jackie. She said yes.

I wrote the first issue over the next few months, and made some necessary tweaks (changing the product from cookies to brownies, after a suggestion from my friend Soyini, and making Bobby less explicitly a stoner, thanks to a note from my writing teacher), and in 2013 Jackie drew, colored, *and* lettered it. We launched a Kickstarter to print that single issue in fall 2013, with a plan on attending Wizard World Portland in January 2014, for which Jackie had received an invitation for a free table. That was our first show tabling and we took 130 copies of our *Breaking-Bad*-meets-*Betty-&-Veronica* book. Later that year we signed with a publisher, and then in March 2015 they re-released the book under their banner and we were off.

There's been ups and downs—have there ever—but in the end, we did it. We made the book we wanted to make, people seem to like it, and we learned a whole lot about comics, and ourselves, along the way. Five years, over 400 pages, countless cities and conventions and bowls of ramen, celebratory beers, podcasts and playlists shared, matching outfits, a million Google Hangout sessions, recipes requested and made, inside jokes, table naps, high fives, Madlib's anthem "Come On, Feet," and a lifelong friendship I wouldn't trade for anything.

Thank you, Jackles, for taking this journey with me.

And thank you, readers, for taking it with us.

Stay sweet,

James aka "Jambles"

THE BITTERSWEET END

Nutmeg has truly been a wild ride and it's still a little unbelievable that it's over. It feels difficult to write a goodbye to something that I've spent 5 years of my life on. It's been a constant when things around me have changed, shifted, been good and bad, and everything in between. When I look back at different issues of the book, I can see those different moments projected back at me through my artwork.

Through all of the ups and downs, I'm so happy to have had James as my partner making this thing. He's the most positive, funny, and kind-spirited person to work with. He's motivated me when I'm not feeling great and reassured me when I'm down on my art. Nutmeg has given me a great lifelong friendship. It's sparked so many opportunities in my life that I wouldn't have had otherwise. I've gone on so many adventures that I may not have gone on. I've made so many friends and grown confidence in myself and my work. I have so many fond memories to look back on.

I'll miss drawing Poppy, Cassia, and all the other girls so much. They became a part of my life and I have that same kind of feeling when you finish a TV show or a game you really loved. You're so happy to have experienced it, but missing the world and those characters brings a real kind of sadness! I'm just so proud of us for making it here to the end and I'm extremely thankful to friends, family, and fans who have supported us along the way. You kept buying the book, visiting us at conventions, and telling us encouraging and positive things along the way. Sometimes those small little things were what we needed to make it through a convention that wasn't going so hot, or to remind us that we were inspiring someone and that's all we needed as a reason to keep going.

Thank you, James, for believing in me and taking this journey! Thank you to our friend and fellow sometimes-Nutmeg-colorist and file prepper, Josh Eckert, for introducing us and putting up with all our craziness! Thank you to everyone reading this, or anyone who's read even just an issue of Nutmeg. It's made this little book of ours feel real and alive.

Be kind to each other,

Jackie aka "Jackles"

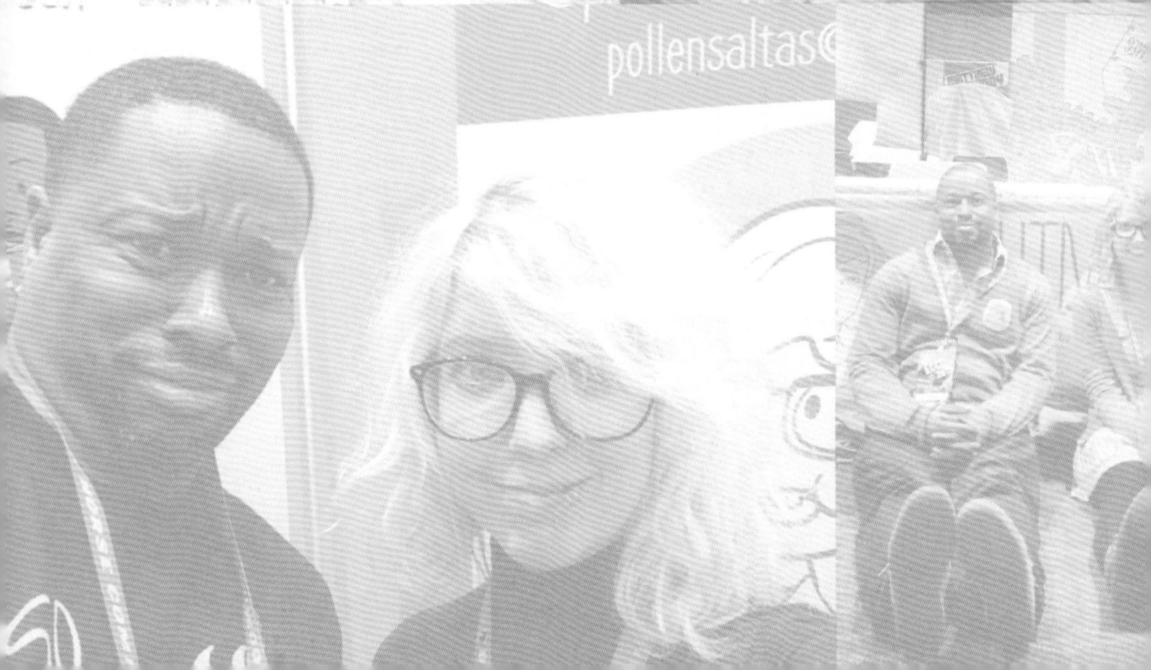
pollensaltas

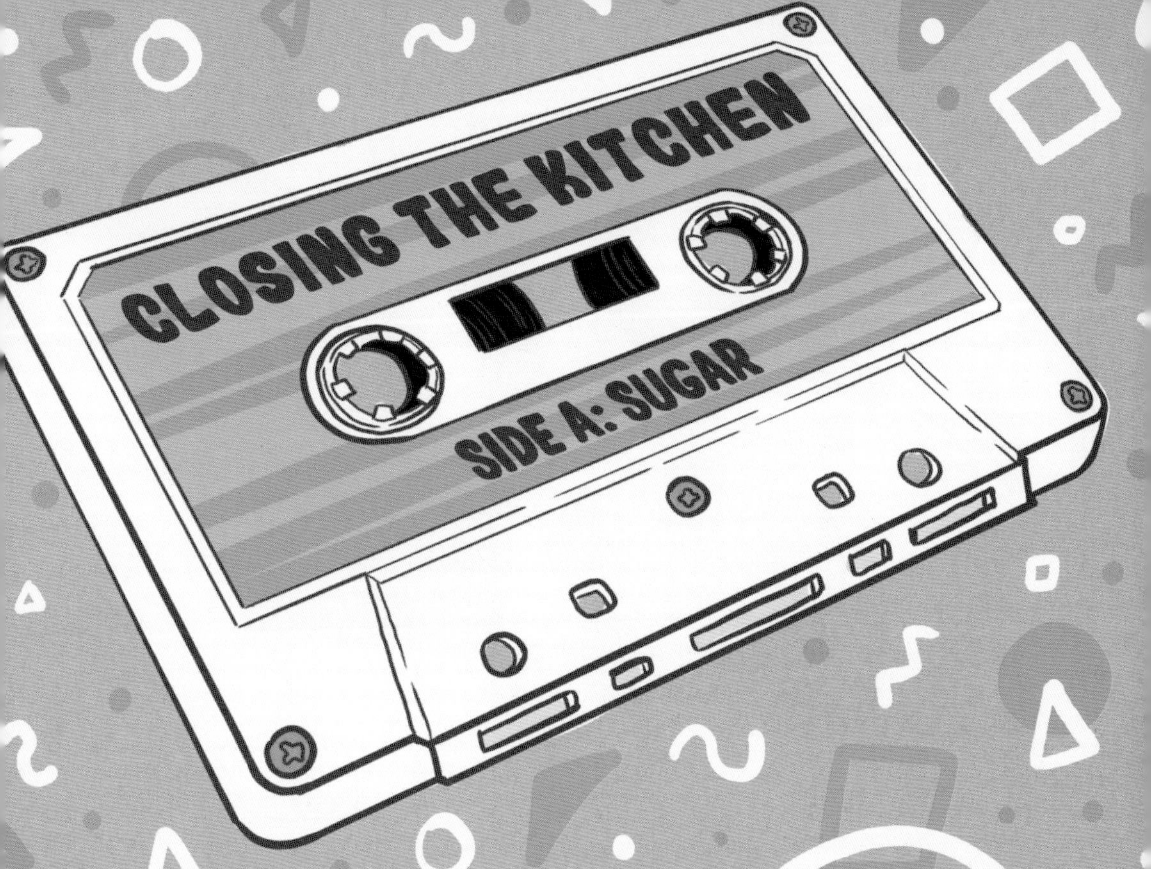
CLOSING THE KITCHEN
SIDE A: SUGAR

CLOSING THE KITCHEN – SIDE A: SUGAR

Go to ***https://spoti.fi/2HyuqIW*** to listen to Jackie's side of the Nutmeg Trade 5 mixtape on Spotify!

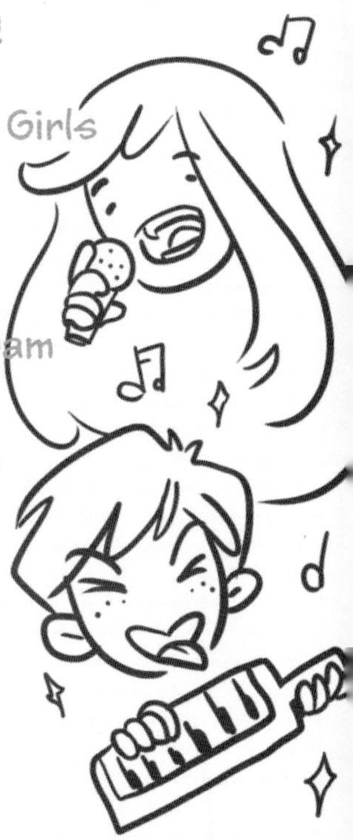

1. Who Do You Think You Are - Spice Girls
2. Bury Our Friends - Sleater-Kinney
3. Regret - St. Vincent
4. Numb - Portishead
5. Running From The Cops - Phantogram
6. Bird of Prey - Natalie Prass
7. Days Are Gone - HAIM
8. If I Had A Heart - Fever Ray
9. Small Poppies - Courtney Barnett
10. Lungs - CHVRCHES
11. I'm Blue - The Shangri-Las
12. Waited 4 U - Slow Magic
13. Go Your Own Way - Fleetwood Mac

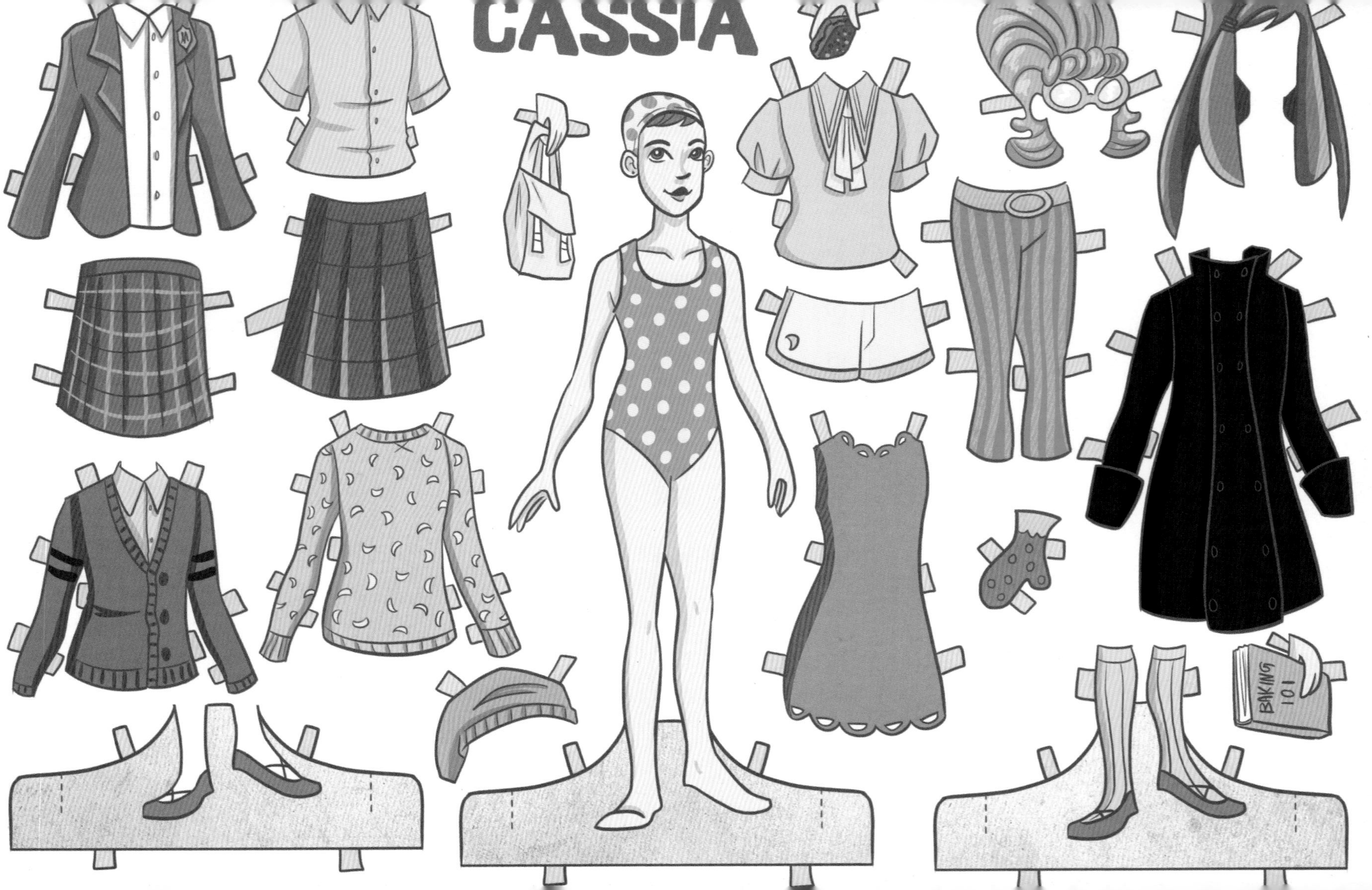
CASSIA
BAKING 101

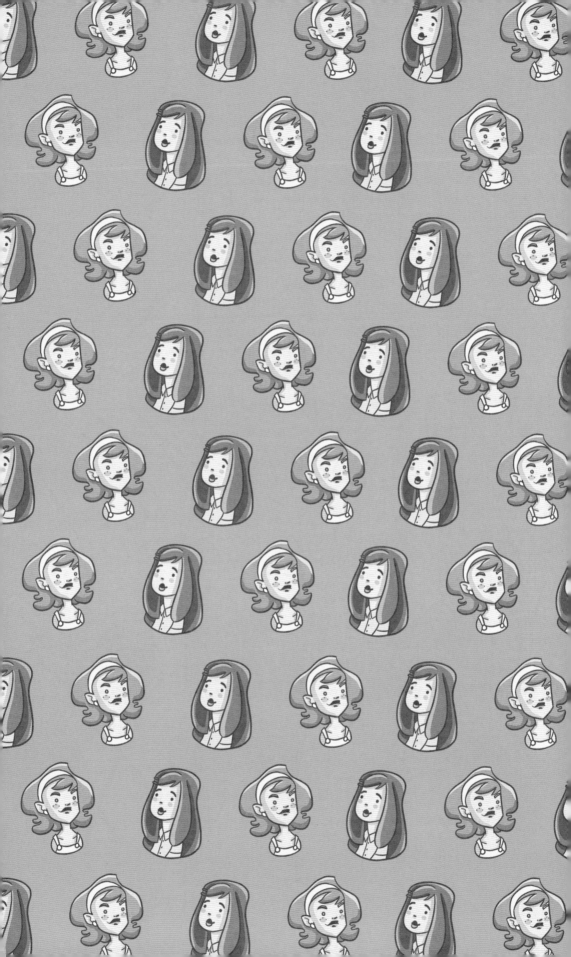

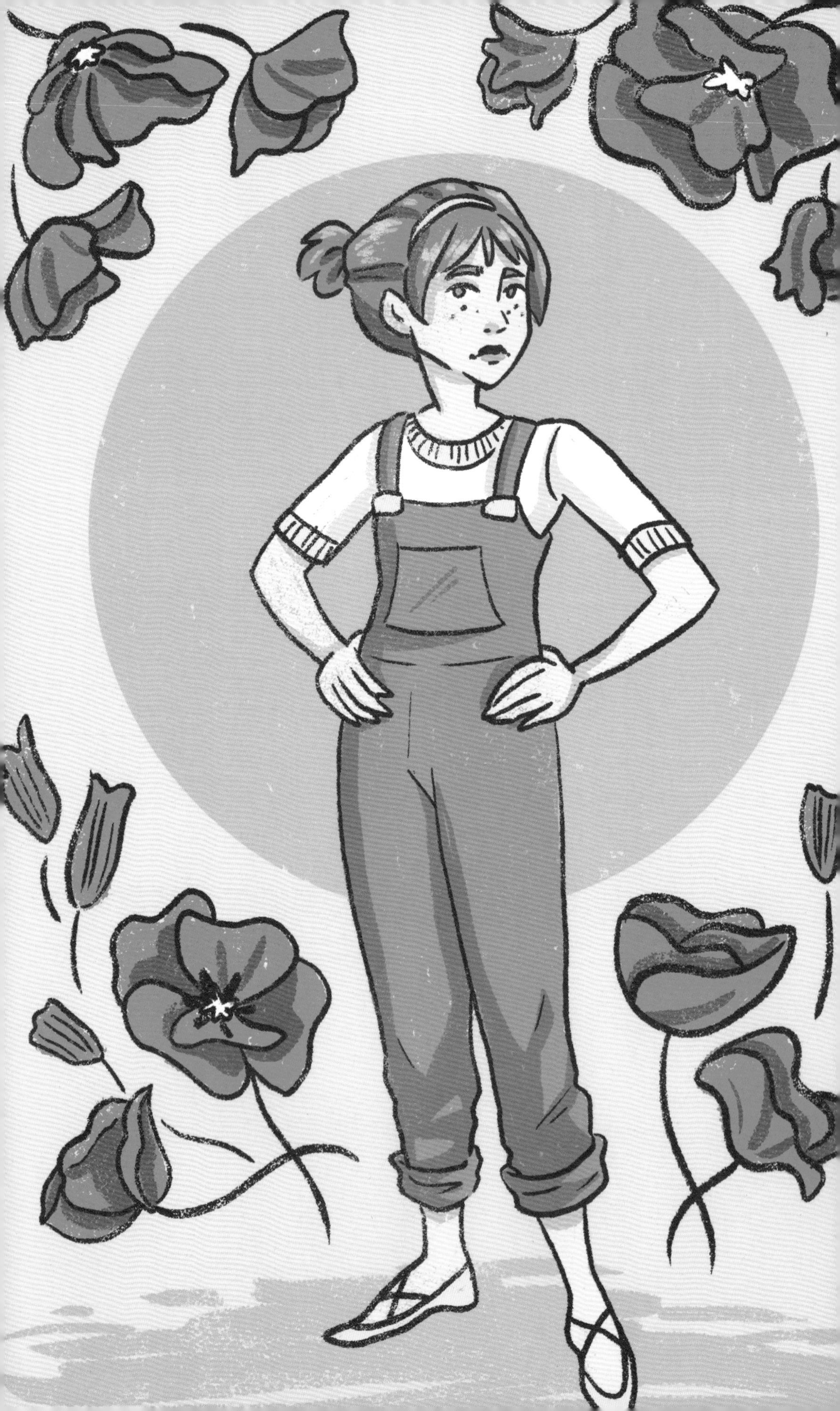

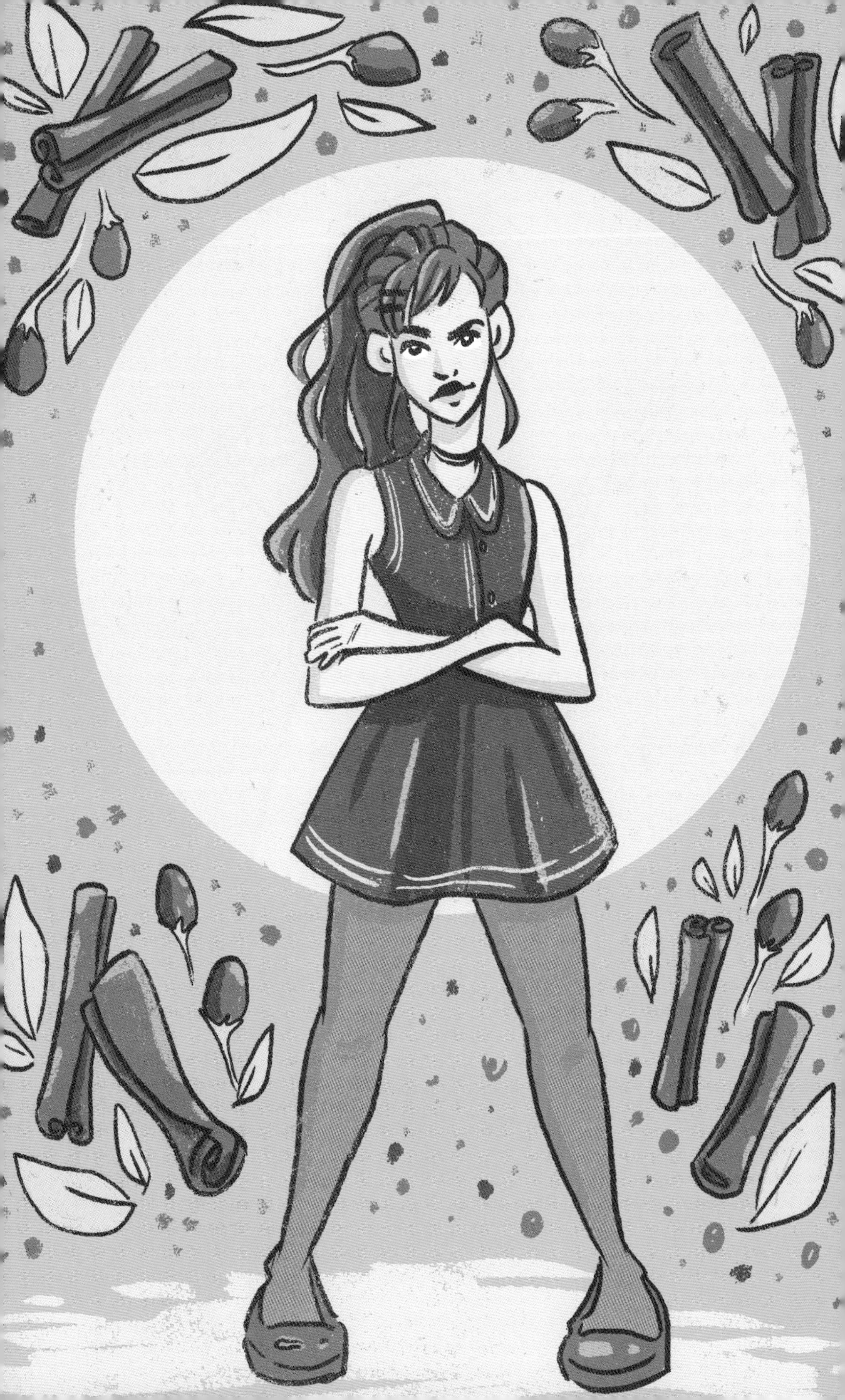

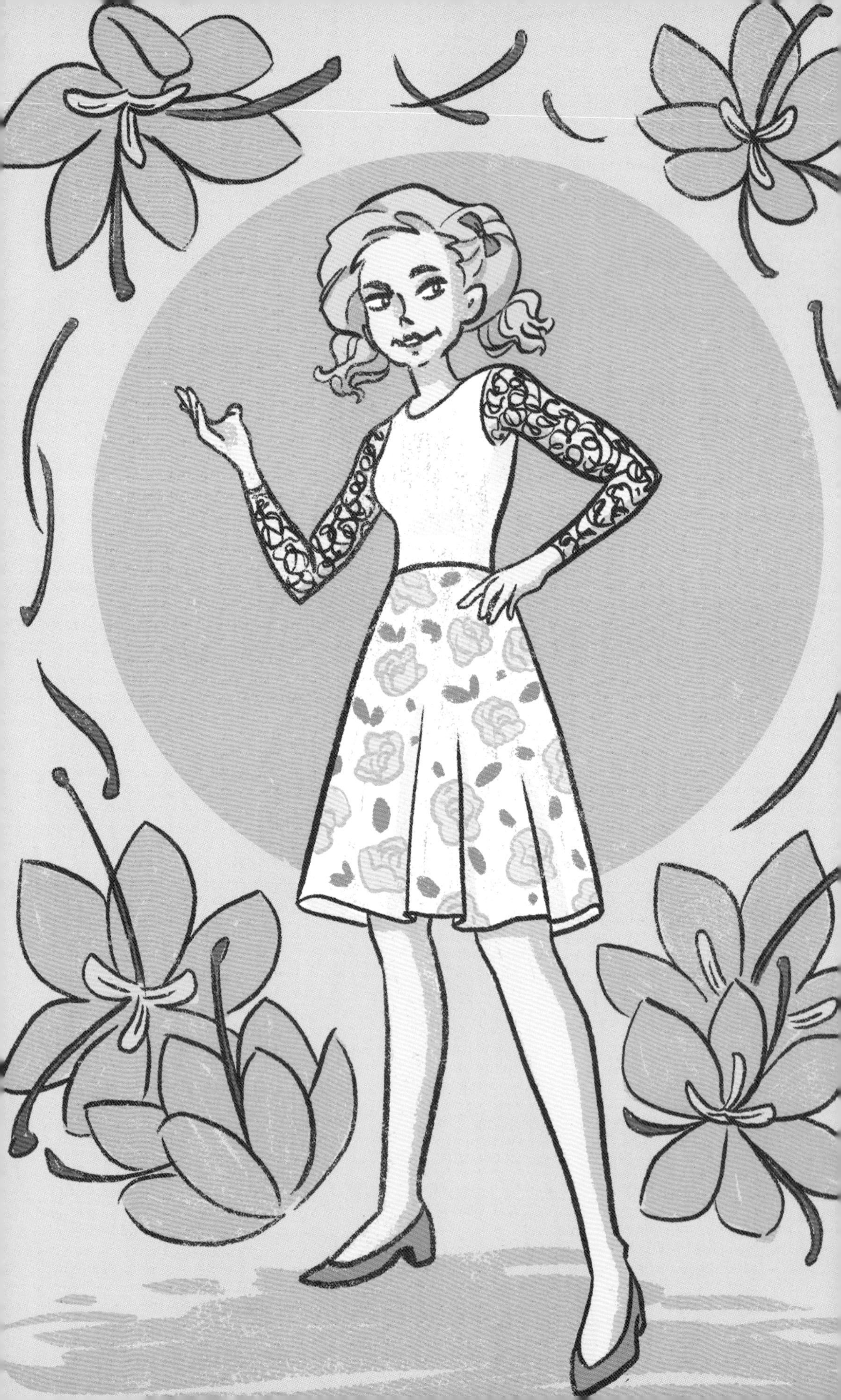

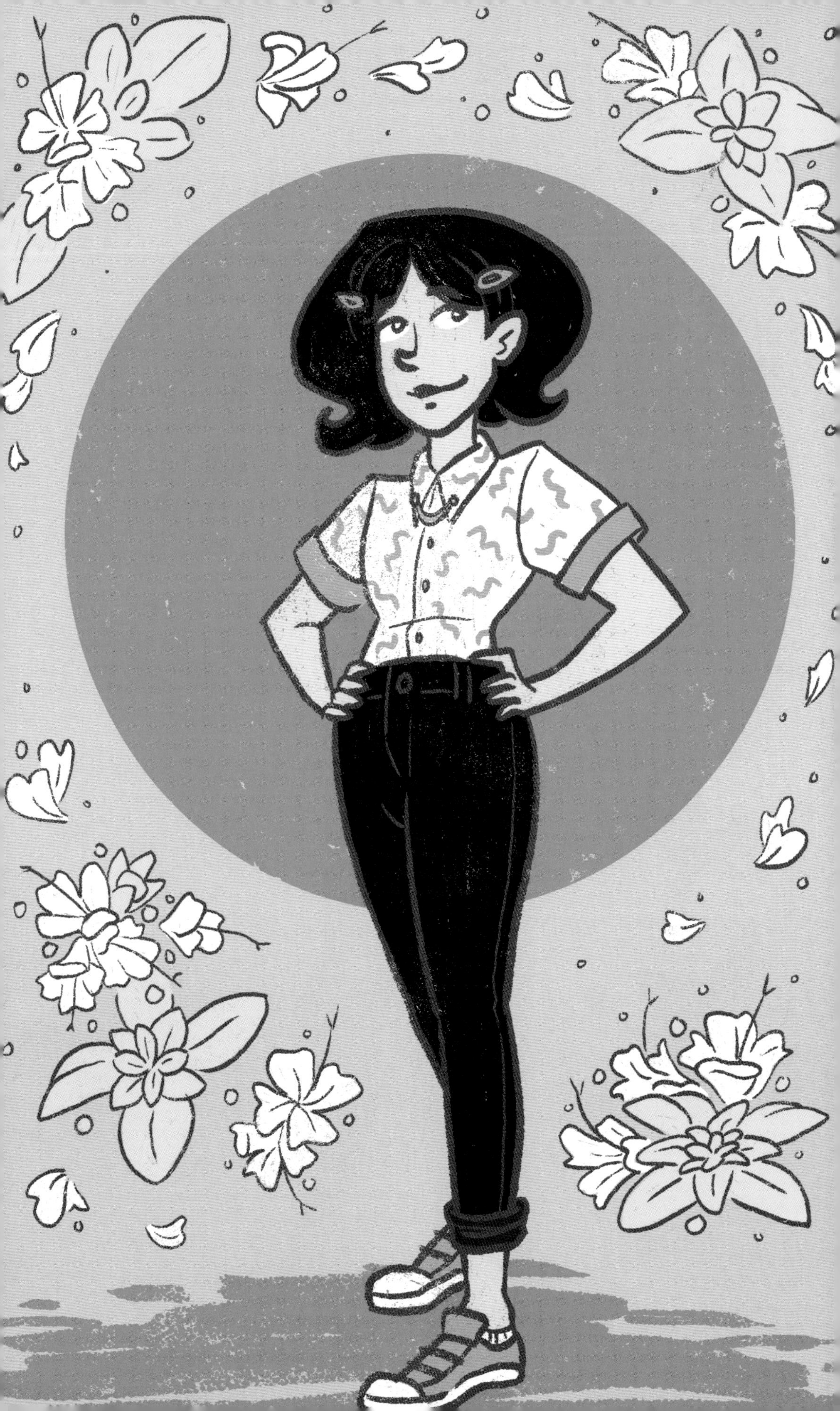

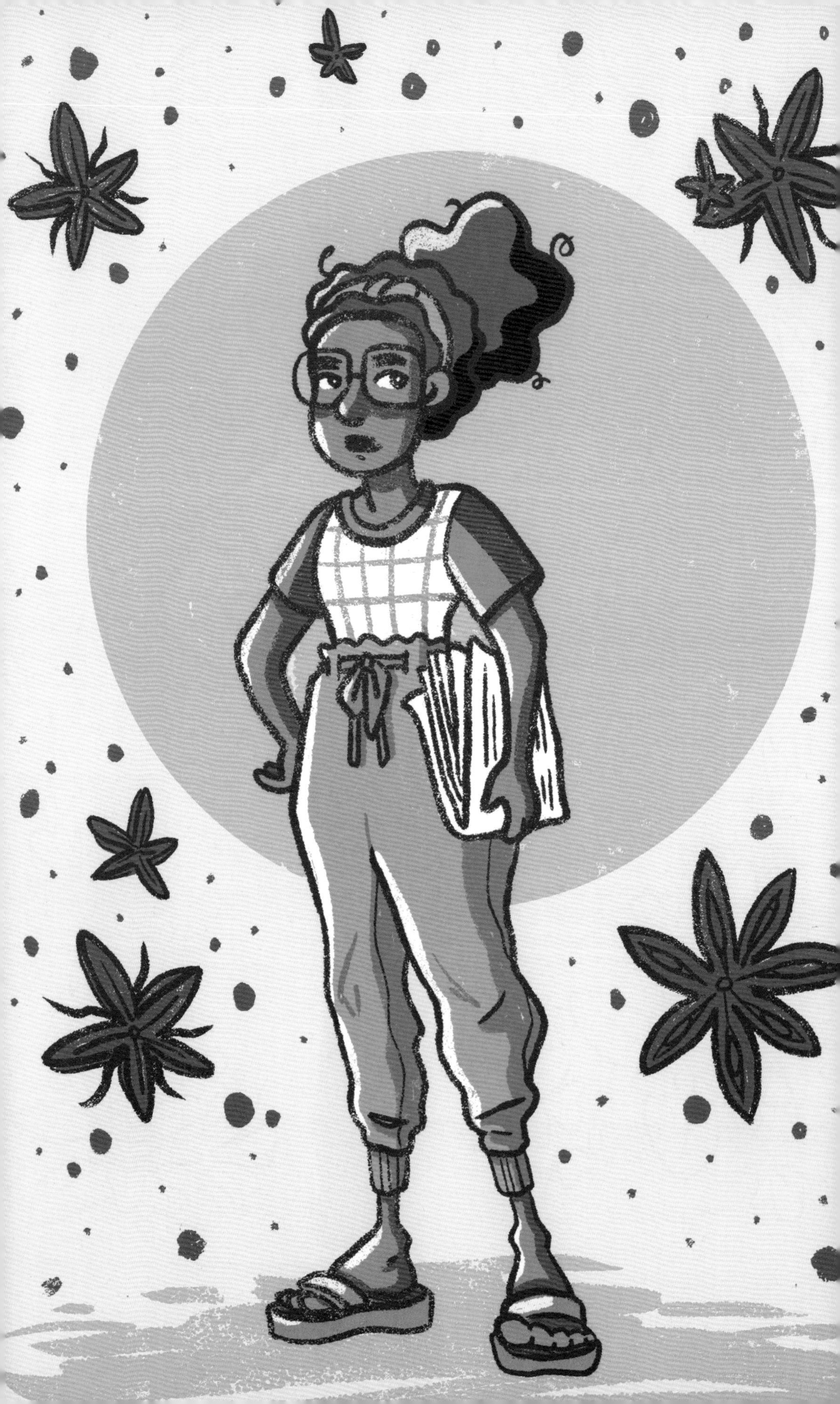

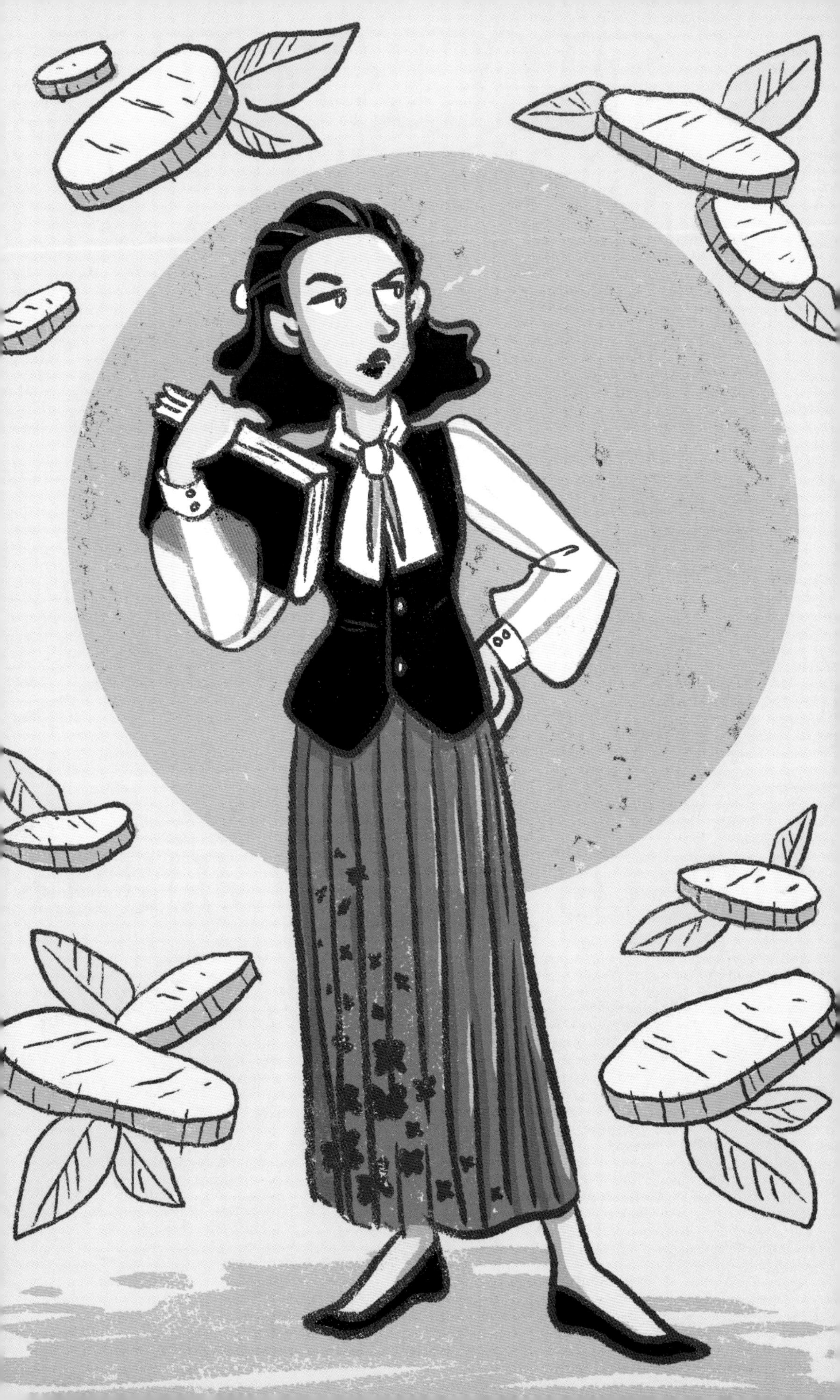

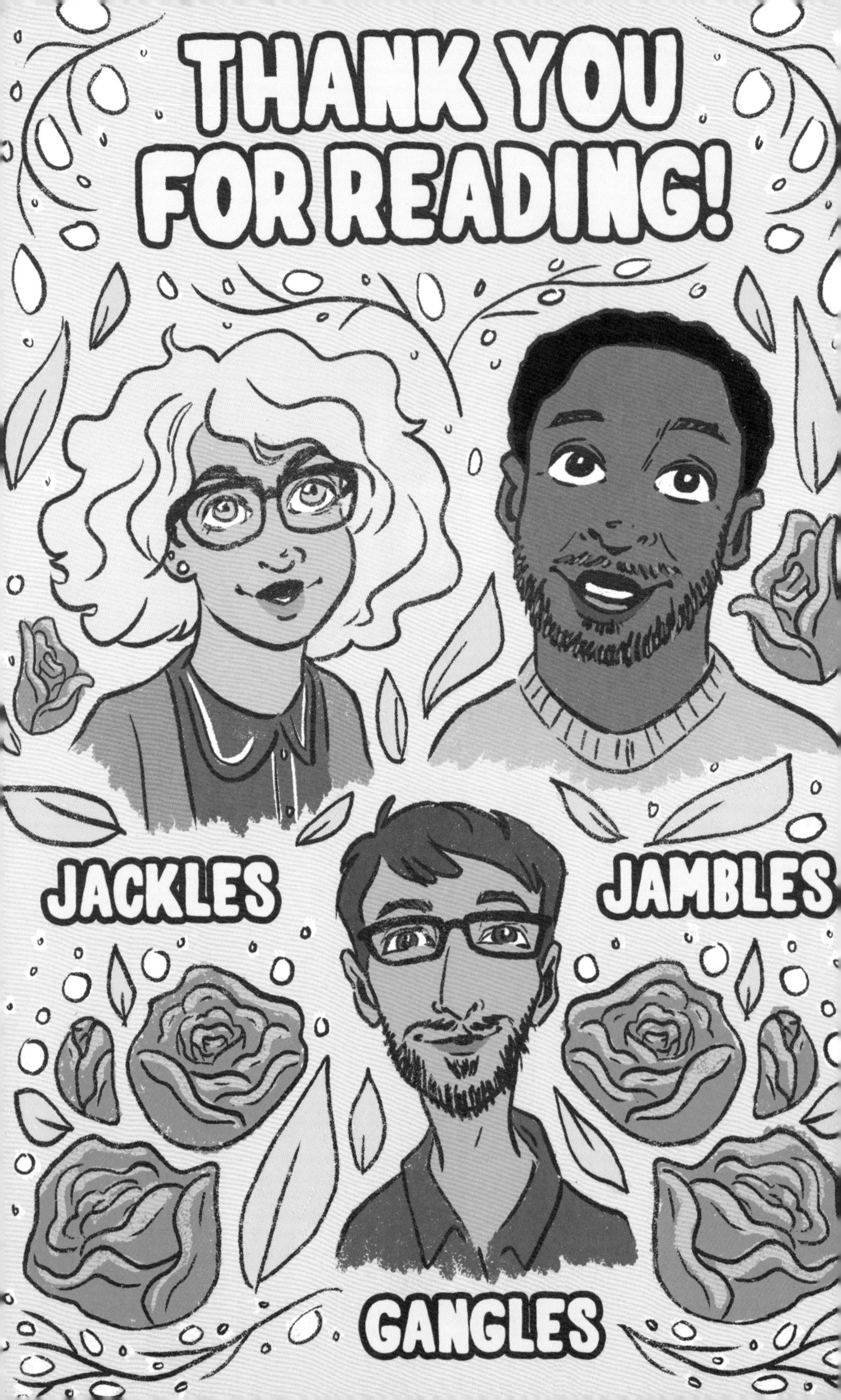
THANK YOU FOR READING!
JACKLES
JAMBLES
GANGLES

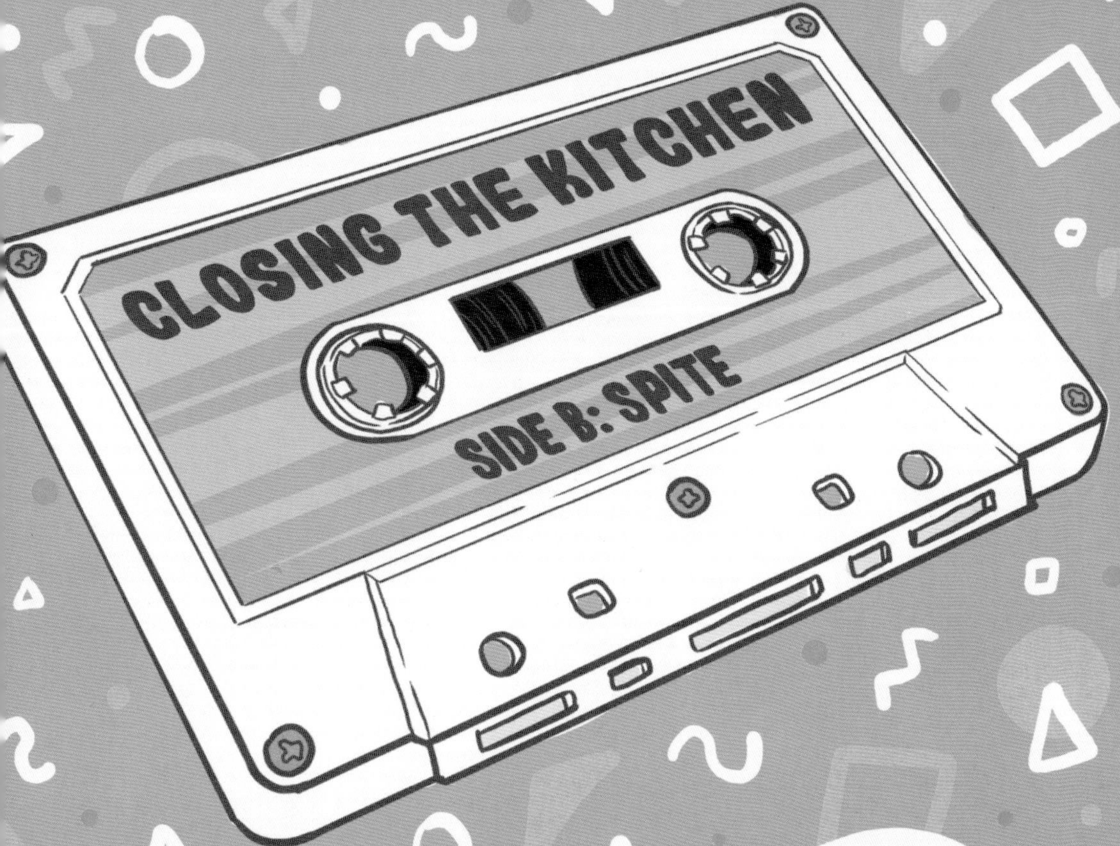
CLOSING THE KITCHEN
SIDE B: SPITE

CLOSING THE KITCHEN – SIDE B: SPITE

Go to ***https://spoti.fi/2B8z4rt*** to listen to James' side of the Nutmeg Trade 5 mixtape on Spotify!

1. Consideration - Rihana, SZA
2. Just A Girl - No Doubt
3. You Don't Get Me High Anymore - Phantogram
4. Party For One - Carly Rae Jepsen
5. Forever - CHVRCHES
6. A Better Son/Daughter - Rilo Kiley
7. Fading Flower - Yuna
8. Concrete Wall - Zee Avi
9. Spice - Ravyn Lenae
10. Pretty Ugly - Tierra Whack
11. Normal Girl - SZA
12. Circles - Izzy Bizu
13. Best Friend - Brandy

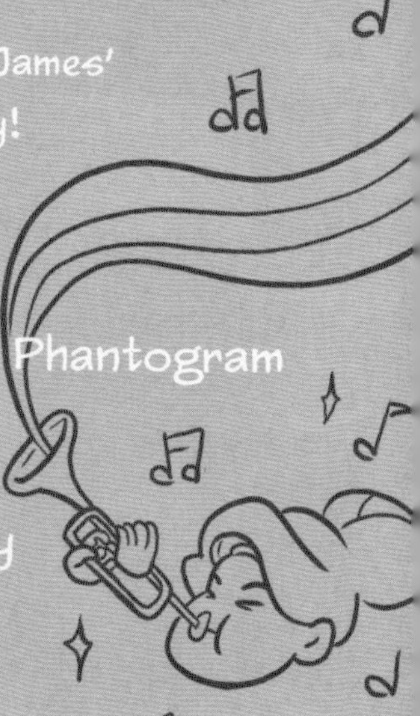

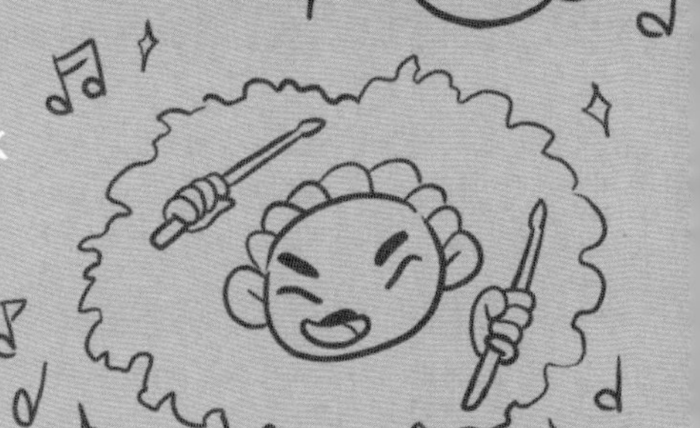

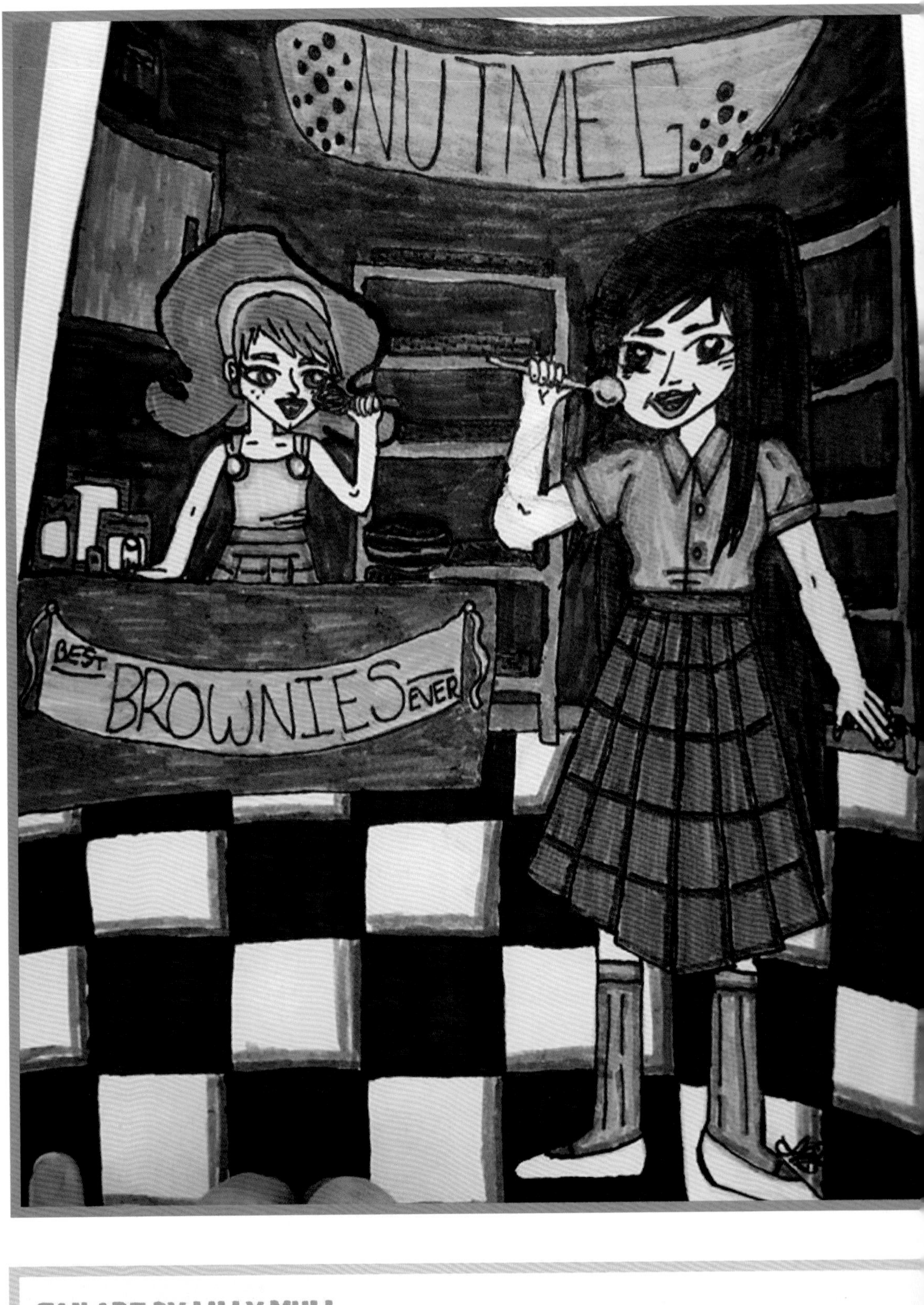
NUTMEG
BEST
BROWNIES
EVER

FAN ART BY LILLY MULL

Lilly Mull is 15 from Greenwood, IN. She started reading comics at an early age and discovered Nutmeg at 12. She loves drawing and wants to do something with creative writing in the future.

PROCESS PAGES

We wanted to take one more opportunity to show some process pages from the last issue of Nutmeg. We hope you enjoy seeing a page come to life from script, to thumnails, inking, and finally colors & lettering.

James F. Wright   *Nutmeg #15*   *"The Good Dine Young"*

PAGE 2:

ONE:
ANISE STARK is seated at her KITCHEN TABLE and sets the NEWPSPAER aside. Also on the table are her half-eaten breakfast, a glass of juice, and her NOTEPAD and PEN.

NO COPY.

TWO:
ANISE takes up her PEN and begins writing on her NOTEPAD. She's narrating (to us) what she's writing down.

1 CAPTION/Anise: What happened was more or less what Ginger wanted.
2 CAPTION/Anise: Even if it isn't exactly what went down.

THREE:
Close on STERLING LONGFELLOW from that black-and-white photo on the front page.

3 CAPTION/Anise: It's good that Sterling Longfellow was convicted.
4 CAPTION/Anise: I never fully believed it was *all* Saffron's fault.

FOUR:
Close on SAFFRON LONGFELLOW now from that same black-and-white photo on the front page.

5 CAPTION/Anise: She was a jerk and a monster, but the journalist in me would rather she
                                        went down for something she actually did.

FIVE:
ANISE and GINGER, days earlier, stand facing each other. Ginger has her hands on either side of Anise's shoulders, looking at Anise with a sort of friendly pity.

6 CAPTION/Anise: When I told Ginger, she scoffed. She said--
7 CAPTION/Anise: "Print the legend."
8 CAPTION/Anise: But I'm getting ahead of myself.

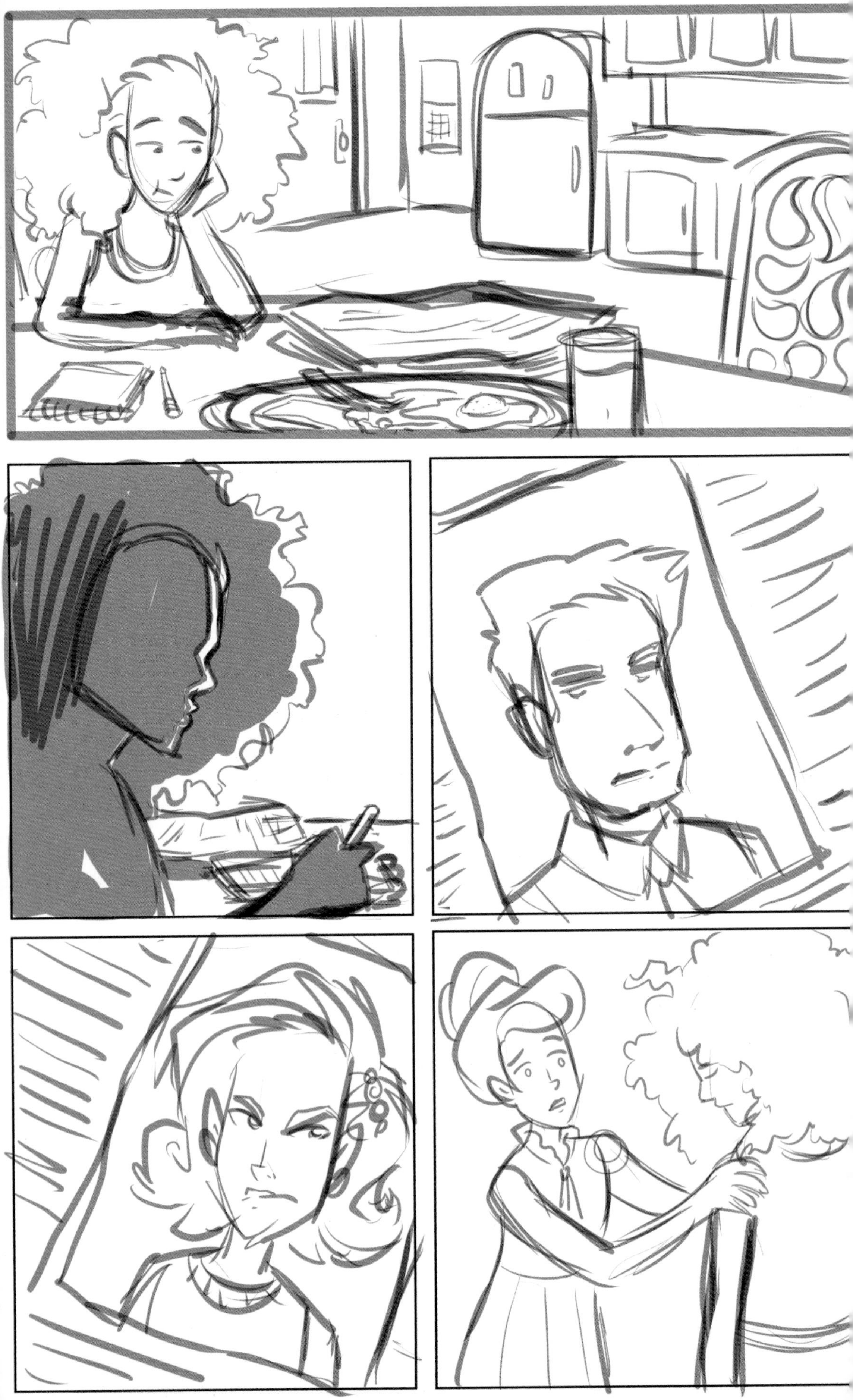

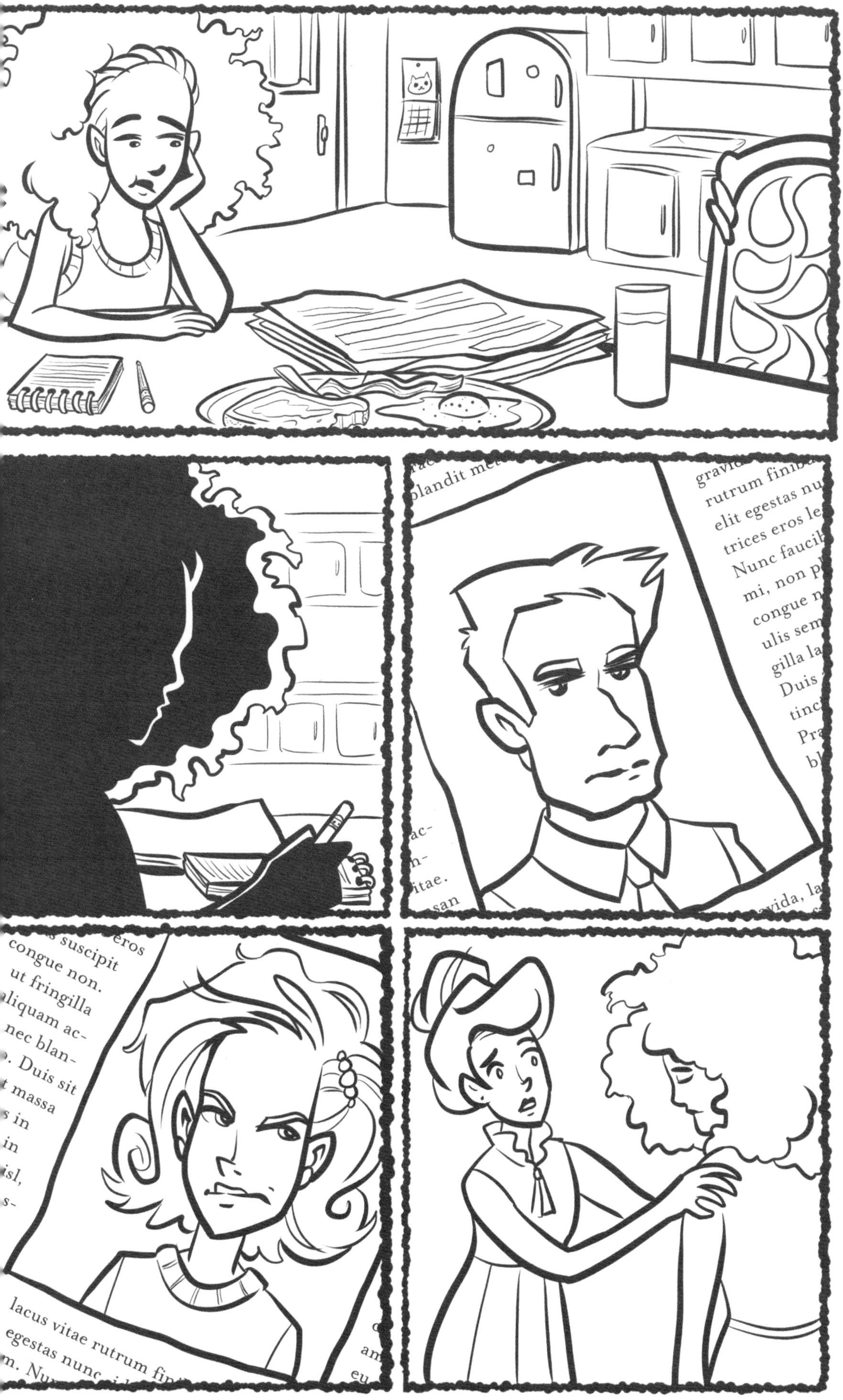
blandit met
rutrum finib
elit egestas nu
trices eros le
Nunc faucib
mi, non p
congue n
ulis sem
gilla la
Duis
itae.
congue suscipit
ut fringilla
aliquam ac-
nec blan-
Duis sit
t massa
lacus vitae rutrum fin
egestas nunc

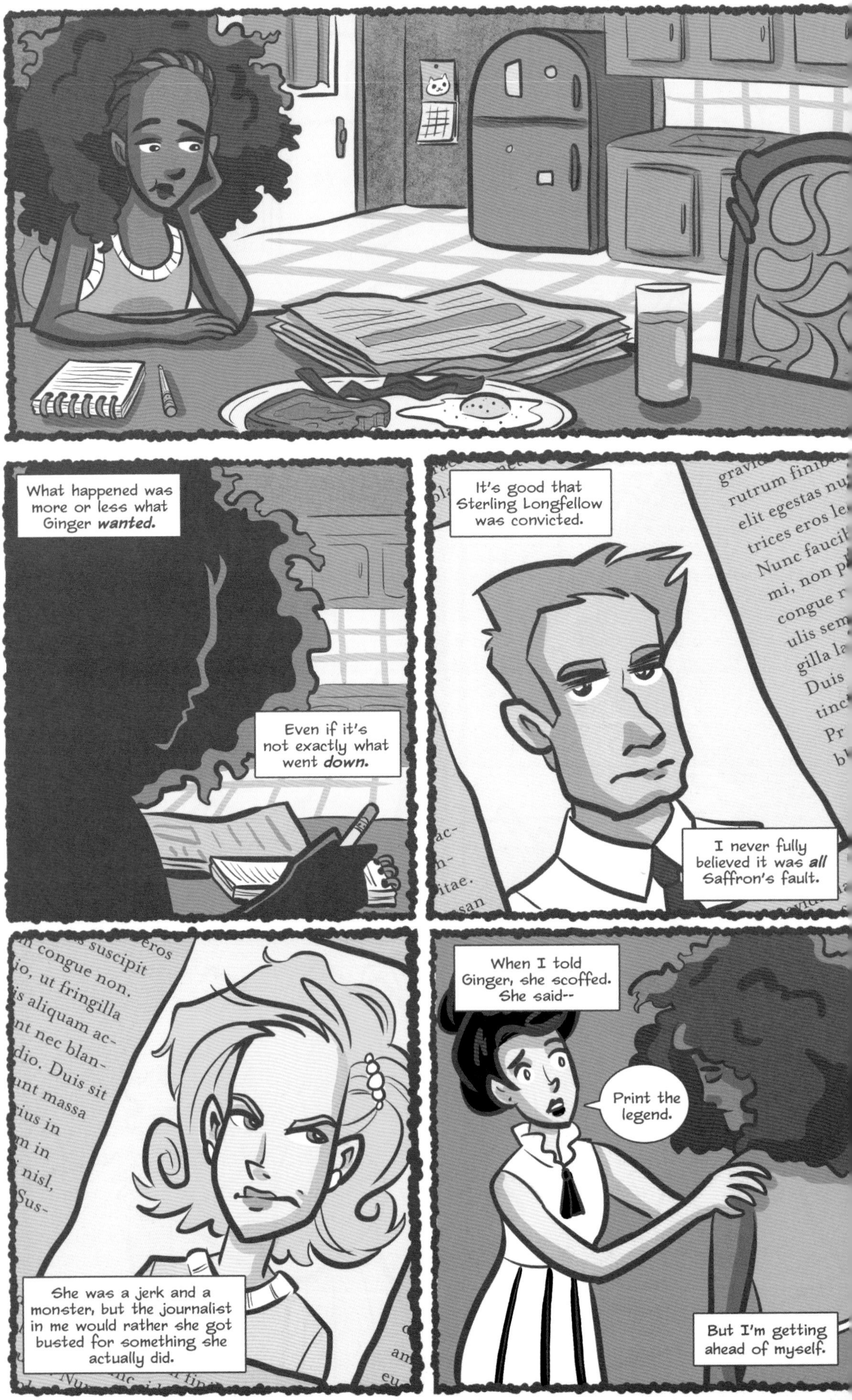
What happened was more or less what Ginger *wanted.*
Even if it's not exactly what went *down.*
It's good that Sterling Longfellow was convicted.
I never fully believed it was *all* Saffron's fault.
She was a jerk and a monster, but the journalist in me would rather she got busted for something she actually did.
When I told Ginger, she scoffed. She said--
Print the legend.
But I'm getting ahead of myself.

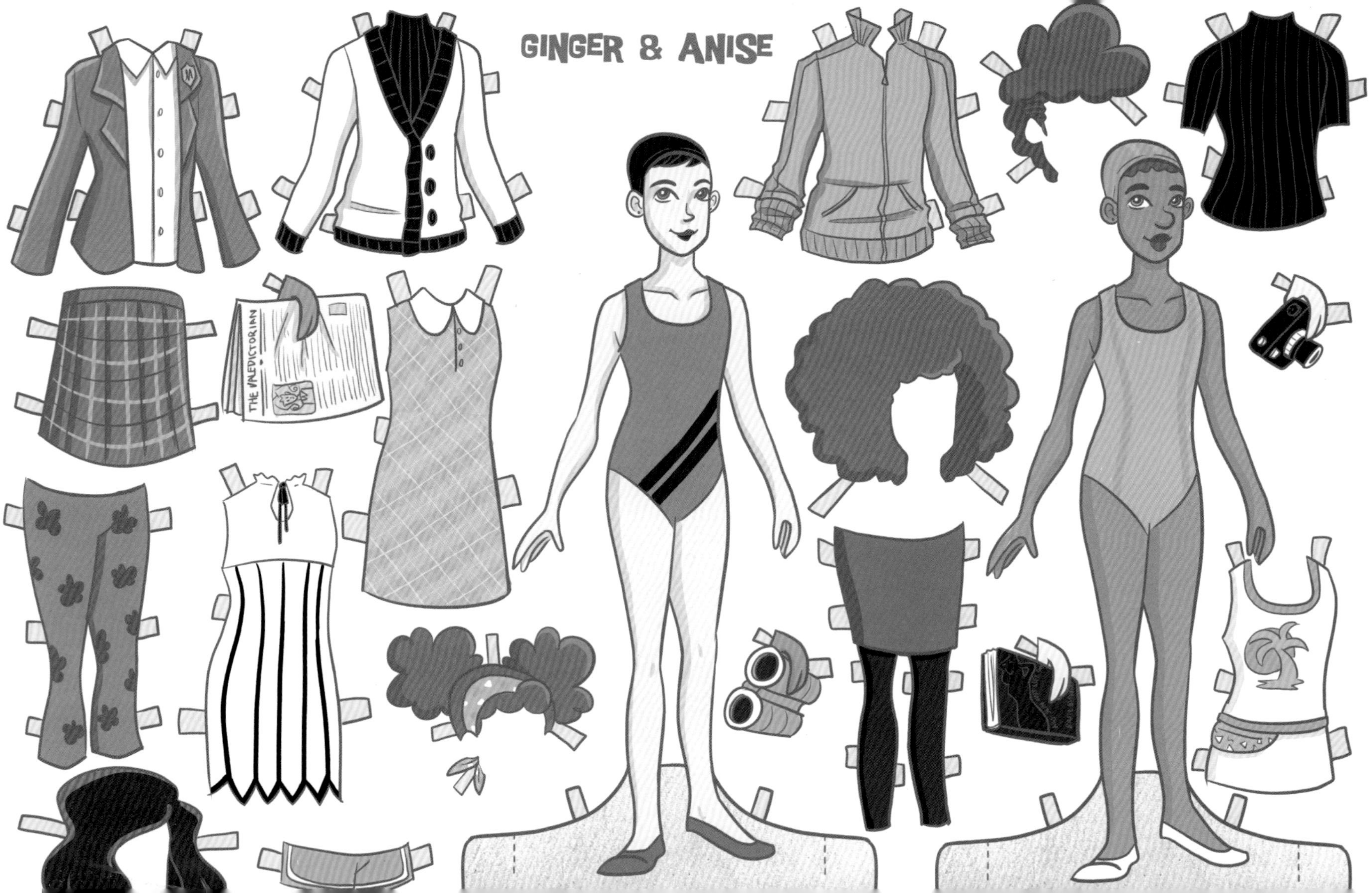
GINGER & ANISE
THE VALEDICTORIAN

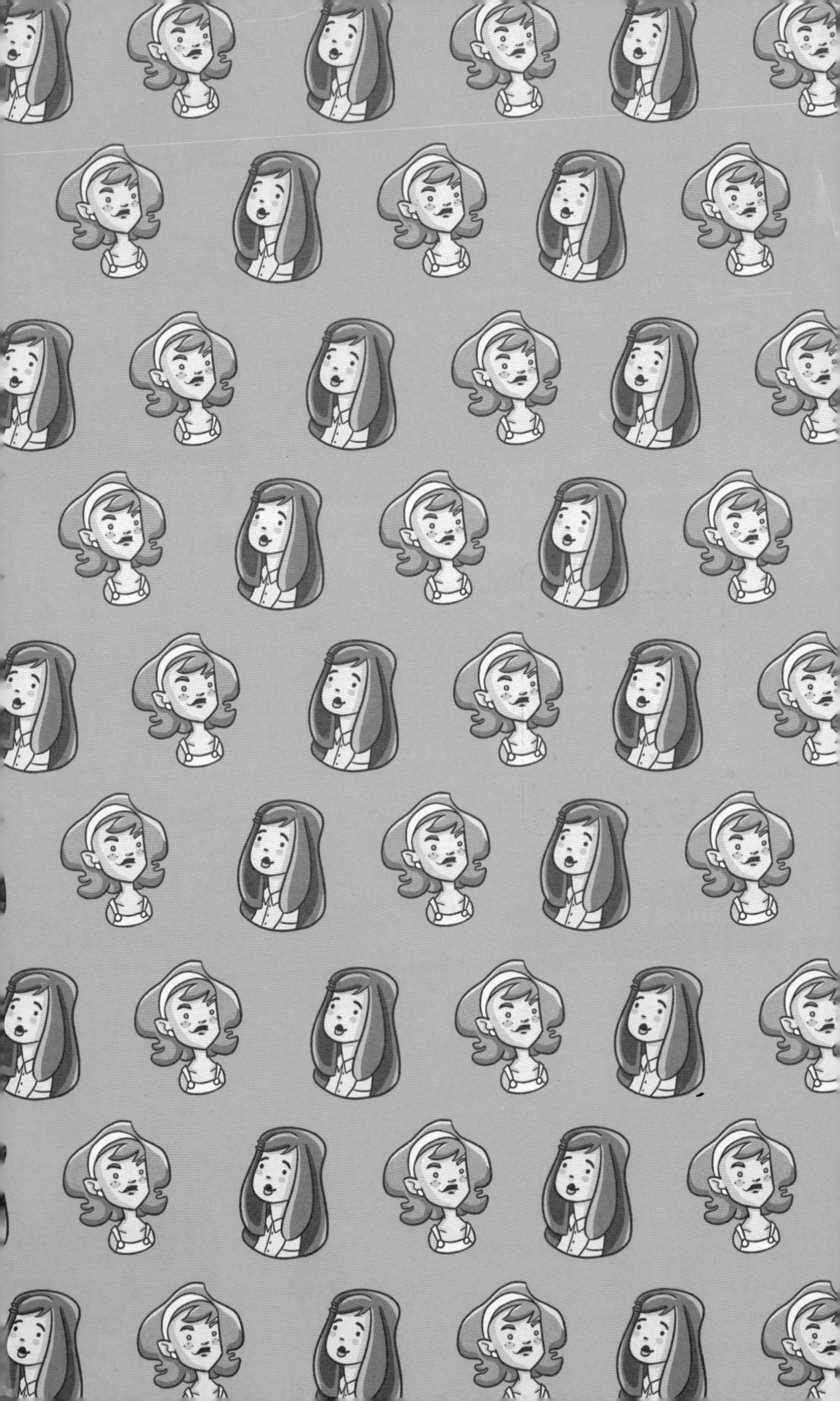